PRAISE FOR FAY WELDON'S
TROUBLE

"An exceedingly wicked novel . . . black and biting . . . [Weldon's] never been better; the evil she describes has never been more insidious."   —*The Miami Herald*

"Weldon manages not only to be witty, but to keep the reader engrossed, tearing along to find out what happens next. . . . She is a master."
                        —Tama Janowitz, *The New York Times Book Review*

"Sex, death, and modern-day Svengalis: Weldon is a master of her own weird amalgamation of satire and horror, and is bliss for those who enjoy simultaneously giggling and gnashing their teeth."
                        —*Paper* magazine

"Deliciously wicked"
                        —*New York Daily News*

"A witty, venomous portrait . . . smart, witty, lively, page-turning, wise, weathered, crackling, withering"
                        —*The Washington Post*

"Fasten your seatbelt before cracking the cover of Weldon's new novel . . . her nimble prose pulls you along at breakneck speed. A hilarious sendup of New Age healing and pseudo-psychology."
                        —*The Orlando Sentinel*

"Another acid-etched portrait of a modern marriage that's as grimly comic as any fairy tale the Brothers Grimm ever told."
                        —*The Hartford Courant*

"This brutal look at modern marriage . . . is a fine example of Weldon at her keen-eyed, sharp-witt~~ed best.~~"
                        —*The S~~...~~*

PENGUIN BOOKS

TROUBLE

Fay Weldon was raised in a household of women in New Zealand, and produced four sons of her own, as if to balance the gender count. She survived a decade of odd jobs and hard times, then wrote the first television script for "Upstairs, Downstairs." Among her twenty novels and short-story collections are *Life Force*, *The Cloning of Joanna May*, *Darcy's Utopia*, *The Life and Loves of a She-Devil*, and *The Heart of the Country*, winner of the 1989 Los Angeles Times Fiction Award. Fay Weldon lives in London.

FAY WELDON

ROUBLE

PENGUIN BOOKS

(825)

PENGUIN BOOKS
Published by the Penguin Group
Penguin Books USA Inc., 375 Hudson Street,
New York, New York 10014, U.S.A.
Penguin Books Ltd, 27 Wrights Lane, London W8 5TZ, England
Penguin Books Australia Ltd, Ringwood, Victoria, Australia
Penguin Books Canada Ltd, 10 Alcorn Avenue,
Toronto, Ontario, Canada M4V 3B2
Penguin Books (N.Z.) Ltd, 182–190 Wairau Road,
Auckland 10, New Zealand

Penguin Books Ltd, Registered Offices:
Harmondsworth, Middlesex, England

First published in the United States of America by Viking Penguin,
a division of Penguin Books USA Inc., 1993
Published in Penguin Books 1994

10 9 8 7 6 5 4 3 2 1

PUBLISHER'S NOTE
This is a work of fiction. Names, characters, places, and incidents either are
the product of the author's imagination or are used fictitiously, and any resemblance
to actual persons, living or dead, events, or locales is entirely coincidental.

THE LIBRARY OF CONGRESS HAS CATALOGUED THE HARDCOVER AS FOLLOWS:
Weldon, Fay.
Trouble/Fay Weldon.
p.   cm.
ISBN 0-670-84148-X (hc.)
ISBN 0 14 01.5916 9 (pbk.)
1. Marriage—England—London—Fiction.   I. Title.
PR6073.E374T66 1993
823'.914—dc20   93–254

Printed in the United States of America
Set in Adobe Bodoni Book
Designed by Francesca Belanger

TROUBLE

PROLOGUE

"Who was that knocking at your front door?" asked Annette, as Spicer got back into bed and entwined his legs through hers.

"Only a gypsy woman," he said. "Dirty and fat and old."

This was in London, ten years ago.

"What did she want?" asked Annette, who was clean, slim, and young.

"She wanted to tell my fortune," said Spicer. "For a fee."

"Did you let her?" asked Annette.

Spicer looked down at her from above. His eyes were brown and intense; his hair was thick and blond.

"Of course I didn't," Spicer said. "Superstitious nonsense! I told her to go away at once."

"She can't have liked that," observed Annette.

"She didn't," said Spicer, "but I wanted to get back to you. She said as she went, 'I'll go, but the bad luck will stay.' She had an angry heart in the first place. Nothing to do with me."

His mouth descended upon Annette's, his hand parted her legs, and she forgot all about the gypsy woman.

"I shall give you half the house for your birthday," said Spicer, eight days later. "I shall give it to you out of my natural love and affection, as it says in legal documents. We will share this house as we share our lives. I will see my lawyer as soon as I can."

"Spicer," warned Annette, "aren't you being precipitate? We've known each other for only seven weeks, and most of that has been spent in bed."

Spicer laughed.

"I'm a precipitate person," he said. "An all-or-nothing guy."

Annette was leaning against an oak tree and Spicer was leaning into her, holding her fast, at the end of the overgrown garden. A little distance away Spicer's son, Jason, by his wife, Aileen, and Annette's daughter, Susan, by her husband, Paddy, played together quietly in the long grasses. Jason had been in the world for two years and Susan for three.

"You know as well as I do, Annette," said Spicer, "that we're going to be married and live happily ever after."

He kissed her on the lips and then drew away from her, but only because he could hear the children coming. Both felt the loss of touch as pain, and moaned. Up above, the green oak leaves shivered in witness.

*   *   *

"But, Annette," said Annette's mother, Judy, on the phone, three months later, "this all comes so soon after your break with Paddy. I'm glad for you, because you've had such a wretched time, but please tell me more about this Spicer."

Annette lay on the bed and Spicer lay beside her.

"He's so beautiful," said Annette, "you've no idea. And he lives in a lovely big house."

"Don't be silly, Annette," said Judy. "And don't say I'm being patronizing and put the phone down. Where and how did you meet him?"

"I met him at a party," said Annette, "and we've hardly been apart since."

"He must go to work," observed Judy.

"It's his own work, his own business; I can go with him. He is heir to Horrocks Wine Imports, established 1793, though there's very little left to inherit."

"Wine's not a good business to be in, in a time of recession," said Judy. "But I expect he had a good education."

"Better than mine," said Annette. "Do you want references for the man I love; is that it?"

"It might be a good idea," said Judy, "and from his first wife too, since you say he's been married before."

"She made him unhappy," said Annette. "Okay? She's depressive, manipulative, and greedy, and tried to turn his little boy against him."

"So now you can look after his little boy and he can give you and little Susan a home," observed Judy.

"Well, yes," said Annette, after a pause. "Isn't that wonderful! Not just that we've found true love but we each answer the other's problems. Please be happy for me, Mother."

"I'll try," said Judy. "I expect I'll manage."

Annette brought the call to an end and with one hand lifted the phone from the bed and half-dropped it onto the floor. The receiver fell off its hook and lay neglected and buzzing at Spicer and Annette while they made love. This was before the advent of the new technology which cuts out the buzz after thirty seconds and instructs the user to redial.

"*E*verything moves faster now," said Annette, some six months after her phone call to her mother. "Do you think it's because there are more and more people in the world, and time has to be shared out amongst them?"

"I am not as fanciful as you," said Spicer. "I'm just a wine merchant."

They sat on the living-room floor watching television. The room had been redecorated; the carpet was thick and clean, all trace of the miserable Aileen removed. Jason and Susan sprawled beside them.

"Shall we have a baby between us?" Spicer asked. "That's one for you, one for me, one for us. That makes a real family."

"I must think about that," said Annette.

"Make me a bacon sandwich while you think about it," said Spicer. "No better food in all the world than the bacon sandwiches you make for me. White, soft bread, thinly spread butter, crisp brown bacon."

"Too much cholesterol, too much salt," warned Annette, but she rose to do Spicer's bidding.

"I shall live forever in perfect health," said Spicer, "because I love you."

When Annette came back from the kitchen, she said, "We must have a baby between us, Spicer; there has to be something to sop up this abundance."

But it was all of ten years before she conceived.

"*A*nnette," said Spicer to his wife ten years and some months later, "I won't be able to come with you to the Maternity Clinic this evening."

"But, Spicer darling," said Annette, "why not? It's Father's Night Extra."

"Because I have matters to attend to that are more important."

"What could be more important than the baby?"

"*I* could," said Spicer, and he left the rest of his breakfast and went to work straightaway without even calling goodbye to Susan or Jason. Nor did Spicer kiss Annette goodbye, as was his custom. The habit of years had been broken: the gears of the relationship shifted and changed.

Annette set about her household duties and after an hour called Spicer at his office.

First sign, beginning

"Mr. Horrocks," said Spicer's secretary, Wendy. "I have your wife on the phone."

Wendy was kind and efficient. She was in her thirties, plain, and a hockey player. She lived with her mother.

"Spicer," said Annette. "How could you speak to me like that? If you knew how it upset me, you wouldn't do it. You being bad-tempered isn't good for the baby."

"Annette," said Spicer, "I am in a meeting," and he put the receiver down his end so that the one in Annette's hand buzzed. Annette and Spicer had been the first in their road to own a mobile phone: now their neighbors possessed newer, lighter, cheaper models. There can be a penalty for being first; especially in technological matters. Annette called Spicer's office again.

"Wendy," asked Annette, "is Spicer really in a meeting or is he just saying that?"

"Mr. Horrocks is just saying it," said Wendy, "but in fact he's very busy. The auditors are due."

"Wendy," said Annette, "has Spicer been a little, well, on edge lately?"

"No," said Wendy. "He's been just fine. Happy as a sandboy, in fact, as usual. Very chatty. We're all so looking forward to the baby. If she's born in November she'll be a little Scorpio."

"I don't know about things like that," said Annette.

"Nor do I," said Wendy, "it's Mr. Horrocks tells me she'll be a little Scorpio. A little stinger."

"Oh," said Annette. "Well, I'll try and get used to the idea."

Wendy said, "When he's got a moment I'll say you called, shall I?" And Annette said, "No, don't worry. It can wait till this evening," and put the phone down, but not before she heard, or thought she heard, Wendy say, "Sometimes I'm really glad I'm not married."

*A*nnette called her friend Gilda. Gilda was seven months pregnant to Annette's five. Annette and Gilda lived parallel lives. They'd been to school and college together. Now they lived down the road from one another and went to antenatal class together. Annette and Gilda liked to see this as destiny, but their husbands said no; propinquity merely breeds propinquity. If now Annette and Gilda both worked in the same TV production company it was not fate, but because Gilda had got Annette the job. Gilda's current task was an investigation into the history of heraldic beasts, and Annette's into the myth of Europa, ravished by Jupiter in the form of a bull. People likened Gilda to Ginger Rogers, and indeed Gilda had red hair and had once been a dancer. But, then, people likened Annette to Meryl Streep for no better reason than that she had a fair skin and small, straight nose, and a vulnerable air.

"Hello, Gilda," said Annette.

"What's the matter?" asked Gilda. "I can tell from your voice something's wrong. Is the baby all right?"

"The baby's just fine," said Annette, "but Spicer won't come to Father's Night Extra at the Clinic and he seems angry with me and I don't know why."

"He was all right when we saw you at dinner on Tuesday," said Gilda. "In fact, he was being very attentive and kind. Perhaps he has troubles at work?"

"His secretary said something about having the auditors in, but so far as I know everything's okay. Profits are down, but aren't everyone's?"

"It depends how far down," said Gilda, whose journalist husband, Steve, was short, thin, and pop-eyed, but kind and intelligent. "Spicer's very protective of you, Annette, especially now you're pregnant. Perhaps he's trying to save you from bad financial news but taking it out on you at the same time. Men do that kind of thing."

"It doesn't feel like that," said Annette. "It feels worse."

"Spicer doesn't have a new secretary? He's still got Wendy?"

"Yes," said Annette. "And I don't think it's anything like that. The sex is still fine between us. It's just that we used always to speak a lot when we made love—each offer the other a running commentary—but for the last few weeks he hasn't liked me to speak. In fact, if I say anything at all he covers my mouth with his hand. This isn't being recorded by the answerphone, I hope?"

"No," said Gilda.

"Because," said Annette, "I don't like talking about things as personal as this in the first place: it feels disloyal. Supposing your Steve ran the answerphone tape and heard me talking about my sex life with Spicer."

"I'm your best friend," said Gilda. "You're allowed to talk to me. Think of the things I've told you!"

"In fact," said Annette, "it's rather as if Spicer were plunging about in the dark, in the silence, and it was nothing at all to do with me. I can't explain it exactly. I don't mind, I quite like it, it's just different. It's mindless. So long as it doesn't go on like this too long."

"Perhaps the baby is the problem," said Gilda.

"But Spicer was the one who always wanted me to be pregnant," said Annette. "One of yours, he said, one of mine, one of ours. And I don't think time has changed that."

"Perhaps Spicer wanted a boy? Men tend to."

"I don't think so. I was the one who so wanted to be told in advance whether it was a girl or boy; Spicer said no, it wasn't natural: he preferred the element of surprise. But to me it always seems peculiar if the hospital know the gender and don't tell the parents, as if everyone were playing some kind of cute game."

"It seems to me," said Gilda, "you're just paying the fetus more attention than you are Spicer, and he doesn't like it. I'll have to go, Annette. My other phone's going."

*A*nnette prepared a special supper for Spicer that evening and put scent behind her ears. Spicer liked Annette to wear scent. Of recent months, Annette realized, she had neglected so to do.

*S*picer returned at seven-fifty-one instead of six o'clock, his customary time. Annette took care not to reproach Spicer or ask him where he had been. Nor did he offer any apologies for, let alone any information about, his lateness.

"I'm sorry I called you at the office, Spicer," said Annette. "I know you like to ring me but not me to ring you. I just sometimes get a little upset if you go off in a mood in the morning."

"Um," Spicer said. "I see you have opened the 1985 St.-Estèphe."

"I made a rather special dinner," she said. "Beef olives. I know you like those. So I thought we'd treat ourselves and open our best wine."

They were in the drawing room. Annette had found some

candles and polished the candlesticks. Their light made the heavy gray curtains shimmer agreeably. She had arranged roses in the vases: red and white. The room seemed delightful.

"I thought pregnant women weren't supposed to drink alcohol," said Spicer.

"Just a glass or so doesn't hurt," she said.

"I thought you'd be at the Clinic," he said. "Weren't you supposed to go?"

"It was Father's Night Extra," she said, "so, if you couldn't be there, there wasn't much point in my going. Steve went with Gilda, though. So I had time to cook us something special. And since Susan and Jason have gone to the cinema, we can have some time to ourselves. Shall we eat now?"

"I don't know why you cooked beef," he said. "I don't eat red meat. It goes against the grain."

"Since when?" she asked. "And what grain?" But he didn't reply. He was not in a jokey mood.

"I'm afraid that, without the meat," Annette apologized, serving her husband's food, "the mange-tout and the new potatoes look a little bleak."

"It takes very little food to keep me going," Spicer said. "Fruit and vegetables; pulses occasionally. In fact, Annette, if you would keep the fruit bowl full, I could help myself when my appetite dictated and then we could do without the formality of the family meals which nobody wants; let alone the dinners *à deux*. They must be as trying for you as they are for me."

*   *   *

And Spicer smiled at Annette politely and rose and went to the living room and, instead of opening the newspaper as was his custom in the evening after dinner, opened a book entitled *The Search for the Father*, which had a whirled pattern of oranges and reds upon the cover, and began to read intently.

Annette cleared the table. The baby kicked. Annette hurled a plate across the room. It broke. Annette went into the living room and snatched the book from Spicer's hand and flung it in the fire.

"For fuck's sake, Spicer," Annette shrieked, "what is the *matter*?"

Spicer regarded his wife calmly, only occasionally looking away from her into the fireplace to watch the book burn. He could have saved it had he wished, but he did not so wish.

"Look at you!" said Spicer. "Take a look at yourself in the mirror, ask yourself what the matter is, and try to calm down. You are quite insane."

"But what have I done?"

"It isn't your fault," said Spicer. "You can't help yourself, I realize that. But shall we go through today's performance? First you call me at my office and try to disturb my peace there; you cannot bear me to escape from you, even for an hour or two; you then call my secretary and try to turn her against me. You spend the morning talking to Gilda on the phone about our sex life—I had lunch with Stephen: it looks as if he's being made redundant, by the way. You're totally self-centered and without loyalty. I do not take kindly to you discussing our intimate life with your lesbian friend. I wonder what hold she has over you? When I come home late you're not even interested enough to ask me where I've been. You're wearing scent, so I know that in your calculating way you have sex with me planned for tonight. You do apologize for calling me at the office, which is something, but then you follow it up with a remark designed to make me feel bad, about how much I upset you. You open a bottle of St.-Estèphe '85 without consulting me—you are so competitive it extends even into the world of wine!—and, worse, do so without the slightest concern for the health of our baby. You have so much ambivalence about poor little Gillian, I'll be surprised if you manage to bring her to term. You don't go to your antenatal class—cutting off your nose to spite my face, because making me responsible for your actions is another way of controlling me, and you can't resist a little extra dig, mentioning that Steve went with Gilda. Poor Steve: he seems to have no will of his own. You must have me all to yourself, so you send the poor kids off to the cinema, regardless of what they want, let alone the fact that I might want to see them. You cook beef although you know perfectly well the only protein I can eat these days is white meat—chicken or a little fish—and you overcook the mange-tout in a way that can only be deliberate. Then you break some plates, follow me in here, where I am peacefully reading, snatch the book from my hand, and fling it in the fire. Is that enough about what the matter is? Now, for God's sake, don't start crying or you'll upset the children. They'll notice your eyes when they get back from the cinema. They're upset enough already. Okay?"

"Gilda," said Annette on the phone early next morning, "I am so miserable."

"What's the matter now?" asked Gilda. "What's the time?"

"It's well past nine," said Annette. "I'm sorry. But I have to speak to someone."

"The baby kept me awake kicking all night," said Gilda. "I've only just got to sleep."

"Well, I didn't sleep at all," said Annette. "I was suffering from terror. That's the only way I can describe it."

"Tell me more," said Gilda. "Here's Steve with my cup of tea. Thank you, Steve. You are so good to me. Okay, Annette, go on. Forgive me if I slurp."

"It's a kind of black pit within the periphery of myself," said Annette. "It's as black and empty as outer space, and everything spins down into it and is lost."

"A black hole," said Gilda. "I used to feel that when Jackson, my first husband, left me and I didn't know how to pay the rent. I think you're describing anxiety, not terror. What's making you anxious?"

"The thought of me without Spicer," said Annette. "He said such terrible things to me last night, and I love him and I'm having his baby. How could he? Then he just went and slept all night in the spare room. He said he was frightened to sleep next to me in case I did him some terrible damage. He said I was a madwoman, and eaten up with hatred of men."

"What had you done?"

"I broke some plates," said Annette, "and threw the book he was reading into the fire."

"Well," said Gilda, "you ought to expect some reaction. If you behave like a madwoman you get called a madwoman."

"He drove me to it," said Annette. "He wouldn't eat the dinner I cooked. And he was late home and wouldn't say why. And I lay alone on the bed all night with a headache and a black hole in my chest, and I must have dozed off, because when I woke Spicer had left the house and gone to work, and without a word, without a note."

"You told me you didn't sleep at all," said Gilda.

"Gilda, this is serious. There was a difference in tone. I can't explain it. I'm terrified."

"It doesn't sound serious to me," said Gilda. "He'll ring later in the morning and apologize."

*A*t ten-thirty precisely the phone rang. Wendy put Spicer through.

"Annette," said Spicer, "I hope you're okay. I left you sleeping. You look lovely asleep: I didn't want to wake you. I hope I didn't upset you last night. I seem to get these moods these days."

"You upset me quite a lot," she said.

"But you're better now? It's all forgotten?"

"Yes," she said.

"I love you very much," he said. "None of it's your fault. You can't help being what you are any more than I can."

"Well, thank you," said Annette.

"Pauline just called. She and Christopher want us to join them at the opera tonight. I said yes. That's okay, isn't it? It's *Figaro*."

"That's wonderful," said Annette. "Mozart is always soothing."

There was a slight pause—

"That's not a dig, is it?" asked Spicer.

"Of course it isn't," replied Annette. "How could it be?"

"It could suggest you needed soothing, which means you're not going to let bygones be bygones. Well, never mind either way. We'll meet up at the Coliseum at seven-thirty, then: eat afterwards. Wear something lovely, especially for me."

"Of course," said Annette. "Don't I always? Spicer, you know you have a really remarkable memory? Last night you went through every single thing I said, in order, finding fault. After I'd stopped being appalled, I was impressed."

"I don't have time to talk now, darling," said Spicer. "Though I'd love to. I have a meeting. But, yes, I do have a good memory. That's Saturn's doing, sextile my moon but, alas, also quincunx your sun."

"What are you talking about?"

"Never mind," said Spicer. "Not your world. Must go. Kiss you."

"Kiss you," said Annette.

"Gilda," said Annette, "you were quite right. Spicer phoned. The black-hole feeling has gone. Last night was incidental, accidental. Put it like this: it was a little bit of emotional flotsam, washed up by the tides of togetherness. In ten years there'd be quite a lot to wash up."

"How poetical," said Gilda.

"Thank you. I'm so relieved," said Annette. "And we're going to the opera. I don't know what Spicer was upset about and I suppose I'll never know, and it doesn't matter."

"I know what it may have been," said Gilda, "and all I can say is I'm sorry. I was about to phone you. I told Steve a bit about what you told me about Spicer and you in bed, and he talked to Spicer about it over lunch, he now tells me. I'm not speaking to Steve, it doesn't matter how many cups of tea he brings me. It was a confidence."

"I knew that," said Annette. "I didn't bring it up. Spicer did mention it. I expect Steve was only trying to help."

"Steve likes everyone to be happy," said Gilda. "That's his trouble."

"It's over now anyway," said Annette. "It did upset Spicer. But all kinds of things seem to upset him nowadays."

"What do you mean by nowadays? How long has this nowadays been going on?" asked Gilda.

"Two, three weeks. I don't know," said Annette. "Two or three years, for all I know. How would I know? Spicer keeps complaining I'm unperceptive. But how can I perceive things he doesn't tell me?"

"Steve expects me to read his mind and tell him what he's feeling," said Gilda.

"If I tell Spicer what he feels he goes berserk," said Annette. "He says he doesn't like to think of me inside his head, so I try to keep out of it. I take nothing for granted. Gilda, have you heard of the word 'quincunx'? Spicer's just used it."

"No."

"Neither have I. I felt stupid. I looked it up. It's a term used in astrology to denote a hundred-and-fifty-degree separation of the planets in orbit: a stressful aspect, particularly in a compatibility chart."

"Nobody could be expected to know that," said Gilda.

"It was a funny kind of word for him to use in a general conversation," said Annette. "And then there was sextile. That's a good aspect, but it applied only to him, not to him and me."

"Don't get paranoid, Annette," said Gilda. "If you worry about every little thing you'll wear yourself out. Perhaps Spicer's just getting you a his-and-hers chart for your birthday."

"Spicer would never do anything like that," said Annette. "He hates all that kind of gobbledygook. The religion of weak minds. Squelchy. So do I. And another thing—"

"Yes?"

"I wish Spicer hadn't called at ten-thirty precisely. It's as if he had it worked out, and was clock-watching. I'll let her stew till ten-thirty, then I'll call. He didn't phone when he first arrived, he didn't wait till after lunch. Those are the times he usually calls. But this wasn't even any old time, it was on the dot."

"Annette, that's insane," said Gilda. "Ten-thirty is as much any old time as any other. It just happened to be on the dot."

"I suppose so," said Annette. "Now I'm feeling uneasy again. There's a subtext I don't understand. Well, I expect whatever it is will emerge: push itself out like the alien in the film, bursting out of the rib cage."

"What a horrid image," said Gilda. "It can't be good for the baby."

$\mathcal{A}$nnette lay down on the marital bed and put Optrex pads on her eyes.

"Mum?"

"Hello, Susan."

"Are you okay? I've brought you a cup of tea."

"Thanks."

"You haven't been crying?"

"Of course not. Being pregnant makes your eyes puffy."

"Yuk. It's time you had new wallpaper in here. This lot's dingy."

"It's how Spicer and I like it," said Annette.

"Why? It's early-eighties drear. Browny dinge."

"Because Spicer and I put it up together the week I moved in with him," said Annette. "There was no money for decorators."

"That's why the pattern's slipped," said Susan. "None of the little flowers match up. It's a mess, and always has been."

"If it's a mess it's because you and Jason were running round our ankles," said Annette, "and tripping us up. Well, you were running: Jason was toddling. We like it the way it is. It's our keepsake: our memento of the beginning."

"That's nice," said Susan.

"And if we tried to take it down," said Annette, "the whole wall would come down with it. We'd have to replaster the room. That wallpaper was too heavy when it went up ten years ago and it's heavier still today."

"That isn't scientifically possible," said Susan.

"Yes it is," said Annette. "It has sopped up pleasure, uxorious bliss."

"What does that mean?" asked Susan.

"Never mind," said Annette.

"I'll look it up," said Susan.

"Look away," said Annette.

*T*he phone rang. Annette stretched out her hand. It was Gilda.

"Annette? Did I disturb you?"

"No. Not really," said Annette.

"I think I know what the matter is," said Gilda.

"What?"

"Your novel," said Gilda. "He's jealous because you're publishing a novel."

"Why should Spicer be jealous of a novel?" asked Annette. "It isn't even a proper novel. It's a novella. I only wrote it for fun. The children were growing up, and work was drying up, and I had some time left over. And it isn't coming out for months and months. No, that can't be the matter."

"Steve says it might be," said Gilda. "Steve says perhaps it's about Spicer."

"Of course it isn't about Spicer," said Annette. "If it's about anyone it's about my parents, and not even them, really. No, that's a silly idea. It was Spicer who gave the manuscript to Ernie Gromback. It was Spicer who wanted it to see the light of day. I wanted to just put it in a drawer and forget it. Do you know Ernie Gromback the publisher?"

"Everyone knows Ernie Gromback," said Gilda. "He's given herpes to at least a dozen people I know."

"That's beside the point," said Annette. "And I'm sure it isn't true."

"Perhaps Spicer assumed Ernie Gromback would turn the manuscript down and put you off writing novels forever."

"Well, Ernie Gromback didn't turn it down," said Annette, "and why on earth should Spicer want to put me off writing novels? It might bring in some money."

"Because he's the kind of man who needs a woman's full attention," said Gilda, "money or not."

"Sometimes I think you don't like Spicer very much," said Annette.

"You asked my opinion and I gave it," said Gilda. "If you didn't want it, why ask?"

"Don't get huffy, please, Gilda," said Annette. "That's the last thing I need. If anyone should be huffy, it's me. You telling Steve about me and Spicer in bed, and still discussing it, so far as I can see."

"Steve and I hate to see you and Spicer having marital problems," said Gilda. "Of course we discuss it. We couldn't bear anything to happen to you. Spicer and Annette go together so well. The names fit. You are central to a whole lot of existences round here. I hope you realize that."

"Spicer and I are not having marital difficulties, Gilda," said Annette. "We are perfectly happy together. I just don't like him being in a bad mood and me not knowing why. If I knew why, I could do something about it. That's all."

"Okay, okay, okay," said Gilda. "Have a good time at the opera."

"*S*cent!" remarked Spicer, in the foyer of the Coliseum. "I'd rather have you natural." And he nipped the skin of her shoulder with his teeth.

"You bit me!" said Annette.

"I am showing my affection," said Spicer, "in a familiarly uxorious way. I thought you'd like it."

"It's just a little public," said Annette. "And surprising. And actually, Spicer, I wear scent for me, not you."

"Surprise," said Spicer, "is the stuff of life. Why, hello, Pauline; hello, Christopher! Pauline, you look wonderful! How is architecture?"

"In the doldrums," said Pauline and Christopher. "How's the wine business, Spicer?"

"Just fine," said Spicer.

"How's the pregnancy, Annette?" asked Pauline.

"Just fine," said Annette. "No sickness, and lots of energy."

"That's because it's a wanted baby," said Pauline. "One day we'll have time and money to have one. Not yet. The future just isn't certain enough. Everyone we know is redundant or bankrupt. But Mozart will soothe us. Civilizations crumble, art goes on forever."

"Good Lord," said Annette. "There's Ernie Gromback and Marion. What are they doing at an opera?"

"Searching for the culture," said Spicer, "they both crave and need. Do you know who they remind me of? Bob Hoskins and his cartoon lady in *Who Killed Roger Rabbit?* He short, squat, and vulgar, she the dream of his delight. Unreal."

"Everyone's delight," said Christopher. "But that's a harsh view of Ernie Gromback. He may be from the people but he's a decent guy and they say he has a nose for a good novel. Others fail but he prospers."

"And besides," said Pauline, "he's our guest."

"Why, hello, Ernie; hello, Marion!" cried Spicer. "Great to see you both!"

"Ernie," said Annette, "and Marion. What a surprise! I didn't know you were operagoers. Last time I saw you, Ernie, you told me you were a Marxist."

"Marx has let us all down," said Ernie. "Now there's nothing left but the New Age. Marion drifts into it, and I drift after her. There's money in it. Didn't Pauline tell you we were coming, Annette? I asked her to tell you."

"I told Spicer," said Pauline, "and I assumed he'd tell Annette: he's usually reliable. What else could I do? Chris only got the box at the very last minute; I was expected to fill it out of the blue. I can't in person keep everyone fully informed. All I can do is delegate. I work too, you know. Why are you all blaming me?"

"Okay, okay, okay," said everyone. "Mozart will soothe us."

"Gilda!"

"Good Lord, Annette," said Gilda, "I thought you were at the opera. Are you okay?"

"I am at the opera," said Annette. "It's half-time or whatever they call it. Gilda, I think I might have left the iron on in the bedroom, and the kids are both out. You couldn't possibly go round and make sure I haven't? The key's under the rose pot."

"You are impossible," said Gilda.

"Why does everyone think that?" asked Annette. "All of a sudden. Or is it just I haven't noticed till now?"

"I mean keeping the key under the rose pot," said Gilda. "That's all. Everyone leaves irons on. Of course I'll go. What are you wearing?"

"My yellow silk dress, with a bronze silk sash thing which more or less hides me being pregnant, and my silver earrings. I look okay. In fact, I look rather good. Pauline came straight from the office in a gray suit and I felt overdressed, but then Ernie's Marion turned up in red jodhpurs, a white lace blouse, a black riding cap, and diamanté earrings, so I felt underdressed. That means I'm probably about right."

"Is Spicer being okay?" asked Gilda.

"I don't know. I just don't know. He said he didn't like me wearing scent and I was stupid enough to say I wore it for me, not him. It wasn't even true: I was just surprised. But I think he must have taken offense: he sat as far from me as he could, and we usually sit together—you know?—if we can. We even hold hands. And then Ernie Gromback annoyed him by talking about books, and falling hardback sales, and paperback deals, and so on, and then Ernie started talking about my novel, which made matters worse."

"What did you call it in the end?" asked Gilda. "*Lucifette Fallen*, wasn't it?"

"*Lucifette Fallen*," said Annette. "That's its title, goddamn it. Hang on while I put in another coin. . . . They think I've gone to the powder room. You can take forever in the powder room at the opera. It's because everyone goes in their best clothes. Ernie said he wanted to bring publication forward to be nearer the baby's birth."

"Is that good or bad?" asked Gilda.

"I've no idea. I said it all sounded unhealthily commercial to me, because I thought that was what Spicer would want me to say, but Spicer said in for a penny, in for a pound—I ought to make as much capital out of the baby as possible, and I could always go into labor in the middle of a chat show and so command maximum media attention."

"Was he being sarcastic?" asked Gilda.

"I don't know," said Annette. "I just don't know. I can't read him any more. So I can't tell you if Spicer is being okay or not: I'm just not having a good time, which is why I'm talking to you. It's all too nervy. Look, I really do have to go to the powder room now. I must go. Please check the iron. I'm sure it's okay. I'd just feel better if you checked."

"I know, I know, I know," said Gilda. "Of course I will, Annette."

"*I*s there a new one-way system or is this taxi taking us the long way home?" asked Spicer.

"There's a new system," said Annette.

"You haven't the faintest idea whether there's a new system or not," said Spicer. "You just want everything to be easy and pleasant. Well, never mind. Here, give me your hand. You're quite right: Mozart is very soothing. Did you see they were advertising a concert of Indian music? No, you wouldn't have noticed. I expect you prefer the familiar tonic scale: Eastern music would pass you by. But I'll try and get to it, if I can find the time and you're prepared to let me out of your sight for an hour or two."

"Spicer," said Annette, "are you sure nothing's wrong?"

"It is really irritating," said Spicer, "to be asked all the time if something's wrong. I can't be laughing and chattering all the time, though I know you'd like me to be. Spicer, life and soul of the party. You don't notice much, do you? From one-way traffic systems, to Indian music, to changes in me."

"What sort of changes?"

"Everyone changes," said Spicer. "And it is normal for spouses to notice, unless they are hopelessly self-centered. Then it may indeed come as both a surprise and a threat."

Two tears ran down Annette's cheek.

"Oh dear," said Spicer, "oh dear, oh dear, oh dear. You do know how to put the pressure on. How many years have I had of this?"

"It must be something in my stars," said Annette, "which makes me so impossible."

"Many a true word spoken in jest," said Spicer.

"I don't feel in the least like jesting," said Annette. "And why this sudden interest in Indian music and astrology? It's hurtful. It keeps me out."

"Good God," said Spicer, "is a man to have no privacy? No space in his own head for his own interests? His own tastes? Must everything be shared? Common-denominated? A very quick way to end a relationship! I hardly think it's your ambition to do that, Annette. There's too much at stake. Look, we've had a splendid evening out at the opera, your fan Ernie's talked prattling nonsense to you nonstop, surely you don't have to be quite so doleful? Sitting in the back of a taxi weeping when you have everything in the world a woman could want? I know you're pregnant, but you mustn't take it out on others."

"I'm sorry, Spicer," said Annette.

"That's okay," said Spicer. "Shall we kiss and make up?"

"*H*ow was the second act?" asked Gilda. "We haven't spoken for days. Where have you been?"

"I've just been rather busy," said Annette. "You know how it is. I'm trying to get this thing on the Europa myth done, but I keep falling asleep. I really can't remember much about the opera, Gilda. I was too worried about what Spicer was thinking to take much notice of it."

"That seems a waste of an expensive ticket," said Gilda.

"I hate it when Spicer's angry with me," said Annette. "I can't focus on anything."

"He does seem to be angry with you rather a lot," said Gilda. "These days."

"He wasn't very nice in the taxi home," said Annette. "But we've been fine since then. Really. In fact, he's been sweet, in a really good mood. I can almost say what I like without thinking first. Almost. Except—"

"Except what?"

"He warned me on Saturday that the moon was full so I had to be extra careful in the traffic."

"What's the matter with that? All kinds of people say that kind of thing," said Gilda.

"But not Spicer," said Annette, "not in normal times. I looked it up in my *Dictionary of Superstitions* and it said there was some justification in the belief that the full moon exacerbated insanity. The moon pulls the tides about, and since the human body is ninety-seven percent water the full moon may well make minimal changes in water pressure on the brain."

"Are you suggesting Spicer's mad, Annette?"

"Of course not. But who's telling him these things? I can see the moon being full could affect the way people drive cars. Okay. But how can Spicer believe that the planet Saturn, which is eight hundred million miles away, in relation to a moon which is racing round the earth, be what gives him a good memory? It's nuts—"

"You're not still worrying about that? You're obsessive," said Gilda.

"I can't help it," said Annette. "I expect it's being pregnant does it."

"Being pregnant makes me happy," said Gilda. "Not anxious. Did you actually look up how many miles Saturn is from the earth?"

"Yes."

"God help you," said Gilda.

"On the other hand," said Annette, "Spicer brought me strawberries from the market early on Sunday morning and came back to bed and we had them with cream for breakfast. And he put his hand on my belly and felt Gillian kicking."

"That's nice," said Gilda. "It can't be too bad."

"It's wonderful," said Annette. "Just wonderful to have him in a good mood again."

"You won't miss Clinic on Tuesday," said Gilda, "just because you're happy?"

"Of course I won't," said Annette. "See you there if I don't speak to you before. I expect it's all nothing."

"I thought whatever it was had passed," said Annette sadly, to Gilda.

They were at the Tuesday-night antenatal class; they lay next to each other on the floor and waited for the relaxation teacher to return from assisting a woman in the Ready-to-Pop class who had gone into premature labor.

"What's he done now?" asked Gilda.

"Don't talk of Spicer as 'he' like that, Gilda," said Annette. "I don't want to be the kind of woman who complains to other women about her husband. I don't want to get into the what's-he-done-now mentality. It's so vulgar."

"This is meant to be a relaxation class," said Gilda. "And listen to you! So uptight! Don't talk to me about Spicer if you don't want to. I didn't ask, you offered. In fact, come to think of it, I'd rather not discuss it either. We can just talk about babies, I suppose, and dishwashers or, better still, not talk about anything at all to each other, ever again."

"Sorry, Gilda," said Annette, and her hand stretched out to hold her friend's, as it lay gently upturned on the wooden floor. Gilda's thick red hair lay, from the angle of Annette's vision, like a kind of flounced skirt around her head. "I didn't mean to snap. I expect I snap at Spicer. I expect that's the trouble. I'm really difficult and neurotic and I just don't know it. I suppose we all think we're perfect and everyone else is to blame: when really we're the source of the trouble." She took her hand away from Gilda's. "I shouldn't hold your hand, I suppose. Spicer thinks we're having a lesbian relationship." Gilda snatched her hand away and lifted her head from the floor, the better to turn and stare at Annette.

"I was joking," explained Annette. "So was he. Oh God, I keep putting my foot in it. Spicer's right. I'm impossible."

"Perhaps you should have some kind of antistress treatment," said Gilda, "for your head as well as your body. I wish Dr. Elsie Spanner would return. This floor is very drafty. And I wish they wouldn't call the other class the 'Ready-to-Pop.' I'm sure it's calling it that which keeps sending women into premature labor. Pop they think and pop they go."

"You mean me see a therapist?" asked Annette. "Spicer and I don't believe in therapy. It's one of the core beliefs of our relationship. Therapists make people self-preoccupied, selfish, and destructive. Spicer's marriage broke up because his wife went into therapy. He thought they had just an ordinary happy marriage, but Aileen started seeing this man, and, the next thing Spicer knew, Aileen told him she was unhappy and Spicer was the cause of it, and so Aileen left Spicer."

"Perhaps it was true," said Gilda.

"But Aileen left Jason as well, because the therapist said she couldn't have a child and be fulfilled at the same time—the child being the fruit of an unhappy marriage. It didn't sound responsible to me."

"You should be grateful to this therapist or you wouldn't be married to Spicer now."

"That's true," said Annette. "You don't think he married me just because he needed someone to help with Jason?"

"For God's sake," said Gilda, "go and see a therapist! Don't ask me. Whatever answer I give, I'll be in trouble."

The class was abandoned, since Dr. Elsie Spanner felt her greater duty was to accompany the woman in parturition to the hospital and help her with her breathing rather than to conduct the class. In the dressing room Gilda said, "Well, so what did Spicer do to upset you? Notice I don't say 'he.'"

Annette said, "My mother came to lunch. It was Monday. She often visits on Mondays. Spicer looked in from the office to see

Spicer—doesn't drink coffee anymore

Spicer, fight w/ mother

her and have a cup of coffee. You know how they get on. It's a relief. She hated my first husband. He was called Paddy. She didn't like that: she said it reminded her of an Irish navvy, and then I'd have to defend Irish navvies. You know how it is. But she and Spicer get on so well I sometimes get the feeling they gang up on me. Certainly they refer to me as 'she' quite a lot. My mother was talking about what it had been like giving birth to me and how quick and easy it had all been. She'd had me in the ambulance; it had to park in a lay-by and the back doors were open; it was early autumn and the morning sun was shining right into her eyes. She often tells that story. And Spicer interrupted and said, 'Did you say morning sun? I thought it was evening.' My mother said, 'I should know, Spicer; I was there!' And Spicer looked at the cup of coffee I was pouring and said to me very angrily, 'You know I don't drink coffee any more,' and just walked out on us both and went back to work. I made excuses for him to my mother; I told her Spicer was overworking and me being pregnant made him edgy—gave him brainstorms. Poor Spicer, I said, he has so much responsibility: myself, Susan, Jason, work, the house, a recession, and only Spicer to look after us all."

"You mean the kind of excuse you make to yourself," said Gilda, "for the way Spicer behaves."

"It's not an excuse," said Annette. "It's true. But my mother stayed upset and went home with her jaw set and her teeth grinding, which gives her headaches, and I felt dreadful. I always feel responsible for my mother's peace of mind. So I made Wendy put me through to Spicer at work and told him he had to call my mother to apologize, and he just shouted at me down the phone and said I should do the apologizing—I was a liar, and psychotic. If I was born in the morning, why had I told him evening? Only mad people made up lies to no purpose."

"Well, why did you tell him wrong?" asked Gilda.

"I just thought evening sounded nicer, I suppose," said Annette. "I can't remember either way. It didn't seem important at the time. I think Spicer might be right and I'm going mad. I really want to see a therapist, but I don't know how to tell Spicer. I'm frightened he'd be angry; he hates people with soggy brains."

"Your brain never used to be soggy," said Gilda.

"I think it's pregnancy," said Annette.

"It might be Spicer," said Gilda. "We must consider that possibility. Spicer confusing you, making you think that what's his fault is your fault. Steve says he does that. Would you like me to ask around about therapists?"

"Yes, please, Gilda," said Annette. "Secret therapy. Find me a man, please. I'm sure I could talk to a man easier than a woman."

"Hello, Mum," said Susan, when Annette got home from the Clinic. "You're early. I didn't expect you for another hour."

"Why are all the windows open?" asked Annette.

"I've been smoking," replied Susan.

"What kind of smoking?"

"Just ordinary cigarettes," said Susan.

"How many?"

"Just one. I still feel sick."

"Good," said Annette.

"Spicer says dope is healthier than tobacco," said Susan. "If I knew how to get hold of it I would, to see if it made you any happier."

"When did he say that?"

"At six o'clock this evening," said Susan.

"Where is Spicer?" asked Annette. "In the study?"

"No," said Susan. "Spicer went out at six-fifteen."

"Did he say where?" asked Annette.

"No," replied Susan. "He looked very smart. Not suit-and-tie smart; leather-jacket-and-Armani-sweater smart. He was wearing aftershave. You don't think he has a sweetheart?"

"No, I don't, Susan," said Annette.

"I was really shocked when he said that about dope."

"I'm glad to hear it," said Annette. "So am I shocked. Could you make me a cup of tea, Susan?"

"Spicer says tea's bad for you. Ordinary tea, that is."

"I'll have some all the same," said Annette.

"Okay. Why was the class canceled?"

"Because everything's collapsing," said Annette, "and it's the end of the world."

"I hate it when you say that kind of thing, Mum. I'll go and stay with my dad if you're not careful."

"Off you go, then."

"No, thanks all the same," said Susan. "I like it here. We can eat in our rooms. At Paddy and Pat's we have to sit up at table and wear clothes that fit. How's your blood pressure?"

"They forgot to take it, in the muddle," said Annette. "I expect Spicer's gone to see a client. To sell them some end-of-bin at a knockdown price. Did he say when he'd be back?"

"No," said Susan.

$\int$picer returned at seven-forty-seven.

"You're home early," he said. "I thought I'd be back before you."

"The class was canceled," said Annette. "That's two in a row I've missed."

"Now, don't start," said Spicer. "It is these constant nagging reproaches: the drip, drip, drip into the ear. No wonder I'm in the state I am."

Annette apologized and went into the kitchen and made bacon sandwiches and low-calorie hot chocolate.

"You know I don't like bacon sandwiches," said Spicer.

"No, I didn't know that," said Annette. "When we first met we ate bacon sandwiches all the time. Don't you remember?"

"I'm sorry, Annette," said Spicer. "I don't."

"Well, we did. I had just left Paddy, and Aileen had just left you. Proper cooking seemed a waste of time we could otherwise spend in bed."

"Then times have certainly changed," said Spicer. "Annette, I don't think it does either of us much good to dwell on an unhappy and messy past. It's the future which should concern us. And in the meantime, I don't eat bacon sandwiches. Bacon's seductive, but pork is probably one of the worst meats."

"In what way, Spicer?"

"Pigs are intelligent enough to know what's going on," said Spicer, "so they suffer more. On the whole, suffering is always the fate of the intelligent. But one can't be party to it, just because it's the way of the world. What is this drink?"

"It's a kind of cocoa without the calories," said Annette.

"As advertised on TV?"

"Yes," said Annette. "As it happens."

"Pregnancy seems to have affected your critical faculties," said Spicer.

"You mean my intelligence?"

"Since you bring the matter up, yes."

"It's quite a problem to know what to give you, Spicer, since you won't drink coffee or tea any more, and seem to have gone off so many foods. Now even bacon."

"These days my system rejects both stimulants and animal foods. I'm sorry if it's an inconvenience."

"Spicer, are you seeing someone else?"

"How do you mean 'seeing'?"

"Having an affair with another woman."

"Annette, you're more than enough for any man to cope with. I would hardly have energy for another. You exhaust me. First the sniping, then the nagging, now come the accusations, the jealousy. I think we'll find it shows up."

"Shows up where? In my astrological chart? The one done for the morning, not the evening? Is she working on it even now? Are you having an affair with an astrologer? Is that it? Because someone somewhere's trying to turn you against me. That's all it can be."

Spicer began to laugh. He ate one square of bacon sandwich, and half the chocolate drink. He enjoyed the first, but not the second. Then he ate the rest of the sandwich.

"I am so hungry," he explained, "I have to give in. Dearest Annette," he said, "I am not having an affair with anyone. Are you?"

"Of course not," said Annette. "I'm pregnant."

"Is that the only reason you're not having an affair with anyone?" asked Spicer.

"Of course not," said Annette. "I love you."

"I love you too, very much, Annette," said Spicer. "And I'd do nothing to hurt you. Your suspicions are without a rational base. I've told you I'm changing, and in many ways. Please just try and accept it. But there are other reasons for a man changing, apart from him having a mistress! Perhaps he begins to be open to his own soul. I am not the same person you married, any more than you are the same person I married."

"You keep saying that," said Annette, "and it doesn't sound like you saying it, although it comes out of your mouth. Your beautiful mouth I love so much."

"Where are the children?" asked Spicer.

"Susan's watching a video and Jason's playing on his computer," said Annette.

"You're so caught up with yourself and your fantasies," said Spicer. "You're letting this whole family go to pieces. I know it's not your fault. Do you think perhaps you need treatment?"

"What sort of treatment?" asked Annette. "Do you mean for my head?"

"Yes, Annette, I do," said Spicer.

"Therapy?"

"Yes," said Spicer.

"But you're so against therapy," said Annette.

"When did I say that?"

"I don't know, Spicer. Way back when, I suppose."

"I can't remember ever being against it," said Spicer. "I think you must have imagined it, or thought that, because you thought something, I thought it too. Somehow we have to get you less inner-directed, more outer-directed: more separated out from me."

"Who would I go and see?"

"You have to be very careful," said Spicer. "There are all

kinds of quacks and charlatans about. And we have to keep you away from the psychiatrists: we don't want you filled up with pills when you're expecting a baby."

"*We're* expecting a baby, Spicer, not just me."

"Please don't start, Annette," said Spicer.

"Sorry," said Annette.

"That's okay," said Spicer. "I know you do your best. I'll have a word with Marion. She's in therapy."

"Marion? Ernie's girlfriend? But she seems so balanced."

"That's because she's in therapy," said Spicer, "I expect."

"How do you know she's in therapy?"

"Annette, for God's sake—"

"I only asked how you knew, Spicer. I wasn't suggesting anything."

"I should hope not," said Spicer. "Marion, of all people! Marion is more than happy with your publisher friend. He has all the money anyone could want, and provides her with the life she needs. She and I were talking about it at the opera, while you were chattering about dust jackets with Ernie. But there is an area of Marion's life which she's had to suppress; she goes to therapy in order to be put back in touch with her inner self, the part Ernie Gromback denies her. Her soul. Okay?"

"Of course it's okay, Spicer," said Annette. "I'm sorry."

"I suppose you can't help it," said Spicer. "I think we'll find you have a Mars/Pluto aspect which is at the root of your possessiveness. It certainly causes a lot of trouble. Shall we nudge the children out of their rooms and all play Monopoly? Try and have some kind of ordinary family life? There may be some areas of it left we can work on. Get back to normal somehow."

"You were late back. I do need reassuring, Spicer. I know I shouldn't, but I do. I don't want to weep onto the Monopoly board and upset everyone, or give away Mayfair by mistake."

"Darling Annette," said Spicer. "At least you can still make me laugh. I was selling bin-ends to Humphrey Watts and his wife, Eleanor, who live round the corner, in the Mews. There are still some people left who don't mind having less than six bottles of the same wine, just as there are still some who don't mind mixing and matching the china at a dinner party, but in these days of recession a man has to seek them out. You have to go to them; they don't come to you. Why, what did you think I was doing? Laying a lady astrologer at a propitious time? That's better. You laugh too. I do love you, Annette."

"Hi, Gilda," said Annette. "I'm so tired, I can't think why. We all played Monopoly last night and I lost. I had houses on all the wrong squares. Spicer had Mayfair and Park Lane. He always does. I went to bed early and fell asleep before Spicer came up. Did you notice the moon?"

"Not particularly," said Gilda.

"It was such a bright night last night. The moon shone through the window onto the bed. I held up my hand in the light and it shone right through my hand: it was blue and translucent. Spooky."

"Are you okay?" asked Gilda.

"I was only telling you because you're a friend," said Annette. "I'm sorry to bother you with it."

"I tell Steve that kind of thing," said Gilda, "but I suppose it's not the kind of thing you'd tell Spicer."

"No," said Annette. "You can get very lonely being married. The word 'corpse' came into my mind when I looked at my hand, but I put it out again. It seemed unlucky."

"Annette," said Gilda, "we may be only just in time. I've found someone wonderful for you to see."

"See? You mean a therapist?" asked Annette. "But I feel okay now. Honestly. I just get in a state with Spicer sometimes. It's being pregnant. It'll be over soon."

"You need some support, Annette," said Gilda. "Steve says you have a lot to cope with."

"I thought Spicer was the one having the trouble coping with me," said Annette.

"On the other hand," said Gilda. "If you're going for Spicer's sake, it might not work. You're supposed to want therapy for yourself: that's what Eleanor says. Do you know Humphrey and Eleanor Watts?"

"I've met them once or twice," said Annette. "They live in the Mews. Spicer sells them bin-ends."

"Really? How odd. They always seem the kind to buy wine by the case. Anyway, Eleanor was on the phone this morning about the street party. How people do muscle in: it's not going to be just us and a Bella Crescent party; now all the Bellas are going to be involved—Mews, Road, Street, Lane, as well as the Crescent. What was I saying?"

"Therapists," said Annette.

"I'm just rambling, sorry." said Gilda. "I'm nervous. It seems such a responsibility recommending a therapist. Supposing they give you the wrong advice? It would all be my fault."

"Apparently they don't exactly give advice. They resolve your inner problems," said Annette.

"What inner problems?"

"You were the one who suggested therapy, Gilda," said Annette. "And now even Spicer says it's a good idea, so I suppose I must have these inner problems, whatever they are. How does Eleanor Watts come to know about therapists? She doesn't seem the kind."

"It's very fashionable, all of a sudden. Eleanor goes to one in Hampstead. They're mostly in Hampstead: there's a real shortage of them down here. Someone ought to fill in the gap in the market. Nice large houses, too big for just families, just right for clinics."

"This house is just right for my family. I love it," said Annette. "It isn't too large at all."

"Don't change the subject, Annette," said Gilda. "Eleanor's man is called Dr. Herman Marks. He's very famous. He writes books on the power of touch. One of his patients has just left, so you're in luck: he has space for another. But you'll have to act fast. Eleanor says she'll mention you to him. She seemed very keen for you to go, I don't know why. Well, I do. Eleanor lives in the Mews. People in the Crescent have bigger houses than people in the Mews, so Eleanor sees a way of upgrading herself, if only by association. She wants you and her to share a therapist. That's the way her mind works."

"Then this Dr. Marks doesn't seem to have done her much good," said Annette.

"Think how much worse she might be without him," said Gilda.

"So now Eleanor Watts knows I'm mad," said Annette. "Honestly, Gilda! Well, I suppose I'd better at least make an appointment. Eleanor buys our bin-ends, I see her therapist. That's the way the world goes round. And at least it's a man. It would be nice to talk to a man, not always women."

"Thank you very much, Annette."

"I didn't mean you, Gilda, you know I didn't. I don't know what I'd do without you."

"*S*picer," said Annette, "I seem to have found a therapist. So don't ask anyone else for names. I don't want everyone knowing how nuts I am."

"You're a bit late," said Spicer. "I asked your friend Ernie's Marion to put forward a few names. She recommends anyone affiliated to the AAP, the Association of Astrological Psychotherapists."

"She would be into all that gobbledygook," said Annette. "I thought you said to be careful of quacks?"

"Don't mock what you don't know about," said Spicer. "The AAP is affiliated to AJAP, the Association of Jungian and Allied Psychotherapists, extremely serious people. Who have you found?"

"A Dr. Herman Marks in Hampstead," said Annette.

Spicer was silent for a little. Then he said, "If that's the way the cookie crumbles, that's the way it crumbles."

"There's very little to say," said Annette, "and I'm sorry for wasting your time. I'm sure there are others far worse off than me. It's just I've been happily married for ten years and now I've become pregnant I find myself catching my husband out in every little thing; I'm even beginning to think he might be having an affair. I know he isn't, but the thought just somehow sticks around, and he's getting fed up with the way I behave."

Dr. Marks laughed: it was a gentle and surprisingly seductive laugh. Annette wondered what it would be like to be engulfed and enfolded by this man, and if there was a Mrs. Marks, and what kind of person she would be.

"Quite probably," said Dr. Marks, "that is a simple matter of projection. You have had an affair, or two, or three, during the course of your relationship with Spicer: now you are pregnant and feel helpless, and your guilt, your unresolved shadow-side, comes back to persecute you."

"You can do something about me, then?"

"My analysis makes sense to you?"

"Yes."

"Then I imagine a cure will easily be found. By cure I mean understanding, peace of mind. You are not a demonstrative person, I can see that. But, then, you are English: it is not surprising or in itself a cause for concern, as it would be, say, for a Mediterranean woman."

"How do you know I am not a demonstrative person? Other people think I am. My husband, Spicer, says I go round touching people far too much."

"You huddle away from me. Touch my hand. What does that make you feel?"

"Trapped," she replied. "Well, you grabbed it. Please let go. You're hurting."

"Trapped," he repeated. "We will work with that, since it's the best we can do."

"Well?" asked Gilda. "How did it go? Is he attractive?"

"I don't know," said Annette. "He was like a great lump of granite, sitting in a wing chair by the fire. He overflowed its edges."

"That doesn't sound like granite," said Gilda.

"You asked what he was like. I'm doing my best. He was about sixty. His face was hairy, as if greenish-gray shrubs were growing out of a mountainside. They came out all over his face: from his nostrils, his ears, over his eyes, out of his scalp, where they at least pretended to be head hair, not foliage."

"You're making this up," said Gilda.

"I'm not," said Annette. "He's just a man with a lot of facial hair. He has a hooked nose and his mouth's crooked. I thought perhaps he'd had a stroke. He spoke mid-European: the kind that's designed to make you feel foolish. He had an old watch on a chain, which he swung to and fro."

"It sounds a nightmare," said Gilda.

"Every now and then he scratched his chin and flakes of skin scattered onto his trousers. The trousers were tweed, so you couldn't see the flakes when they landed."

"And you took this person seriously?" asked Gilda.

"He asked me to touch his hand and I did. He twisted it and

grabbed my wrist. His hands had liver spots and were horribly strong. I still have marks: I reckon they'll be bruises tomorrow."

"Was he helpful?"

"How do I know? I might be in a worse state if I hadn't been to see him. He doesn't seem to have a gender: he's too foreign. Sometimes I think he's making a pass; at other times I think how stupid and vulgar of me to think any such thing. There is a kind of attraction but it's not a male/female thing. He is just a very powerful person."

"But he did make you feel better?"

"I think so. I did some confessing. And that was only the first session. It was rather like lancing a boil."

"Confessions? What about?"

"Well, you know. Various things. A person."

"Who?"

"I'm not going to tell you who, Gilda. It's all over now."

"While you were married?"

"Yes."

"Did you have a fling with Ernie Gromback?"

"Of course I didn't, Gilda. You're insane. Far too close to home."

"I just wondered."

"Nobody you know and nobody you'll ever know," said Annette. "Just promise you won't tell Steve. It was in the summer, when Spicer was away in France and everything was just stupid. You know how I hated Spicer going away without me: you know how I miss him, how lonely and edgy I get. Sex grounds me, that's all. It wasn't love, anything like that: it was just sex."

"In the first place," said Gilda, "I don't know how you had the nerve. And in the second place, I don't know how you were stupid enough to tell Dr. Herman Marks. Supposing he tells Eleanor Watts and she tells her husband and he tells Spicer over a drunken bin-end?"

"But what you tell a therapist is completely confidential," said Annette. "They're like priests."

"I hope you're right," said Gilda.

"Anyway," said Annette, "I could always just deny everything."

"Is this Dr. Marks married?" asked Gilda.

"I think so. There were two brass plates on the door: Dr. Herman Marks and Dr. Rhea Marks. She had so many letters after her name! MD, MBBS, MRC, AJAP, AHTN. I remember those. My father had the first two. I used to polish the brass plate outside our door. Dr. Rhea had far more letters than Dr. Herman did. I wondered if that made him jealous, and then I thought, no, they're therapists. They'll have been so analyzed out themselves, they wouldn't have an unreasonable emotion left in them. I expect they're blissfully happy. Except he does do rather a lot of hugging and touching. I wouldn't like it if I were her. When he stood up he was at least six foot five, and his arms were like a gorilla's. He put them round me."

"Wasn't that horrible?"

"No. It was like being embraced by a cross between a father and a bear. It makes you feel safe and drowsy. When he's hugged all the air out of you he lets you go. But thank God he didn't mention astrology. Gilda, do you know anyone who's into astrology?"

"Ernie Gromback's Marion talks about star signs nonstop."

"Ah."

"But I don't think Spicer's having an affair with Marion," said Gilda.

he wants to keep lives separate doesn't want to hear abt therapy

"Neither do I," said Annette. "He loves me too much. I've made a real effort not to be paranoid, and I reckon I'm succeeding."

"*A*nnette," said Spicer that night, "the fact is that I do not want to hear about Dr. Herman Marks: what he said to you, or you said to him. You have to keep some areas of yourself apart from me, the way I do with you. We are separate people. You just descend upon me hook, line, and sinker: you squash me into the ground."

"It's true," said Annette, as lightly as she could, "that I've put on a lot of weight lately, but most of it is the baby. Our baby." But it was Tuesday night. Spicer had returned at two minutes past seven and was not in the mood for jokes. "And anyway," she said, "I thought marriage was about togetherness."

"Your vocabulary," said Spicer, "comes straight out of a woman's magazine. Togetherness!"

"You know what I mean," said Annette.

"I don't," said Spicer. "Explain it to me."

Annette declined, saying she would wait until Spicer was better; Spicer said there was nothing wrong with him, only with her; her demands were unreasonable, but she was so afflicted in the Seventh House it was not surprising. She had had an unhappy childhood and was taking it out on Spicer.

"But, Spicer darling—" said Annette.

"Don't call me darling: it rings false."

"But, Spicer, your childhood was far unhappier than mine."

"This is not a competition, Annette. And it is no laughing matter."

"If I'm laughing it's because this is silly," said Annette. "In the childhood-tragedy stakes you win hands down, Spicer. I still have both my parents: you lost your father when you were four and your mother went insane and rushed round screaming till they shut her up."

"Annette," said Spicer, "sometimes your insensitivity takes my breath away."

"I'm sorry, Spicer. I was trying not to be too heavy about it, that's all."

"Your mother is still most certainly around," said Spicer, "and hasn't yet done you the favor of dying. How you hate her, poor woman."

"What is the matter with you?" asked Annette. "I don't hate my mother at all."

"I've heard you say so many a time, Annette."

"Sometimes she annoys me, in the way mothers do, Spicer," said Annette, "and I may have said things against her—and confided them in you because you are my husband—but I love my mother, I don't hate her."

"I don't think you know what you say or how you feel," said Spicer. "Your Neptune is afflicted by Pluto and you live in a state of perpetual confusion. We have found out a great deal about you in the last few weeks. Now we have the correct time of your birth, all kinds of things become clear." And he went into the study to read.

"Dad! Is everything all right?"

"Just fine, Annette. A friendly call. How're things with you?"

"Fine. Any changes back home?"

"Everything much as usual," said Giles Thomas, Annette's father. "Your mother wants new carpets. Do you think we need new carpets? They are getting shabby."

"If it was me, I'd take away the carpets and polish the floor-boards, and have rugs."

"Wouldn't that create dust?"

"Yes, it would, Dad," said Annette. "But you could take Mum away for a week while it settled."

"I couldn't afford that if we had new carpets. Interest rates are down again. People rejoice when interest rates go down: they don't think what it's like for retired people who live on fixed incomes."

"But you're managing?"

"Of course we're managing, sweetheart. Don't worry about us. How's the baby?"

"Flourishing," said Annette. "So am I."

"Spicer?"

"Just fine. Reading at the moment, in the study."

"So what are you doing?" asked her father.

"Trying to focus on the Europa myth. This producer friend of Gilda's is trying to link the failure of the GATT talks with Europa's rape by Jupiter in the form of a bull—the bull being the U.S."

"Does it work?"

"I'm doing my best to make the connection. It's just that being pregnant makes you keep falling asleep. Dad, what was I like when I was a little girl?"

"You were the sweetest thing, Annette. The light of all our lives. Bright as a button, chattered all day. You were an only child and a late one; you were worth waiting for. Why? What's the matter? Is Spicer being difficult?"

"Of course not," said Annette. "It's just sometimes nice to hear, and I know you'll always say it."

"Because men can react strangely when their wives are pregnant," said Giles Thomas. "I loved your mother dearly, but even I—"

"Yes, I know about that, Dad," said Annette.

"So keep an eye on him," said Giles Thomas. "Boys will be boys, but there are limits."

Annette went into the study.

"Spicer," she said. "We have been together for ten years. I would have thought you'd have known what I was like by now. Why do you need an astrological chart to tell you? And who is this 'we' you keep talking about which is not you and me?"

"None of it is anything to do with you," said Spicer.

"But it is," said Annette. "Is this other person a woman?"

"The gender of the other person is immaterial," said Spicer, "since they are a skilled professional. You're a feminist; you should be the first to agree."

"An astrologer is a professional?"

"Of course," said Spicer.

"And my chart is bad news?"

"Yes," said Spicer. "Insofar as it relates to mine."

"Then it is to do with me," said Annette. "If you believe this nonsense."

"Annette," said Spicer, "I am trying to read."

"In what way is my chart bad news?"

"You are badly afflicted in both the Fourth and Seventh houses. The house of childhood and the house of marriage. The unhappy, lonely child of elderly parents, a mother badly treated by a faithless husband—we know all that to be true, don't we?"

"It hardly registered like that, Spicer," said Annette.

"Your Pluto being afflicted by your Neptune," said Spicer, "you're so confused, hardly anything registers. Look at us. Your total lack of sensitivity."

"Spicer, what is the matter? Please!"

"Don't upset yourself. You're so excitable, these days. I thought pregnancy was meant to calm women down. The matter is that your moon in the First is quincunx your moon in the Seventh; you simply have no idea how to be a wife. Well, the unhappy daughter seldom has."

"I am a good wife, Spicer. And a good mother."

"Really? Do good wives nag? Are they obsessively jealous? Do they break plates and burn books? Do they blab the secrets of the marriage bed to all and sundry? You have wonderful qualities, Annette, and I love you dearly, but let us not suppose you are without faults. As for being a good mother, you have a kind heart and a good nature but your idea of cooking is a bacon sandwich. Your idea of child-rearing is to let the kids watch TV all day. They are increasingly withdrawn and disturbed. It's quite a worry."

"If it's all written in the stars, Spicer," said Annette, "there's nothing we can do about it, so why worry? I have to have an afflicted whatever it is, to show up in Susan's and Jason's star charts as a persecuting mother. And my parents had to be what they were, in order to prove my affliction."

"Everything's interconnected, Annette," said Spicer. "I'm surprised you don't recognize that."

"How can I recognize anything if it's written in my star chart that I won't? And how can anything surprise you about me, now you know what I'm like before we even begin?"

"Annette, you are becoming upset about nothing at all. Our compatibility chart shows up problems, that's all I'm trying to say. I'm tired. I say things I don't mean because you provoke me. I wish you wouldn't say 'star chart'; you do it to mock and deride. The proper description is 'natal chart.' Now, please, Annette, leave me alone."

"Well, Spicer," said Annette, "if it makes you feel better, I'll be down to the nearest fortune-teller the moment I can."

"You are impossible," said Spicer. "There's the phone. How any woman can spend so much time on the phone beats me."

"Annette?"

"Ernie!"

"You busy?"

"No. Just talking to Spicer."

"I hope he's saying nice things," said Ernie Gromback. "Is he in the room?"

"No, Ernie, he isn't," said Annette. "He's in the study and I'm in the hall. But it makes no difference. I won't say anything to you I wouldn't say if he was by my side."

"That's what worries me about you, Annette," said Ernie. "You won't. He is in your head. I thought you were looking peaky the other night."

"I thought I was looking rather beautiful," said Annette.

"You are always beautiful, Annette," said Ernie Gromback. "But you were distracted. Distracted people are not productive. I need my writers to be productive."

Ernie worried abt. her productivity

"So this is a business call?"

"Of course," said Ernie Gromback. "I have had an offer from a German publisher who wants to do *Lucifette Fallen.*"

"That's wonderful," said Annette. "Will there be much money?"

"Very little," said her publisher. "It's a first novel, a foreign sale, and translation costs are high. But I thought it might cheer you up to know."

"I'm perfectly cheerful as it is," said Annette. "Do you know anything about astrology?"

"As little as possible," said Ernie Gromback. "But everyone's into it. Marion's writing a book on the nature of Sagittarians. I'm a Sagittarian. I talk too much and am faithless. I think of you a lot, Annette."

"Goodbye, Ernie," said Annette.

"Goodbye, Annette," said Ernie.

"Who was that?" asked Spicer. "Your lesbian friend?"

"It was Ernie Gromback," said Annette.

"What did he want?"

"He's sold *Lucifette Fallen* to the Germans," said Annette.

"Trust the Germans," said Spicer. "And trust that little runt to disturb a peaceful evening. That last dig of yours, Annette, about fortune-telling? Shall we go back to that? Astrology is nothing to do with fortune-telling. It is a wonderfully useful diagnostic and therapeutic tool, in the hands of intuitive and sensitive people. And thank God there are some around."

"And I'm still not to know the name or gender of this wonderful and sensitive person," asked Annette, "who means so much to you?"

"I've been advised to tell you as little as possible," said Spicer. "Though in fact she may want to see you some time."

"She," said Annette. "I knew it. You're having an affair with her."

"I knew you'd be like this," said Spicer. "No wonder I put off telling you. She's my therapist."

"Your therapist? You have a therapist? You?"

"There is nothing sexual in my relationship with her," said Spicer.

"I should bloody hope not," cried Annette. "And why does this astrologer/therapist want to see me, and why should I go, and why do you want one in the first place, Spicer? What's the matter with you?"

"The matter is, Annette," said Spicer, "that, because of scenes like this, and the perpetual stress of the rows you precipitate, my blood pressure has become dangerously raised, and I am in danger of falling dead with a heart attack or stroke."

"Your blood pressure? But you're too young!"

"Stress can kill at any age," said Spicer.

"But this is dreadful! What do they say at the surgery? What does Dr. Winspit say? Is it going to be okay?"

"I'm not seeing Dr. Winspit about this. I'm seeing a homeopath."

"I don't believe this," said Annette.

"I shouldn't have confided in you," said Spicer. "I might have known this is how you'd react. No sympathy, no understanding: nothing except hysteria."

"Spicer, you have my every sympathy. I'm just terribly worried. You don't believe in alternative medicine. Who on earth recommended homeopathy? Your therapist? This astrologer?"

"Well, yes," said Spicer.

"And who recommended the therapist?"

"Marion," said Spicer.

"Spicer!" cried Annette. "Marion's an idiot. You know she is!"

"I knew it wasn't wise to tell you," said Spicer. "My therapist said you'd react like this. If I so much as talk to another woman, you curl up with spite and jealousy. Therapy and homeopathy helped Marion's asthma when conventional medicine failed. I started getting headaches, my vision was blurred. I took Marion's advice; that's all there was to it. I don't want to live on doctor's pills for the rest of my life."

"But what is this homeopath doing for you, Spicer?" asked Annette. "Is it working? That's all that matters. I'm sorry, I didn't mean to raise my voice. I was just taken by surprise."

"She's given me drops," said Spicer, "which I place on my tongue every morning and every evening."

"She?"

"Annette, leave off! I can feel my blood pressure rising already. Half human race is female."

"I'm sorry."

"Try not to make me choleric," said Spicer. "It'll kill me."

"Choleric's a funny word," said Annette. "Where did you get it from? I suppose it's a homeopathic term. Kind of medieval. Are the drops working?"

"My blood pressure is down, yes, though scenes like this don't help."

"It isn't a scene. It's just me reacting. What sort of drops? What's in them?"

"I don't know," said Spicer. "All I know is you have to make sure they get to the tongue without first coming in contact with any other part of the body, or they don't work so well."

"Like sex without foreplay," said Annette. "A shock to the system."

"Quite so," said Spicer.

"Could be good, could be bad," said Annette.

"Let's go to bed and find out," said Spicer. "I'm glad that's out in the open. I'm glad I've got it over. Now let's get back to normal."

"Is making love good for blood pressure?" asked Annette.

"Best possible thing," said Spicer.

"I suppose it will give me time to let all this sink in," said Annette. "Think things through."

"The important thing for you, Annette," said Spicer, "is not to think too much. Just accept. Come upstairs."

The phone rang.

"Don't answer that," said Spicer.

"I won't," said Annette.

"Pay attention to me," said Spicer.

"I will," said Annette, and they went upstairs to the bedroom, and the phone went on ringing.

"Wait till I take my drops," said Spicer.

"I will," said Annette. "Spicer, I suppose the therapist and the homeopath aren't the same person?"

"Let's say they're part of the same gestalt," said Spicer. "Annette, will you help me? My eyes cross if I try to do it myself. Thank you."

"What's a gestalt?" asked Annette.

"A German word for a whole made up of parts which you could separate out but on the whole it would be better not to," Spicer said.

"So they could be the same?"

"Actually, yes, they are. She is both healer and astrologer. Now, don't make a fuss."

"She's not making a lot of money out of you?"

"My God," said Spicer, "a man's health is not to be measured in monetary terms."

"Of course not," said Annette.

"Nor is his mind, or his soul."

"Sweetheart," said Annette, "I love your tongue, I love your teeth, I love your mouth, I love all of you. How often do you see her?"

"Four times a week at the moment," said Spicer, "while the crisis lasts."

"Oh," said Annette.

"The nicer you are to me, the sooner the crisis will be over," Spicer said.

"Of course," said Annette. "I wish you'd tell me her name."

"Let it be, Annette," said Spicer.

"I can always sleep in the spare room," said Annette.

"I wouldn't put it past you," said Spicer. "You are inconsistent enough. I can't rely on you for anything."

"Other people find me perfectly consistent and reliable," said Annette.

"Other people, other people!" said Spicer. "I don't like your habit of appealing to these convenient witnesses. What other people?"

"I'm sorry," said Annette.

"Your apologies are accepted," said Spicer. "Rest assured my therapist/astrologer/homeopath has conventional medical qualifications and I am in excellent hands; it's just that at the moment I'd rather be in yours. The great thing about you being pregnant is that your breasts are finally a proper size."

"Yes, but there's this bump beneath them," said Annette.

"I'll forget it," said Spicer, "if you will. Put on your white pleated silk nightgown. I like so to take it off. You are so beautiful, even with your bump."

"I'm not sure the white nightie will fit over the bump," said Annette. "But I'm willing to try."

"Don't talk all the time, darling. Stop thinking. Just *be*."

"Can I just say one more thing?"

"If it's neither critical nor reproachful," said Spicer.

"I wish you'd told me earlier you were going to see a therapist," Annette said.

"I have told you," said Spicer.

"But isn't it just what Aileen did?"

"That's a silly comparison," said Spicer. "Aileen wanted to end the marriage. I want the opposite for ours. I want to live in peace and tranquillity."

"Help me put the nightie on," said Annette. "Just a little tug at the back. I love your hands, Spicer. I always have."

"I love all of you, Annette," said Spicer. "You're like the sea; I love to drown in you. But, like the seas, you have your moods: sometimes you can be dangerous. So I must learn to navigate you. Is that comfortable?"

"Well, not totally any more," said Annette. "You are quite heavy on the bump."

"Turn on your side, then. Is that better?"

"Well, yes, but then I can't see you," said Annette. "I like to see you: the expression of your face. I like to watch you loving me."

"But by liking to see me we have to stay very decorous, very missionary, Annette."

"Something's lost, something's gained," said Annette. "I'll turn on my side. Not too hard, not too violent, please. I wouldn't want you to shake the baby loose—"

"Babies are well locked in," said Spicer. "Nature sees to it. Other women don't make this fuss. Don't make me feel guilty or none of this will work."

"Sorry, Spicer," said Annette. "If I bring my knees up—wonderful, wonderful—you've always been wonderful, like nothing else, no one else."

"Then why can't you be more secure in me?"

"I am, I am," said Annette. "I shouldn't have spoken the way I did to Gilda: I didn't mean to be disloyal."

"You speak far too much to Gilda," said Spicer.

"I'll try not to in future," said Annette.

"Gilda isn't a real friend: she just wants someone to gossip about."

"I expect so."

"The way you go on about me," said Spicer, "makes me wonder about you. You are sure it is my baby?"

"Of course I am, Spicer."

"Because I have to have you all to myself," said Spicer. "I couldn't bear to share you."

"Only you, Spicer, only ever you."

"Not like Aileen."

"Never, never like Aileen," said Annette. "Spicer, not so rough. Spicer, whatever you like—but you are tearing my best nightdress."

"It's too tight over the bump; why did you wear it? Please don't talk, it distracts me—turn over, talk into the pillow if you have to—"

"I don't want to turn over," said Annette.

"Why not? I love every bit of you, every part of you," said Spicer.

"I want to be able to say that too," said Annette. "To your face, not to a pillow."

"Do as I say," said Spicer.

"Oh, very well," said Annette.

"I love you," said Spicer into his wife's ear. "So much love must be good for the baby. It couldn't possibly harm it: that's what Rhea says. There, I've told you. Dr. Rhea Marks, my therapist. Annette, I'm coming, I can't help it, you moved so suddenly— come with me—please—"

"I am, I am. There."

"There. Oh my God. I love you, Annette."

Spicer brought Annette some orange juice and sat in the blue basket chair by the bed.

"You were faking, weren't you?" said Spicer.

"I was not," said Annette.

"Yes you were. I can always tell."

"I'd quite like to go to sleep now, Spicer," said Annette.

"You never talk when I want to talk," said Spicer. "You always talk when I'd rather you didn't."

"I expect I'm afflicted in my planets. Ask Dr. Rhea Marks. She'll tell you all about it."

"Sulky, sulky!" said Spicer. "Rhea told me it would happen. Spouses feel resentful if an outsider, as they see it, comes into the marriage. But of course it isn't like that."

"Isn't it?"

"Good God, no," said Spicer. "Is your seeing Dr. Herman

Marks coming between you and me? No. The opposite is true. Weren't we together just now? You were wonderful. He's already dispersed some of the frigidity."

"But I've never been frigid," said Annette. "What do you mean?"

"Lilith is cold," said Spicer. "Lilith is the devourer of children, the hater of men. Lilith stops women coming. See Dr. Herman as Saturn: only Saturn can deal with Lilith."

"What are you talking about, Spicer? You're frightening me."

"You mustn't be frightened," said Spicer. "I'm coming back into bed. We have to drive Lilith out. You were faking."

"I was not so, Spicer," said Annette. "I want to go to sleep. Please. I'm pregnant."

"Spoilsport. Talk to me."

"Very well," said Annette. "Is Dr. Rhea young and attractive? Or is she the female equivalent of her husband?"

"She's kind of in the middle," said Spicer. "I do not have a sexual relationship with her. Okay? And I've never even met her husband. It seems such a waste for the baby to have your breasts."

"It won't be for long," said Annette. "Then you can have them back. Do you see her in the house in Maresfield Gardens?"

"Yes. But it's on a lease from the AJAP. They have to move out soon."

"The AJAP?" asked Annette.

"The Association of Jungian and Allied Psychotherapists," said Spicer. "Very reputable, very respectable. She was well recommended. I'm not a fool."

"If you go to the same house, how come you haven't met her husband?" asked Annette.

"I like your knees," said Spicer. "I've always liked your knees. Part them just a little. If I haven't met her husband it's because antisynchronicity is almost as strong a force in the universe as synchronicity."

"I must say," said Annette, "this is rather like being in bed with a stranger. I've never heard you talk like this."

"All the more exciting," said Spicer. "We have layer upon layer with which to encounter each other. You are so hot between your legs since you've been pregnant. It's almost worth it."

"I suppose Dr. Herman and Dr. Rhea won't get together to discuss our cases?" asked Annette.

"I wouldn't think so," said Spicer. "It wouldn't be ethical. Why, have you got something to hide?"

"No," said Annette.

"That's just as well," said Spicer. "I'm coming in you now."

"*G*ilda?"

"What is it, Annette? It's very early to ring."

"I'm sorry," said Annette. "But I have to tell someone."

"Could it possibly wait, Annette? Because I'm having breakfast with Steve, and he doesn't like me on the phone when he's in the house."

"Oh, very well," said Annette. "Don't worry. It can wait. It's probably better if I don't tell you. Spicer's coming out of the bathroom now, anyway, so I can't talk either. If you and me were earning more than peanuts and Steve and Spicer were househusbands, would we be the way they are about using the phone?"

"I don't think so," said Gilda.

"I don't think so either," said Annette. "Bye."

"*I*s something the matter, Spicer?" asked Annette.

"For God's sake, Annette," said Spicer. "I am sitting in my dressing gown, drinking orange juice, and reading the morning paper, like any other husband. What should be the matter?"

"You don't look at me, you don't speak to me. You're angry."

"I am not in the least angry. I will put down my paper. Speak to me, I will speak back."

"When you thought I was born in the evening, did I seem a nicer person?" asked Annette.

"Let us say you had fewer life problems," said Spicer. "And so did I. The evening sun was cuspate. But your morning sun remains firmly in Virgo; it hasn't even begun to move over into Libra."

"I see," said Annette. "Is that bad?"

"Nothing in astrology is bad in itself," said Spicer. "But Virgos have a problem with their sexuality. They hold back. Librans are more giving. They don't have to fake."

"Good Lord," said Annette. "Who'd have thought it!"

"Which of course is not a source of grief for the Virgo," said Spicer, "on the contrary, but can be to the Sun-Aquarian who marries her."

"I really wish," said Annette, "my mother had kept her legs closed a little longer, at least until evening."

"Try not to be so insensitive," said Spicer.

"I'm sorry," said Annette. "Besides the sun in the wrong place, what else?"

"For God's sake," said Spicer, "I'm trying to explain that nothing in astrology is 'wrong.' No one is to blame. It is just useful to locate the problem areas. We now find your moon is square my Neptune in my Seventh; this does suggest marital upsets."

"But you're to blame as much as me if it's your Neptune, not mine."

"You're simply trying to provoke me, Annette. You are being stupid on purpose."

"I'm sorry," said Annette. "I just don't seem able to get my head round astrology."

"It's not an easy subject. It took Rhea years to get her degree."

"Her *degree?*" inquired Annette. "Who on earth gives degrees in astrology?"

"There are very reputable associations in existence which supervise training and issue qualifications," said Spicer. "It's a growing field."

"You're telling me!" said Annette. "Anyway, I'm put very firmly in my place. Tell me, if I'm so stupid and insensitive, how do I get to hold down a job of work and get a novel published?"

"Your job of work," said Spicer, "brings in a little pin money. You do it in your spare time. It's Gilda's work anyway: you just do the overflow. As for you being the artistic and creative one in the family," said Spicer, "that's another of your fantasies. Your idea of art is a novel called *Lucifette Fallen,* which you manage to get published by a dwarf who thinks he'll get cheap wine from me in return."

"I never claimed to be artistic or creative, Spicer," said Annette. "I never even mentioned the words. I'm a researcher by nature. You're the imaginative one. And the title was your idea, and I'm sure Ernie Gromback doesn't want his wine cheap. Why should he? He's rich enough."

"Everyone wants their wine cheap. When I said call the

bloody book *Lucifette Fallen* I was joking. You took me seriously and went ahead with it. I could hardly believe it."

"You were being ironic? And you let me go ahead? Laughing at me?" wept Annette.

"One thing I have learned from Rhea Marks," said Spicer, "is that it is best to allow people to take the consequences of their actions. For one spouse to intervene to protect the other is in the long run counterproductive. Marriage doesn't mean that life learning stops. Though Sun-Virgos do all they can to make it."

Annette went upstairs to the bathroom and vomited. Spicer followed her.

"Are you okay, Annette?" he asked. "It's important for us to get these feelings out into the open: we have to speak the truth to each other. It is one of the things that Dr. Rhea stresses."

"Please go away and let me be ill in peace," said Annette.

"Now, why does that sound so familiar? Of course, Aileen! How a man does repeat the same mistake! Aileen was a Virgo, just as you are."

"Please don't compare me with Aileen," said Annette. "I keep getting a terrible headache, Spicer. Something's going wrong with the baby."

"I'm the one who's ill," said Spicer. "But Virgos do love to compete. If there was anything wrong with you, they'd have picked it up at the Clinic. That's why you go."

"I haven't been to the Clinic for three Tuesdays in a row."

"You pretend to care about this baby," said Spicer, "but at best you're ambivalent. That's why you don't go to the Clinic. I feel quite drained after my conversations with you. Rhea says this is because you represent the suffocated and suffocating mother. First Aileen, now you."

"Spicer," said Annette, "I am doing my best to make this relationship work."

"Are you?" asked Spicer. "I really wonder. Your problems conceiving? An unconscious rejection of the baby: hatred of the husband? That's what it feels like to me."

"I'm going back to bed," said Annette. "I feel really ill."

"And I'm going to work," said Spicer. "Present you with a little truth, Annette, and your reaction is to sulk. It's the children I'm sorry for. But, not having had the experience of a happy childhood, how can you hope to re-create it for your own children? At least you're in therapy: there may be some hope for the rest of us. Otherwise, God help us."

"*O*h God, Gilda."

"Now what's the matter?"

"I've just had a very strange dream," said Annette.

"But it's the middle of the morning," said Gilda.

"The morning sickness was so bad I was exhausted and went back to bed," said Annette.

"You've hardly been morning sick at all so far," said Gilda, "and it's far too late to start now."

"Well, I had a row with Spicer and I was. Not exactly a row: just home-truth time. He's seeing a therapist: she's the one who's been turning him on to astrology."

"So that's it," said Gilda. "At least it's not a mistress. They do say treatment stirs things up. That's why he's been so moody."

"She's also a homeopath. She's mending his mind, casting his star chart, and mine, and giving him drops for high blood pressure."

"Steve said something about Spicer's blood pressure," said Gilda. "I expect it's all all right. But it can't be nice having another woman helping out in quite so many respects."

"It isn't," said Annette.

"Are the drops working?" asked Gilda.

"Spicer says so," said Annette.

"That's something," said Gilda. "But you have to be careful, Annette. Therapists tends to think all illness is caused by stress, and stress is caused by the spouse, so, to cure the patient, get rid of the spouse."

"I think you're rather oversimplifying matters," said Annette.

"I'd never let Steve go to a therapist," said Gilda.

"Spicer does what he wants," said Annette.

"You can say that again," said Gilda. "What was the dream?"

"I dreamt I was having a row with him and he bit me on the shoulder."

"Like a vampire?" asked Gilda.

"More like a love bite," said Annette. "It hurt and I woke up. Oh, how extraordinary!"

"What's extraordinary?" asked Gilda.

"I do have a love bite on my shoulder and it is hurting. Spicer must have done it last night. Sorry, Gilda."

"That's okay," said Gilda. "Any time. But is quite so much sex good for the baby? See you at the Clinic tonight. Now, do you mind if I get on with buttering my toast?"

"*H*ello, Annette."

"Hello, Mum."

"All well?"

"Everything's fine."

"What did they say at the Clinic?"

"Everything's running to plan."

"Because I thought on Monday your wrists were a little puffy. Did they say anything about that?"

"They picked it up," lied Annette. "They're very careful. They decided any puffiness was well within normal limits. Now, don't worry, Mum: everything will be just fine."

"And how's Susan? Are you spending enough time with her? She isn't still sulking in her room? You should take her out and about. No reason why mothers and daughters shouldn't be friends. You don't want her to feel neglected even before the new baby comes along."

"I'm very conscious of the danger, Mum. But Susan's a very self-sustaining girl. And she has a lot of friends up and down the Crescent."

"And Jason? I mustn't forget little Jason. He does tend to keep himself to himself rather, I've noticed. Not the most sociable little chap."

"He has a new friend, Tommy by name. They shut themselves in his room and play video games."

"Tommy? What sort of boy?"

"Really nice," said Annette. "Peaceful."

"It all sounds a little convenient, Annette. It isn't good to let these intense one-to-one relations develop between children."

"I don't think it's all that intense," said Annette.

"How do you know?" asked her mother. "If the pair of them shut themselves into his room? And do you check the games? They can be really unpleasant, I hear. But it's the fashionable way to bring up children, I suppose. The hands-off method. How's dear Spicer? He did seem a little stressed last time I saw him—you shouldn't let him be so rude to you. But he did ring me up in the afternoon, and was sweet to me. Really affectionate. He's a good man, Annette. I hope you value him properly. A good husband's hard to find."

"I know that, Mum."

"Because men can get a little stressed when their wives are pregnant. When I was carrying you, your father had an affair."

"Yes, I know that too, Mum."

"Our marriage limped along after that: we managed, but things were never really the same. Of course, you children never got to know. Your father and myself were careful to present a united front. And I wouldn't bring any of this up, Annette, except I do worry for you and Spicer, and I wouldn't want to happen to you what happened to me."

"Honestly, Mum, Monday lunch was just a fluke," said Annette. "You can't expect Spicer to be the life and soul of the party all the time. It was really stupid of me to forget he doesn't drink coffee any more."

"You shouldn't drink coffee either, Annette," said her mother. "It's bad for the baby. It isn't good of you. Sometimes you surprise me by your selfishness. But you were like that even as a child: what Annette wants, Annette has to have. If Spicer's stopped drinking coffee, it's probably to set you an example."

"I expect that's what it is, Mum," agreed Annette. "Honestly, we're just fine. Don't worry."

(handwritten note in right margin) making excuse for S mum of her mom

"*A*nnette, why haven't you called me?"

"Oh, hello, Gilda. I've been busy, I expect."

"Because you weren't at the Clinic," said Gilda.

"I know," said Annette. "I felt kind of depleted. I didn't want to be somehow examined and found wanting."

"You sound really low."

"I'm just fine."

"No, you're not," said Gilda. "I can tell from your voice."

"Gilda, you won't tell anyone what I told you last time? You do understand it's confidential?"

"Of course I fucking understand it's fucking confidential. What's the matter with you?"

"Don't be so emotional," said Annette.

"You are so *English*," said Gilda.

"You're English too."

"But I don't feel it," said Gilda. "I was born an outsider. You always want to be an insider. You like to be accepted."

"Gilda, I don't know why I didn't ring you before. It's a great relief talking to you. You make me laugh. I just kind of get muddled in my head all the time."

"That's why you're in therapy," said Gilda. "It will get better."

"Dr. Herman Marks says I'm very English. I always thought it was a compliment, but apparently in a woman it means cut off, repressed. I had the oddest dream about him. We were waiting for a whole lot of vague people to leave his consulting room so we could make love. But we never quite got there. You know how these dreams are. I'm not really in therapy either: I've only been to see him once. All the touching and hugging somehow got him into my head: but he's disgusting, really."

"When are you going again?" asked Gilda.

"This afternoon. Gilda, I shouldn't tell you. I meant not to. Everything gets so gossipy."

"Thanks a million, Annette."

"I don't mean you gossip—oh God, everything with you gets so involved."

"Steve says that too. He says it's my lesbian past. He is quite convinced I have a lesbian past, and I expect he has told Spicer. That kind of thing quite turns men on. All I did, when I was fifteen, was share a bed with a prefect who touched me all over, most beautifully, and I won't say I didn't like it, because I did. Okay? Shall we now forget my being overemotional, et cetera, et cetera?"

"Sometimes I'm glad I'm a repressed Englishwoman, Gilda," said Annette. "And you won't tell Steve what I said about you-know-what, because what's happened, which I didn't mean to tell you, is that the therapist Spicer has been going to see is Herman Marks' wife, a Dr. Rhea Marks, the one with all the letters after her name. They share consulting rooms."

"Oh my God, Annette," said Gilda.

"You don't think this phone is bugged?"

"No."

"Because I saw a TV program about private detectives," said Annette, "and it's the easiest thing in the world to bug telephones."

"Who would want to do such a thing?" asked Gilda.

"Spicer, of course," said Annette.

"Annette, Spicer is right, you've gone nuts."

"You mean Spicer told Steve I'd gone nuts?"

"Not exactly," said Gilda.

"It's as if I'm not standing on the proper ground," said Annette, "but on a rug, and people keep snatching it from under my feet."

"Don't cry, Annette. Shall I come round?"

"No, you'd better not," said Annette.

"Why not? Wouldn't Spicer like it, because of my lesbian past?"

"I'm so muddled, Gilda," said Annette.

"I can tell. What time are you seeing this Dr. Herman Marks again? Because the sooner the better."

"It just seems so peculiar," said Annette, "that I'm going to the husband, and Spicer's going to the wife. And Spicer knowing but doing nothing to stop me. Is it ethical?"

"I don't see much wrong with it," said Gilda.

"Not in itself," said Annette. "But wouldn't they be tempted to talk to one another about their patients?"

"It does happen," said Gilda gloomily. "All London knows about Ernie Gromback's herpes, because a gossip columnist happened to be sitting in a restaurant at the next table to a group of therapists discussing case histories, with names. But I'm sure the Drs. Marks aren't like that. They're original Hampstead types, from the sound of them, and old-fashionedly professional. So no one except themselves would understand the jargon they spoke. What do you think she looks like?"

"She didn't seem to make much impression on Spicer," said Annette. "It doesn't sound exactly sexy: a New Age homeopathic therapist/astrologer. But I suppose one never knows. What I can't stand is Spicer being so gullible. He never used to be. I hold Dr. Rhea Marks responsible for sapping his intellect."

"Annette," said Gilda, "if you take my advice, you won't speak against his therapist, or he'll side with her against you."

"But I'm his wife."

"For a man to be close to his therapist might be worse than his having a mistress. An affair without sex. A meeting of minds. What could you do about it? Nothing. There are no laws against it; nobody to socially disapprove; nobody to cut dead in the street."

"I do see," said Annette, "that I might have a real problem."

"Is that Dr. Herman Marks?" said Annette over the phone. "This is Mrs. Horrocks speaking. I have an appointment with you this afternoon, but if you don't mind I think I'll cancel. I'm not feeling very well."

"All the more reason to come and see me," said Dr. Herman Marks. "A young woman in the full flood of pregnancy should be the happiest, healthiest creature in the world. If such a person is ill, the distress seeps out from the mind, not the body. I will see you at three this afternoon. I went to some trouble making space for you, as you will understand. There are many calls upon my time from people in serious need."

"Believe me, I understand that."

"As we arranged, Mrs. Horrocks. Annette. So I'll see you at three, as we planned."

"Yes, Dr. Marks."

$\mathcal{A}$t two-fifty-two Annette knocked on the door of the Drs. Marks, and was admitted by a woman in her mid-thirties. She had a sweet face and a gentle, welcoming smile. Her lashes were colorless, her eyes protruded, her face was without makeup, her clothes indeterminate dove-gray, and her mousy hair was pulled back in a bun. Her movements were graceful and her demeanor was peaceful.

"I will show you into my husband's surgery, Mrs. Horrocks," said Dr. Rhea Marks, "although you are a few minutes early." Her voice was agreeably soft, low, and tentative. "We do like patients to arrive at the appointed time."

"It is difficult to time one's arrival to the dot," said Annette, "traffic being what it is, and random."

"Patients sometimes just park and sit in their cars outside and wait," said Dr. Rhea Marks, "and take the opportunity to relax, or meditate if they are in touch with their inner being, until the proper time."

"I came by public transport," said Annette.

"What a nuisance for you!" said Dr. Marks sympathetically.

Annette sat in the leather chair facing Dr. Herman Marks' desk. The Persian carpet was worn. The room was hot and the ceiling yellow from cigarette smoke. She fell asleep.

"Oh, Dr. Marks, you startled me!"

"Do please call me Herman. Otherwise I might mistake myself for my wife, and that would never do. Two Drs. Marks in one house! When I married, my wife was my student—the merest miss. Now she outstrips me in everything, including doctorates. You were asleep, my dear. How flattering. How at home you must feel!"

"Well, I'm awake now, Dr. Marks. If you don't mind, I won't call you Herman. It seems so informal."

"You are very nervous today, I can tell. In a very English mood," said Dr. Herman.

"I told you I was not feeling very well," said Annette.

"And how does this mysterious 'not well' affect you?"

"I have a permanent headache," said Annette. "There seems to be a kind of space in my head where things aren't connecting."

"You put it very well," said Dr. Herman. "Things 'not connecting.' Well, we will help if we can. Do you often get these headaches?"

"No."

"But you have today. I wonder why?"

"I'm not getting enough sleep," said Annette. "And when I do sleep I get dreams which wake me up. Or else it's the baby kicking. I don't know."

"And I figure in these dreams?"

"Well, yes, come to think of it."

"In what way?" asked Dr. Herman. He bent towards her. The hairs in his nostrils were black, thick, and curly. There was gray in his hair but not in his nostrils.

"Do we have to go into all this?"

"I think perhaps we do," said Dr. Herman. "And in some detail. You must learn to trust me; not to hold back. There is no blame in our sexual fantasies. You have already trusted me with many confidences. I really would prefer you to call me Herman. See me as a father, be a good daughter: call me what I ask."

"I could call you Dr. Herman," said Annette.

"Thank you, Annette," said Dr. Herman. "That is a satisfactory compromise. Many of your troubles stem from your being the daughter of a perhaps too loving father."

"That simply is not the case," said Annette. "He seemed to love me just about right. Still does."

"These memories are often buried," said Dr. Herman. "It does not mean they are not there, simply that you have overlaid them. See what has just happened? I instructed you to call me Herman. At first you refuse; then you change your mind and obey, from which I deduce that you see me as the father, you oblige me with your obedience. You were unwilling; but how easily I am able to override you."

"I just wanted you to stop going on about it," said Annette.

"You just wanted the father to stop," said Dr. Herman. "How often do we not hear that story?"

"Now, hang on a minute," said Annette.

"I think you protest too much, Annette. You identify me with your father; then you dream of me in intimate terms: now, what are we to make of that? It was almost the first thing you told me. Practically bursting out of your lips."

"Actually, I've got too bad a headache to make much of anything, Dr. Marks. Dr. Herman. But I can promise you I was not the victim of child abuse at the hands of my father."

"At the hands of your father? Or something worse than hands?"

"Do you have any aspirin?" asked Annette.

"Perhaps we should take your blood pressure," said Dr. Herman. "If you are having headaches. Just stand here beside me. There is no need to be nervous of physical contact. I am not your father in the real world, though in your dreams you fantasize that I am."

"I can go to my own doctor to have my blood pressure taken. Really, I'd rather."

"But will you? Since you are avoiding treatment for both yourself and your baby?"

"How do you know I'm avoiding treatment?"

"You see! I am right. You are ambivalent about your baby. So others must look after it! Roll up your sleeve, please: I will wrap this black collar round your arm. The sleeve higher, please. It won't roll up any further? Then I think you should take your blouse off altogether. When I have taken your blood pressure, I will need to listen to your heart anyway. Don't be prudish. I am a medical doctor. I have seen many a bare bosom in my time, even younger and prettier than yours—what are you ashamed of?"

Dr. Ing getting her to take off blouse

"*G*ilda," wept Annette, "please come and help me."

"Where are you? What's the matter?"

"I'm in a phone box at Finchley Road Station."

"What's happened?"

"Gilda, it's terrible. Awful. I'm in such a state."

"Shall I get hold of Spicer?"

"No, just you. Quickly, please."

"*O*h, thank you, Gilda. You are so kind," said Annette.

"Just lie and soak in the bath, Annette. It will stop you trembling. Are you hurt anywhere? He didn't actually rape you?"

"Oh no, no," said Annette. "Of course not. His wife was in the house."

"Well, what?"

"First he made me stand there without anything at all on top—"

"Not even your bra? Most doctors let you keep your bra on when they take your blood pressure."

"He forgot about my blood pressure as soon as my blouse was off. He kept saying he wanted to listen to my heart," said Annette. "Then he complained about the little wired metal rose in the center of my bra: he said it was interfering with the electronics of his stethoscope, so would I take the bra off, and I felt stupid not wanting to, as if I was seeing sexual implications when there weren't any. What made me think I was so attractive anyway: pregnant women aren't exactly fanciable by all and sundry, are they? A breast's a breast in a medical context. So I took it off, but then he said there was something wrong with his stethoscope after all, and I just had to stand there while he found another, not sure whether I was meant to put my bra back on. There comes a moment when modesty is almost more suggestive than anything else. Then he did listen to my heart, and to my back while I coughed. He said my heart was okay. So what else was new! Then he felt my nipples, and said they were very engorged, and not very attractive, and my husband could hardly like them in that state. Then he pinched them, first one, then the other: he told me to see if they'd retract—"

"Why didn't you just kick him in the balls and run?"

"I was kind of paralyzed. It was so hard to believe. I thought it might be genuine, some kind of middle-European nipple test. How was I to know? He told me he was just making sure they"

A was assulted by Dr. Herman

were healthy," said Annette. "That it was extra estrogen, not malignancy, which was smudging them."

"So you just stood there?"

"I was so taken by surprise," said Annette. "He seemed to be suggesting the reason I had marital difficulties was because Spicer must find me unattractive."

"What marital difficulties?" asked Gilda.

"I have no idea. It was just somehow assumed I had them," said Annette. "And I thought perhaps he's right. Perhaps Spicer doesn't fancy me any more. Then I thought, no, that's absurd, the way Spicer's been carrying on lately: if I'm tired it's because of Spicer. So I fought back, Gilda. I said, why are you trying to humiliate me? And do you know what he said? He said because the more I identified him with my father the better. He said he had to rework the trauma and then I'd be better."

"Oh dear God," said Gilda.

"And I was still puzzling over that when he began to palpate my breasts—you know how the nurse does it at the Clinic, checking for lumps so you don't have to have the mammogram and be slammed up between those metal plates. By that time, he was standing behind me. And I somehow came to, and said, what are you doing, is that really necessary? He just snapped that it was, because pregnant women can get a galloping form of breast cancer, did I know that, so I had to be checked. I couldn't work out whether he was a doctor, my father, or this horrible man with black hairs coming out of his nostrils. Then those long, long arms were hugging me from behind: the way he'd done the week before, but now he was talking this junk about undoing the trauma; about how I had to love the touch of the father in adult life, as I had learned to loathe it in infancy; and this long, hard thing was pressing into my back, so I shrieked and turned round and hit his face, and grabbed my clothes and ran. I suppose that counts as an indecent assault, but who'd ever believe me? He'd just deny it and say it was therapy. His wife was in the hall, arranging roses, can you believe? Dr. Rhea Marks. The one Spicer so adores. I bet she'd been listening in. I pushed past her and let myself out the front door, and she just stared after me. I had to stop to put on my shirt, can you believe it? In the street? Then I ran on down to the station and called you. I don't think anyone saw me. Are my nipples really so horrible?"

"They look quite ordinary to me," said Gilda, "though they have kind of spread, I suppose. Some women at the Clinic have far worse. Theirs are kind of chocolate-brown, yours are coffee."

"That's something," said Annette. "I suppose."

"You don't think you imagined it?" Gilda asked. "Women do fantasize about doctors."

"Of course I didn't imagine it," said Annette. "Would I imagine phrases like 'the homeopathy of humiliation'? 'The rebirth of response'? I'd be ashamed even to make them up."

"I don't know, Annette. It does seem unlikely, but, then, so does being assaulted by a therapist. The human brain is very strange, especially when it's pregnant."

"Whose side are you on?"

"Yours. I was just theorizing," said Gilda. "For all we know, what Dr. Herman Marks was doing is a perfectly accepted form of therapy. It sounds reasonable to me. Sexual rehabilitation via the therapist. A cure for child-abuse trauma. Identify the therapist with the father, relive the original experience as an adult, and bingo."

"It sounds disgusting to me," said Annette, "especially as I wasn't traumatized as a child."

"That's what you say. But supposing this doctor is right, and you've buried the memory? And now he's cured you anyway. You'd never know. Well, if it's orgasms, orgasms, orgasms from now on in, I suppose you will. Are you going to tell Spicer?"

"I don't think he's going to want to know," said Annette.

"I can always tell Steve," said Gilda. "And Steve will go round and beat Dr. Herman Marks up. He would if it happened to me."

"Spicer will only think I led him on," said Annette. "He'll only blame me. Or he'll say I was fantasizing. Perhaps I was? But what was I doing at Finchley Road Station trembling and with my bra in my pocket if it didn't happen?"

"It's a hot day," said Gilda. "Your bra might have got too tight and you just took it off."

"I'd never have taken off my bra just because it was hot," said Annette. "My breasts have got so big they bounced all the way down the hill. I hated that. Of course it really happened."

"I'll bring you some champagne," said Gilda.

"Well, just a glass. More would be bad for baby," said Annette.

"What was your blood pressure," asked Gilda, "as a matter of interest?"

"He never got round to taking it," said Annette. "And the other reason I can't tell Spicer is because you're right: he'd be more anxious to protect Dr. Rhea Marks than he would me. If he didn't believe me, he'd be angry because I was causing unpleasantness; if he did believe me, he might decide to rescue Dr. Rhea Marks from Dr. Herman. She wasn't exactly pretty: just sort of helpless, and she has a very little voice, with which she puts you in your place. And I can just see her gazing up at Spicer with her pale pop-eyes, and flattering him by talking about his soul."

"I suppose not many people talk to wine merchants about their souls," said Gilda.

"Probably not," said Annette. "I'd better get dry and go home, and face whatever happens next."

"*A*nnette?"

"Oh, hi, Spicer."

"You were a long time answering," said Spicer on the phone. Have you just come in?"

"Yes," said Annette.

"Where were you?" asked Spicer. "Out gadding with your beloved Gilda? I had your friend Ernie on the phone. He was trying to get hold of you. You didn't even put the answerphone on."

"I forgot," said Annette.

"If you forget, there's very little point in owning one, wouldn't you think?"

"I was out seeing my therapist," said Annette. "I got nervy."

" 'My therapist'! I knew it would happen," said Spicer. "You have joined the ranks of the ladies-in-treatment. Now at last my Annette can hold her head up in the cafés and coffee shops! She will be equal in the beauty parlors and the hair salons. Oh, to be a lady of leisure, and the doors of the soul held open wide."

"You're very lyrical, Spicer, considering it was your idea I went in the first place."

"I think you misremember it, Annette. You misremember so much."

"Anyway, Spicer, you go to a therapist too."

"It's hardly the same," said Spicer.

"I don't understand why not," said Annette. "Unless it's different for men."

"You're very sharp and edgy today, Annette," said Spicer. "Let me put it like this: men, unlike women, seldom seek therapy for trivial reasons. Rhea Marks is a Jungian, a transcendentalist. Herman Marks, her husband, is an eclectic: a behaviorist. I am seeking treatment from the first, you from the second. How did you get on with him this time?"

"Not very well, actually," said Annette. "I don't think I like him very much. In fact, I think I'll stop seeing him."

"Oh dear, oh dear," said Spicer. "Oh, the whims and fancies. First I will, then I won't. You do find it difficult to persist in anything, Annette. Not even our baby's welfare has done anything to steady you down."

"For God's sake, Spicer—"

"If you're going to be unpleasant, there's very little point in ringing you."

The phone buzzed. Spicer had cut her off. Annette switched the yellow button over to save the battery. She sat down. She could see her ankles: they were indeed puffy. She took off her shoes. The phone rang again.

"Spicer?"

"No, Mrs. Horrocks," said Wendy. "It's me. Mr. Horrocks said to say he's sorry he had to go and asked me to tell you to call Mr. Gromback at once. Apparently *Oprah Winfrey* are interested and Mr. Gromback needs a yes or no from you as soon as possible."

"*Oprah Winfrey?* You mean the TV show?"

"Yes. She's over here doing a series on literary women worldwide."

"But that's extraordinary. Why should they want me?"

"I don't know why, Mrs. Horrocks. Mr. Horrocks just asked you to call Mr. Gromback. Isn't it exciting!"

"I suppose so. Can I speak to Spicer?"

"He's in a meeting. I always watch *Oprah Winfrey* if ever I'm ill, which is hardly ever. Mr. Horrocks says he doesn't know who in God's name she is, but I bet he does. Well, everyone does. Must go!"

"*E*rnie?"

"Thank God you called back, Annette," said Ernie Gromback. "Where have you been? Where do you housewives get to? I was worried. You're meant to be resting."

"As it happens," said Annette, "I was out being indecently assaulted by a mad therapist."

"There's a lot of it about," said Ernie Gromback. "Anyone can do a weekend course and set up in business. Or not even bother with the course. Marion's thinking of setting herself up as a counselor."

"She's not!"

"She threatens to," said Ernie. "But enough about Marion; are you okay?"

"Just about," said Annette.

"Not traumatized?"

"No," said Annette. "I don't think so. It was a long way this side of rape."

"Spicer didn't say anything about it," said Ernie, suspiciously.

"Spicer doesn't know."

"Funny kind of relationship you and Spicer have," said Ernie Gromback.

"It's a very good relationship," said Annette, automatically. "We're very close and we love each other very much."

"Now that's settled," said Ernie, after a short pause, "Oprah Winfrey wants you to be on her show next week. Literary schmiterary, but she'll shift a book or two."

"But, Ernie—"

"Look, publishing's hit hard times. This is a first novel. You turn down Oprah Winfrey, you do Gromback, Little & Peach a bad turn. And yourself. I have a feeling you need all the good turns you can get."

"But why would anyone be interested in a book called *Lucifette Fallen*?"

"Some researcher picked up an early review. 'The Archetype of the Matrimonial Row: God and Lucifette,' subtitle 'Lilith in Her New Appearance.'"

"Why haven't I seen this review?" asked Annette.

"Because it came out in some nutty, New Age journal," said Ernie Gromback. "Winfrey must have got hold of a proof copy. Probably by way of Marion. Marion's into the New Age. She goes to a self-discovery group; so do all sorts of TV people. Drives me nuts. I'm the only rational man left in the universe; everyone else has gone Carl Gustav. Personally, I'd rather put my faith in a rabbi, but even they are gazing into crystals these days and telling their fortunes by the stars."

"*Lucifette Fallen* is nothing to do with the stars," said Annette.

"It's all cosmos, darling," said Ernie. "All cosmos. At any rate, I'm glad they think it is. There's money in the New Age."

"Can you be more precise about the magazine?" asked Annette.

"I'll put it in the post to you," said Ernie Gromback. "*Jungian Eclectics, Astrologian Psychonuts,* I can't remember. So I'll ask the *Oprah Winfrey* people to get back to you as soon as possible. That's decided?"

"But, Ernie," said Annette, "I don't think Spicer would like me going on a chat show. We never look at things like that on TV."

"Does Spicer want you to earn any money out of this book or not?"

"Well, frankly, Ernie," said Annette, "possibly Spicer doesn't. And possibly I don't, because I can see trouble ahead, and family is more important to me than anything else, and I love Spicer, as you know."

"Perhaps it's because you're pregnant," said Ernie Gromback, "that you're slightly out of your mind."

"I am so not," said Annette. "I've waited so long to have this baby, and I mean it to be born into a happy, settled family. Now, you know all that, Ernie."

"I suppose this baby of yours is Spicer's? It isn't mine?"

"Ernie!" protested Annette.

"Well, Annette?" asked Ernie Gromback. "It's a reasonable question."

"Babies have a gestation period of nine months," said Annette. "The last and indeed the only time you and I had any association of a carnal nature was two years and one month ago."

"You make it sound rather bleak," said Ernie, "but at least you've been counting. So have I, if you want to know. And I wish

Ernie A had an affair 2 yrs ago

Spicer would be better to you, but what can I say? Do this one small thing for me, Annette, since you won't do anything else— appear on *The Oprah Winfrey Show*, in the full flower of lovely motherhood, tribute to Gromback's knack for picking talent. Literary talent, that is."

"But what angle are they going to take?" inquired Annette. "I'll have no control over any of it. Supposing my mother sees the program, and thinks *Lucifette Fallen* is all about her and my dad. Which it is. Oh God, Ernie, couldn't I just unwrite this novel? And it has such an embarrassing title."

"The title works, Annette," said Ernie Gromback. "I rather doubted it would, but since *Astrojunk* has picked it up you were spot on in your judgment. So you're going to say yes to *Oprah Winfrey*?"

"I'll think about it, Ernie," said Annette. "I'm going to look dreadfully pregnant and I've had such a terrible day."

"Husbands are for telling about terrible days," said Ernie Gromback. "Keep it for Spicer, since that's the way you want it. When exactly are you having this baby?"

"In November," said Annette.

"Ah, a little Scorpio," said Ernie.

"What?"

"A little Scorpio," he said. "Marion has me well trained. I'm on the cusp between Scorpio and Sagittarius, did you know that? Wildly attractive but a sting in the tail! Marion's a Gemini. We were born for each other; but Scorpios simply have to scuttle from out of their rocks from time to time to see what they're missing. Marion knew that when she took me in. Perhaps in the spring, when your waist has returned, and you're a world-famous author, I could scuttle past your door and you would look out from your Virgoan isolation—"

"Ernie, I have to go," said Annette.

"But never forget the sting in the tail," said Ernie Gromback. *"Oprah Winfrey?"*

"Oprah Winfrey, Ernie," said Annette sadly. "I can see I have no option."

"Not really, no," said Mr. Gromback of Gromback, Little & Peach: Gromback since 1982, Little since 1921, and Peach since 1810, and doing nicely, even in this year of recession.

"*A*nnette," said Spicer, "I'm trying to read."

"But you haven't had your supper, Spicer," said Annette. "Straight in the door, hardly a word to anyone, and into your study. Aren't you hungry?" The evening sun shone in the window and made all things gold.

"I had some fruit," said Spicer. "That's all I need."

"Don't get too thin," said Annette. "Your shoulders are so broad and nice as they are. What are you reading?"

"Not a book I think you'd understand," said Spicer.

"*Cutting Free from Hurtful Ties,* by Chalice Wellspring," Annette read over Spicer's shoulder. "Am I one of the ties that hurt? Does that include wives?"

"Annette," said Spicer, "the book is a study of the internalized negative figures that can sabotage everything that a man attempts to do. The inner enemies. If you wish to take on the role of enemy in my life, there is no way I can prevent you. But I will then have to do my best to escape you. You certainly represent something phenomenal in my life—last night in my dreams I was Jonah inside the whale; the seas were tumultuous, terrifying."

"I was the whale?" asked Annette.

"Annette, please just go away and leave me in peace, for God's sake! If you see yourself as the whale, that's your problem. Most women would have realized they were the sea. Get on with your own life. It's busy enough, to all accounts."

"No. I won't go away," said Annette. "I'm your wife. I want to know. I have a right to know. Okay, so I'm this inner enemy, just suppose. What does the book tell you to do about it?"

"Invoke the High C," said Spicer. "Now, you won't understand that, you'll just laugh, as the ignorant and antagonistic do. The Inner Enemy all too often takes the form of the seducer, the doubter: the one who mocks. Not surprising you're prepared to hold your husband and family up to ridicule by appearing on a TV show in an advanced state of pregnancy."

"I'm not laughing, Spicer," said Annette, "or mocking. If you are cutting the ties that link you to me, if you are detaching yourself from me, then this is very painful for me indeed. Don't you understand that? That it hurts?"

"How you center everything upon yourself," said Spicer. "You are hopelessly egocentric. A man can be tied to many things, from drink to drugs to rubber fetishes to money, let alone wives. Good Lord, Annette, can't a man even read a book someone's recommended without your coming over all paranoid?"

"Who recommended this book?" asked Annette. "Dr. Rhea Marks?"

"Yes," said Spicer. "She did. As it happens."

"I went to see Dr. Rhea Marks' husband today," said Annette, before she could stop herself, "and he indecently assaulted me. Perhaps he does that to all his patients. Perhaps Dr. Rhea's decided to get rid of pathetic old Herman Marks and Spicer Horrocks would do very nicely, thank you. Wine merchant in prime of life,

A tells S abt. assult ⇒ offers no sympathy

energetic in bed—merely persuade him to cut the ties that hurt, and *voilà*!"

"Perhaps I'd better ring your mother," said Spicer.

"Why?"

"Because you're insane," said Spicer. "Your mother may know better than me how to deal with you when you're in this frame of mind. I frankly have no idea what to do for the best."

"You could close the book and talk to me," said Annette.

"Very well," said Spicer. "I can see I have no choice. But it doesn't endear you to me. Now, can we take these things one at a time? First, Dr. Herman Marks indecently assaulted you? Really? In what way?"

"I don't even want to say—you are so out of sympathy with me," said Annette.

"You can't make these accusations and then just leave them in the air," said Spicer. "People get into real trouble doing that. You need to be more careful, Annette."

"Don't bully me like this."

"What form did the assault take?" Spicer asked.

"He made me undress," said Annette.

"Made you? Really? How does someone make someone else undress?" asked Spicer. "Tell me!"

"On pretext of a medical examination," said Annette.

"Annette, he is a doctor, and you are pregnant," observed her husband.

"Forget it," said Annette. "Let's just say I had to run out of his room half-naked and then out of the house, past his wife."

"Oh dear God," said Spicer. "Poor Rhea. This madwoman running out of her husband's consulting room, shrieking rape. Is this what pregnancy does to women? First obsessive jealousy, then accusations, now fantasies of sexual molestation?"

"I knew you wouldn't believe me," sobbed Annette. "You always side with my enemies."

"Enemies? A middle-aged middle-class housewife with enemies?" inquired Spicer. "Only if she's a paranoiac. Now, shall we get back to your earlier statement? That Dr. Rhea Marks has decided to get rid of her husband and selected me as a substitute? You do see that this can only be the product of a distressed mind?"

"I know it sounds stupid, Spicer, and I'm sorry," said Annette, "but why else is she trying to break up our relationship? How can you believe all the nonsense she speaks? She's the one who's destructive, not me. She feeds into your vanity, she flatters you. Something going on I don't understand. Perhaps she procures patients for her husband."

"You have to stop making these allegations, Annette, or you'll end up in prison," said Spicer. "And the more you insult Dr. Rhea Marks, who is extremely helpful, supportive, and positive, the more difficult things will get between you and me. So please, for God's sake, stop. Let me make you a cup of tea. You distress yourself so."

"But things between us aren't difficult, Spicer," said Annette, as she sipped her tea and dabbed her eyes. "Or they weren't before you started going to see Dr. Rhea Marks."

"Not for you, perhaps," said Spicer. "What about me? Could you really believe the rows, the scenes, make me happy? I was becoming ill, Annette," said Spicer. "The stress of being married to you was showing. My blood pressure was up. I could have had a stroke, a heart attack, any minute: thank God I got to Dr. Rhea in time. I'll always be indebted to Marion for getting me to her."

"If you're really ill, and not just a hypochondriac, go to a proper doctor," said Annette. "Get your blood pressure lowered by pills. Or get someone else to measure it, who isn't taking your money."

"Is that your only response? No concern, no love; just to suggest doctor's pills which always do more damage than they do good. You should hear Dr. Rhea on the subject. She's turned her back on the orthodox medical establishment. She's seen too much of it. Now, don't start crying again. I spoke to Rhea today," said Spicer. "She feels she needs to see you, in the hope of bringing you to some understanding of just how drastic my situation is. Just how ill I am: how careful you have to be."

"I'm too stunned to cry any more," said Annette. "Why should I see someone who obviously has such a low opinion of me? Who reads my star chart and says it's shit? I suppose yours is the cat's whiskers."

"It certainly isn't afflicted in the way yours is. My planets cluster in air signs. Yours are mostly earth, and in the bottom half of your chart. Well, there's nothing wrong with that. It just means I am intuitive and imaginative, while you are practical. We balance each other, more or less."

"But I drag you down," cried Annette sadly. "Deject you and undermine you."

"I didn't say that," said Spicer. "But I do think we should go together to see Dr. Marks. She'll have a thing to two to say to you. I'll keep you out of Dr. Herman's way, if only for his sake."

"Very well, Spicer," said Annette. "Make the appointment."

"*G*ilda," said Annette. It was ten past two on a Friday afternoon.

"Hi, Annette," said Gilda. "Why are you whispering?"

"Because I'm in Dr. Herman's room using his phone. It's okay. He's gone to Austria, or somewhere, for a conference. Spicer's upstairs with Dr. Rhea. On the way he said I was very brave to see her, considering what she knew about me."

"That wasn't very nice of him, Annette," said Gilda.

"He's in a funny mood," said Annette. "Dr. Rhea opened the door sort of excited to see me, I don't know why. You just get a feeling. She was on some kind of power trip. Then she wiped the smile off her face and said I was to wait while she saw Spicer for twenty minutes, then she'd see me for twenty minutes, then both of us together, and she showed me in here to wait. There's a chart on the wall of how to search the breast for lumps."

"Didn't you ask her why she wanted to see you?" inquired Annette.

"Yes, I did," said Annette. "I was quite bold. I said to her the minute we were in the door, what are we in, some kind of marriage therapy?"

"What did she say?" asked Gilda.

"She just said, oh, we don't like to call it that, and led Spicer upstairs. She's wearing a kind of pleated navy-blue dress with a white collar. It's perfectly horrible: the kind of thing a nun would wear on her afternoon off. And an old yellowy cardigan."

"What are you wearing?"

"Tights and my old Calvin Klein mustardy top. I'm trying to look serious. Spiritual, even."

A in Dr. H's office, waiting for Rhea, talking to Gilda, convincing herself that she

"What's Dr. Herman's room like? Apart from the breasts. Does it give you the shivers?"

"There's a big wing chair, a greasy patch either side where his head touches it. The ceiling's yellow from cigarette smoke. There are locked bookcases."

"It would give you the creeps," said Gilda, "in the circumstances."

"I think perhaps I did imagine what I thought happened," said Annette.

"But you said he had an erection and it pressed into your back," said Gilda.

"It could have been a pipe in his pocket or a slide rule or something," said Annette. "He was behind me. It might have been some kind of crystal device these nutters use to heal you, I don't know."

"I think the simplest explanation is best," said Gilda.

"But it felt long," said Annette. "Too long. Mind you, it did occur to me that's the kind of length it would have seemed if I was a child and he was a grown man."

"You mean your father?" asked Gilda.

"I simply cannot believe any such thing about my father," said Annette, "but perhaps an uncle. Who's to say?"

"So either way," said Gilda, "Dr. Herman's let off the hook. Either you imagined it, or if you didn't it's a legitimate therapy and you'll end up sexually liberated."

"Yes," said Annette.

"You never struck me as sexually unliberated," said Gilda. "In fact, I remember things from our student days when you were decidedly liberated."

"Just shut up about those," said Annette.

"And you were trembling and crying in that telephone box," said Gilda.

"I think they call that abreaction," said Annette.

"They're brainwashing you," said Gilda.

"I just want to live happily ever after with Spicer," said Annette, "and if I have to turn my head inside out it's worth it. I've got to go now. Spicer's coming downstairs. Gilda, I'm petrified. I don't know why. I just get intimidated by doctors."

"Well, now," said Dr. Marks cheerily, "what do you want to tell me about your relationship with your husband?"

"I thought you were going to tell me about it," said Annette. "That's why you wanted to see me."

"It would help me if you told me how you saw it first," said Dr. Rhea.

"He seems upset at the moment," said Annette. "I don't know why. And he blames me for everything that goes wrong, and he's giving me a really hard time. But I'm sure we can work through it. Marriages go through bad patches and come out the other side, don't they? We've been happy before and we will be again. I'm pregnant and not at my best. I expect I imagine things that don't happen: Spicer says I do. Everything will just click back into place as soon as the baby's born. Spicer and I need each other, always have. Until we met, both our lives were messy. After we met, we got things together. I stopped raving, Spicer stopped drinking. It was love at first sight. We met at a party and went home together and never left each other's side thereafter. Though we both had to get unmarried to third parties to do it. We still call each other on the phone every day. Well, Spicer calls me. He doesn't much like me calling him, because he can be busy: it interrupts the flow of money-making thought, he says. And the children are in private schools; so the money has to flow. We try and give them stability. Spicer and I hate being apart. He has to go away in the summers to France, to see the vineyards: then we both feel desperate, lonely. We're just intertwined. We're so lucky to love each other. Lots of couples aren't like that. By ourselves Spicer and I are nothing: together we add up to something. Well, a lot. Friends rely on us; our families; Spicer's aunts: we're central to so many people, you've no idea. Things have just got to work out." Annette fell silent.

"Ah," said Dr. Rhea Marks, and she got up and stared out of the window. "You must realize, Mrs. Horrocks," said Dr. Rhea after some reflection, "that Spicer would get on perfectly well without you. After all, he has his own friends, his own work, his own interests, his own income."

"Oh!" said Annette, and she giggled.

"And no doubt the same applies to you," said Dr. Rhea.

"Do you really think so?" asked Annette, and she giggled some more.

"Spouses are often far less dependent upon each other than they imagine," said Dr. Rhea. "The close relationship can turn destructive; in response it is not unusual for one partner to develop an image of themselves as dependent."

"My feeling more dependent than usual is nothing to do with being pregnant?" asked Annette.

"Oh no," said Dr. Rhea. "Your feelings of dependence are to do with your close connection to the child: they are the mere reflection of embryonic dependency, which little by little becomes the basis for your unconscious and conscious maternal solicitude."

"Well, thank you very much," said Annette. "If what you mean is I'm just catching it from the baby."

"You are more lighthearted than your chart suggests," said Dr. Rhea. "You giggle a lot."

"Nerves," said Annette. "What you say is quite shocking to me, but I'll try and take it seriously."

"Of course, Spicer, being male, experiences the primordial mysteries directly and indirectly as provocative: a force that sets him in motion and impels him towards change. It is a matter of indifference whether the transformation of the male is caused by positive or negative fascination."

"I'm not altogether indifferent," remarked Annette, "to changes in Spicer."

"But of course in Spicer we notice the emergence of something soullike—the anima—from the archetypal feminine, the unconscious, represented by yourself; so the relation of the ego to the unconscious changes. What you describe as a bad patch, Mrs. Horrocks. It may be more profound than this."

"That sounds bad," said Annette.

"The transformative character fascinates but does not obliterate. It sets the personality in motion, produces change and ultimately transformation. The process is fraught with danger, even mortal peril. Spicer will fight for the preservation of his ego: you, the feminine, are determined to retain his ego as your mate."

"I see. Well, I don't really, but I expect we'll weather it," said Annette. "Haven't we been talking for twenty minutes? I forgot my watch. I'm beginning to miss Spicer."

Dr. Rhea thought for a moment. "Spicer tells me you have been suffering from sexual fantasies of a markedly destructive nature."

"He told you this?" asked Annette.

"He is open with me, of course," said Dr. Rhea. "Don't reproach yourself. The spontaneous processes of the collective unconscious are at their most demonstrable in mental disorder."

"Mental disorder? Are you telling me I'm nuts?"

"My dear," said Dr. Rhea, "don't be distressed. Of course not, or only as the world will see it. You are simply open at the moment to the elementary character of the archetypal feminine. The affected individual doesn't in reality have visions, they occur as an autonomous natural process. You will have these visions: you will communicate them to your husband. The structure of the transformative character, that is to say Spicer, already relates to a personality embracing the spontaneity of consciousness, that is to say yourself. It is a fascinating phenomenon, Mrs. Horrocks."

"Good," said Annette. She polished her nail with her thumb. Her fingers were quite stiff and swollen.

"Spicer's dreams indicate the degree of transformation. The Western symbol group of the Terrible Mothers—night, abyss, sea, watery depths, snake, dragon, whale—all the symbols color one another and merge. Devouring water, rending earth womb, abyss of death, hostile snake of night and death, whale, sea—all aspects of the negative unconscious; which lives in the nocturnal darkness beneath the world of man and threatens catastrophe."

"Poor Spicer," said Annette. "Though I wish you wouldn't call him Spicer, and me Mrs. Horrocks. It smacks of possession. He is my husband. He has been dreaming of whales, as it happens."

"It's understandable that you are resistant. Spouses often are. You fear the anima in Spicer, he the anima in you. You to him are like the enchantress who turns men into beasts. He sees himself as Odysseus, the successful suitor you as Circe invited to share your bed. But danger is all around: to be changed into a pig is the fate of those who displease Circe. Your anima is negative, your intention to poison his male consciousness, as he sees it, like Circe to endanger it by intoxication—"

"Is that why he's gone off drink?"

"You have a frivolity, Mrs. Horrocks, that isn't altogether helpful to your own cause. You are putting up barriers to understanding. Very well, I will speak in language you understand."

"What is my own cause?" asked Annette.

"To keep your husband, Mrs. Horrocks."

"I don't think I am in any danger of losing him," said Annette. "Tell me, do you have children?"

"No. But we are not thinking about me, we are thinking about you."

"I'm thinking quite hard about you," said Annette. "You'd be surprised."

"You may not realize quite how ill your husband is. He collapsed and nearly died in this very room on his first visit to me."

"He didn't mention it to me," said Annette.

"Perhaps he thought he wouldn't receive much sympathy. Your husband's view is that there is so great an unconscious hostility to him that you welcome his illness—indeed, have brought it about."

"Your view or Spicer's view? His illness or the one you've put into his head?"

"And please try not to be hostile to me. I am here to help you both, if I can. My concern is primarily with Spicer: he is my patient and therefore my responsibility, as you are not. But because of your relationship you and he are interlinked. That is why I needed to see you."

"And my star chart isn't sufficient to tell you all about me?"

"It can tell me a lot but not everything," said Dr. Rhea.

"I see," said Annette. "And Spicer can get on very well without me. That's the conclusion you've reached."

"Spicer and I have discussed it between us, and, yes, we have more or less come to that conclusion," said Dr. Rhea. "Spicer is not the man he was when you met him. We all change: you as well."

"Don't tell me what is perfectly obvious, Dr. Marks," said Annette. "And when Spicer so nearly died, or so you say, how exactly did you save him?"

"I am medically trained, as is my husband. We were able to revive Spicer with an appropriate remedy. A natural stimulant."

"You didn't think to call an ambulance?" asked Annette.

"There was no need," said Dr. Rhea. "The danger was over. Hospitals do more damage than most people realize. The body is a self-healing entity. Statistics show that heart-attack victims, simply left to themselves, have a better survival rate than those who are rushed off to hospital. It is the journey which kills, and powerful drugs introduced into a system already under stress. I am a qualified medical doctor, Mrs. Horrocks; I do know what I'm talking about. Now, I understand your hostility to me—most spouses profoundly resent the therapist—so don't see yourself as unusual. The spouse sees therapy as an interference in the life of the marriage: but sometimes a therapist will intervene to help a marriage survive which would otherwise fail, if the therapist judges that is the best option. You feel threatened: of course you do. I understand that."

"I don't *feel* threatened," said Annette. "I *am* threatened. And not even free to ask a second opinion. Are you telling me I'm the cause of Spicer's alleged heart attack? And telling that to Spicer too?"

"Why 'alleged'? Why are you so resistant to the idea of his illness?"

"Because he hasn't been to see our doctor."

"He has changed his doctor, Mrs. Horrocks. I am his doctor, and his counselor."

"Don't forget astrologer. Got him all ways, haven't you?"

"You have a very treacherous Mercury, Mrs. Horrocks. You present yourself as a doubting Thomas, the fool who mocks, the enemy of the self. A great deal of negative energy can shelter behind mirth. You have an afflicted Mercury in the Tenth House."

"So it's just stress that's harming Spicer's heart; not a history of drinking, or smoking, or genetics, anything like that? Not even a negative Mercury? Just stress, that is to say me?"

"The spouse," said Dr. Rhea, "is in most cases the primary source of stress."

"So Spicer's illness is my fault?"

"We are not talking about blame, Mrs. Horrocks," said Dr. Rhea.

"You don't like me very much, do you?" observed Annette. "Or is it just that you love rocking the foundation of other people's lives?"

"On the contrary, I am surprised I like you so much," said Dr. Rhea, "even though you are temporarily so hostile to me."

"It'll all be in my star chart," said Annette. "I wonder what your motives are in doing this to me? Are you jealous because I'm pregnant? Or because I've written a book? Perhaps you're a would-be novelist? Perhaps you've tried and you can't, so you sit there earning a living by writing living fictions, altering the narrative of other people's lives, changing it in their heads—writing your scenario about Spicer getting on perfectly well without me. For God's sake, Spicer and I would both be lost without the other! We have a very special, very solid relationship."

"It has been deteriorating for years," said Dr. Rhea. "But you haven't perceived it."

The baby gave Annette a blow beneath the ribs. It had woken up.

"But this is appalling," said Gilda to Annette. They were lunching at Antoine's. Gilda picked at a roast-pepper pâté, Annette at a tomato-and-feta-cheese salad.

"At first I thought it was funny," said Annette, "and then I saw it was appalling. When she called Spicer in, having totally devastated me, I said, as lightly as I could, 'According to Dr. Rhea here, the next step for us is divorce.' Spicer said, 'No one said anything about divorce: divorce is just a scrap of paper.' And Dr. Rhea said, 'I am glad Mrs. Horrocks can take it so lightly: a separating out would in the circumstances perhaps be advisable.' To which I said, 'Well, in my mind you're either together or apart; it's only eggs get separated out.'"

"You shouldn't have been so flippant," said Gilda. "She'll really have it in for you now."

"But at least Spicer said he'd like to give us another try: if I could be sexually more responsive it would help. And she talked about the generative earth and the phallic penetration of the primeval hill, which was consciousness rising out of the unconsciousness, the foundation of the diurnal ego."

"Was she talking about him buggering you? It sounds like it," said Gilda.

"I have no idea. I hope not," said Annette. "But I daresay that's how Spicer registered it."

"Why do you hope not?" asked Gilda.

"Because, forget the diurnal ego, all he's doing when he buggers me is confirming the shitlike nature of my existence," said Annette. "Rubbishing me."

"Hush," said Gilda. "Not so loud. I don't see why you have to see buggery like that. I quite enjoy it."

"Well, I do see it like that," said Annette, "and that's that. The nonmaternal end of me, as it were. The reluctant hole. Unnatural love. The slippage into pleasure/pain—into death, not life; into grunts, not murmurs; into silence. Then Dr. Rhea gave us this stuff about the uroboric primeval serpent, and the luminous principle, and I agreed to give it another try, as expected to."

"What, the marriage?"

"By that time 'the marriage,'" said Annette, "seemed to be a kind of luminous principle in itself, not just a couple of words which described Spicer and me living together. And I was the one who was somehow burrowing under it, wearing it away, with dark archetypal flood water, and I had to be stopped."

"But Spicer isn't doing anything wrong?"

"No. Spicer is just emerging like a moth out of a chrysalis of unknowing."

"And Spicer takes all this seriously?" asked Gilda.

"I told you she has sapped his intelligence in some peculiar way," said Annette. "But what was most nightmarish was the way his loyalty seemed to be towards her, not me. And his saying I was sexually suffocating and he was an unhappily married man."

"He's trying to punish you," said Gilda. "He doesn't mean it."

"But why should he want to punish me?" asked Annette.

"For the same reason she's doing what she is. Because you can make things where there was nothing before. You're having a baby and you've written a book and they're screaming with envy in their souls, the pair of them. And he's frightened of death, and if he has to ditch you to save his life, he will."

"It does seem to boil down to all that," said Annette. "But what can I do about any of it? Too late! I was born the way I was, and it served Spicer very well for ten years: now this!"

Annette pushed away her plate. Gilda asked for duck and red cabbage.

"What was your feeling?" asked Gilda. "What was the subtext? Is she trying to make or break the marriage?"

Annette thought for a little.

"To break it," she said. "As Spicer and I left, an exciting thought seemed to come to her. She waved her hands in the air. She had serpent rings on her fingers. She said that, since the majority of Spicer's planets were in the creative and romantic constellation and mine were in the active, the relationship was all but impossible. 'Thank you so much, Dr. Marks,' I said, and she quickly amended it to 'needs a great deal of work.' So let us just say that she hopes it doesn't work, so she can be vindicated in her belief in astrology."

"I wish you'd eat more," said Gilda.

"I've lost my appetite," said Annette.

Gilda ordered toffee pudding for herself and a black coffee for Annette.

"*A*nnette," said Spicer, "there is a side of me you simply don't understand."

"I'm trying to understand it, Spicer," said Annette. "What's the time?" she asked.

"Two-thirty," said Spicer.

"Afternoon or night?" asked Annette.

"Night," said Spicer. "Have you been taking sleeping pills?"

"Of course I haven't," said Annette. "They'd be bad for the baby."

"I don't know how you can sleep while there's so much going on." Spicer turned off the ceiling light and turned on the bedside lamp.

"Did you say something?" asked Spicer.

"No," said Annette.

"It sounded to me rather like 'It's because I'm so earthy and practical.'"

"I wouldn't be so smart-alecky, Spicer," said Annette. "I just sort of groaned, I think."

"I hope so," said Spicer, "because I can do without the wise-cracks. Especially at this time of night."

"Spicer," said Annette, "if it's two-thirty in the morning, where have you been?"

"Walking, thinking, dealing with my shadow-side."

"Is that the whale?" asked Annette. "Sorry, I was joking. You must mean the uroboric primal principle."

"I wish you wouldn't talk about what you don't understand, Annette."

"I'm sorry. Can you tell me what 'uroboric' means?"

"The uroboros is the circular snake biting its tail," Spicer said.

"I see," said Annette.

"I don't think you do," said Spicer. "It's the symbol of the psychic state of the beginning. I am a creative man, Annette."

"Of course you are, my darling," said Annette.

"A romantic."

"I know, my sweet," said Annette.

"My conscious ego takes on the female role, just as yours does the masculine. That's the case for everyone."

"So?" asked Annette. "What's the problem?"

"There are power struggles going on inside me. In the creative, romantic male the mother archetype in the collective unconscious tries to take over, so I find myself fascinated by certain things. I can't help it."

"What sort of thing, Spicer?" asked Annette.

"It's known as uroboric incest," said Spicer. "I believe."

"Dr. Rhea tells you all this?"

"Yes. It's dangerous, perilous, Annette," said Spicer. "It can lead to madness, or death. God, I wish I were married to someone who understood me."

"Just come to bed, Spicer. You seem terribly distressed about nothing."

"You're so dangerous to me, Annette."

"I don't feel dangerous, Spicer," said Annette.

"I think I'll sleep in the spare room," said Spicer.

so damn aggravating!!

"*A*nnette," said Spicer.

"What's the time, Spicer?" asked Annette.

"I don't know," said Spicer. "But it's not quite dark and not quite light. I couldn't sleep. Move over so I can get into bed. You are so beautifully warm and soft. Female."

"I should hope so," said Annette.

"But in that very fact lies the threat. How can I locate my anima when you've stolen it all?"

"Spicer," said Annette, "couldn't you just stop seeing Dr. Rhea Marks?"

"It's natural for you to feel threatened," said Spicer. "She told me you would be. I think she's right about us separating out. At least for a time."

"But why?"

"Because I am going on a journey, and you're incapable of keeping me company."

"A spiritual journey?"

"Yes," said Spicer.

"I see," said Annette. "Towards the oneness, the wholeness, the ineffable light."

"Don't mock," said Spicer.

"I suppose Dr. Rhea Marks would keep you very good company on this inner journey? Having first pointed out the way."

"I should have stayed in the spare room," said Spicer. "You're beginning again."

"If you want to go and live somewhere else, Spicer," said Annette, "please do. Go and meditate to your heart's content, or should I say 'soul'? And I'll have the three kids, or would you do Jason the honor of taking him with you? Though I suppose he'd he wants Separation

get in the way of your soul's development. And we just part, do we? A property settlement? All that?"

"Annette, you're leaping ahead. Of course I don't want us to part permanently. I'm only suggesting a temporary separation, while I sort things out. And how could there be a property settlement? There's no property to settle."

"There's the house," said Annette.

"It's my house, sweetheart," Spicer said.

"Don't sweetheart me," said Annette.

"If it upsets you so, we won't even contemplate it," said Spicer. "Don't sob like that. Here, let me hold you close. I won't leave you. I'll never leave you."

"Oh, Spicer, don't frighten me so," she wept. "And how could you talk about our sex life to Rhea Marks? It's so disloyal."

"So that's what's upsetting you," said Spicer. "You talked about it to Gilda, why shouldn't I talk about it to Rhea?"

"I wish you wouldn't call her Rhea. Kiss my eyes to stop me crying."

"There," said Spicer. "That's your eyes. Now your ears."

"Please no," said Annette. "It makes me feel I'm going deaf."

"You can't let go," said Spicer. "Why can't you just let go? If you'd let go I wouldn't be in the state I am."

"I'm sorry, Spicer. If only I knew what you meant," said Annette.

"Do it to me," said Spicer. "Put your tongue in my ear."

"There might be wax in there," said Annette.

"Oh God," said Spicer, "why did I marry so repressed a woman?"

"It's in your stars, I expect," said Annette. "No, Spicer, I don't mean to make you angry. I'll do whatever you like."

"But I want you to want it," said Spicer. "You're not wearing your nightie."

"None of them fit any more," said Annette. "They're uncomfortable."

"The bump's grown," said Spicer. "I can't get near you. Come on top of me."

"No."

"Why not?"

"My breasts are swollen," said Annette. "You might feel overwhelmed: whatever it was you complained of to Dr. Rhea. Your anima being taken over. Archetypes creeping out of my you-know-where. Swept away by floods. And my nipples are blotchy and you might see too much of them and go off me. Dr. Herman hated the sight of them."

"I don't mind. It's only temporary. Isn't it?" asked Spicer.

"I don't know. They didn't go like this with Susan," said Annette. "I worry dreadfully."

"Now you are putting me off. I shouldn't really be doing this, anyway."

"Why not?"

"I need to be in control. I went to the spare room. You lured me out. Now you've got the better of me," said Spicer.

"How do you mean I've got the better of you? How did I lure you?"

"It's so seductive. Giving in to needing you, you needing me. Eve with the apple. Sex," said Spicer.

"It isn't just sex, Spicer. It's love. Isn't it?"

"It's a diversion from important things," said Spicer. "It's a distraction."

"But I'm your wife, you're meant to," said Annette. "I need you. Put your hand here."

"You're so wonderful," said Spicer. "I can feel you needing me. Come on top of me."

"All right," said Annette. "But I'm such a funny shape."

"It's the shape we made by doing this," said Spicer. "It's our punishment and our justification."

"I've had my punishment and I don't need any justification," said Annette.

"Stop talking," said Spicer, so Annette did.

"Now turn over," he said. "That's enough of that."

"You won't see her again, will you?" Annette asked. "Please stop seeing Dr. Rhea, please come back to me properly, all of you."

"I don't want to think about it," said Spicer. "Not at the moment. Rhea's unimportant. Lean your forehead against the pillow; then you're at the proper angle. That's wonderful. I'm not hurting the baby?"

"No. Just gently, though."

"I'm never sure you really like it this way," he said. "Why not? It doesn't hurt if you relax."

"Because it lacks dignity," said Annette.

"Sex isn't dignified," said Spicer. "That's its point."

"It ought to be dignified," said Annette. "Since its end result is to produce children with souls."

"Rhea says we should try speaking less when making love," said Spicer. "Then it might work better."

"Isn't this working? It seems to be working for me."

"But it won't for long enough," said Spicer. "We ought to be able to go on for hours."

"Who says?" asked Annette. "Dr. Rhea Marks?"

"I can't hear you," said Spicer. "Your voice is muffled by the pillow."

"It probably wasn't important," said Annette.

"If you can't say anything nice," said Spicer, "don't say anything at all."

"Let me turn over so I can see your eyes," said Annette, "and the shape of your lips when you talk."

"I'll think about it," said Spicer. "I'd rather just move the pillow."

"If you want me to stop talking, you could turn me over and kiss me," said Annette.

"I don't like kissing," said Spicer. "Mouths are for toothpaste and toothbrushes."

"I blame the dentists," said Annette. "They're in our mouths, and the gynecologists are in our cunts, and the epidemiologists are after our cocks—yours, that is—and the surgeons are after our hearts, and now the therapists are after our souls. I wish they'd leave us alone."

"How about the Pope?" asked Spicer.

"He just wants the human race to outbreed the professionals," said Annette, "so there are so many mouths, cunts, cocks, hearts, and souls in the world no one can possibly decipher them, and they flow undiscussed to God. I'm on his side."

"And the TV people? The media?"

"They're looting our lives for narrative," said Annette. "Please be careful of the baby. It's somewhere in there."

"It's walls and walls away from me," said Spicer. "Nature looks after that, or I wouldn't be doing this. The tendency would have been bred out. You're very hot in there, though. Hotter than usual."

"I'm sorry," said Annette.

"I like it," said Spicer. "Let's hot it up some more."

"Please not so hard," said Annette. "You've changed the angle somehow."

"So you told *The Oprah Winfrey Show* to bugger off?" said Spicer.

"I tried to, but Ernie Gromback put the pressure on, so I said I'd do it."

"Bitch," said Spicer, and all the spirit went out of him.

S made at A for
taking Oprah W. show

"Please come back inside me, Spicer," said Annette. "I miss you."

"How can I?" asked Spicer. "See what you've done to me? I have a soft banana instead of a cock."

"I'm sorry," said Annette. "I didn't mean to. What's wrong with *Oprah Winfrey*? It's a TV special about literature and life, not the kind where husbands and wives appear together for everyone to jeer at."

"Bad enough having our lives looted for a novella," said Spicer, "without you talking about it on TV. For God's sake, don't start crying. Sex for us always ends up like this. You crying, me incapable."

"But it doesn't," said Annette. "It never has before. Or only once or twice, in all our ten years. You remember everything wrongly."

"I don't know what's the matter with you," said Spicer. "Why do you do it to me?"

"Can't we just go to sleep?" said Annette.

"I don't feel like sleep," said Spicer. "You've made sure of that."

"But you need dreams to report to Rhea Marks," said Annette. "How can you dream if you don't sleep?"

"You're so cunning," said Spicer. "You don't like me seeing Dr. Rhea Marks, so you steal my potency."

"You mean you're Samson and I'm Delilah," said Annette, "and when I mention *The Oprah Winfrey Show* I'm cutting your hair?"

"Yes," said Spicer. "But I'm not defeated yet, though you'd like me to be. Now I'm going to bring the temple down around your ears. Turn over onto your front."

"Please don't," said Annette.

"I have to find my shadow-side," said Spicer, "and confront it. See, I'm strong again."

"But why?" asked Annette. "Why are you doing this?"

"Because I must find my anima within your animus. Because I need dark, difficult depths. Because you are the cleft in the hill and I am the tree. Because, if this is the only way I can, this is the way I will."

"But, Spicer, there it's too small and it hurts and I hate it."

"Too bad. If it's the only way it works for me, what else can we do? Now just shut up. You don't want to wake the children. At least I hope you don't. Dr. Rhea isn't too sure."

"ivorce him," said Gilda.

"It isn't as bad as that," said Annette.

"It sounds like marital rape to me," said Gilda. "Sodomy without consent."

"You could get to like it," said Annette. "You could be

trained to like it. But you wouldn't like yourself for liking it, if it wasn't your idea in the first place."

"Take him to court, prosecute."

"Gilda, what's the matter with you? Yesterday you were telling me to lie back and enjoy it. Poor Spicer. He's upset about me doing *Oprah Winfrey*. It was my fault. I just wasn't tactful."

"You mean upsetting and hurting you is what turns him on?"

"It isn't like that, Gilda. I think it was because I wouldn't let him do what he wanted that he went to see Dr. Rhea Marks in the first place. The blood pressure's just an excuse. If he was really ill he'd go and see a proper doctor."

"So him seeing Dr. Rhea is your fault too? You drove him to it?"

"No one's talking about fault," said Annette. "I shouldn't have told you."

"If Spicer's talking about your sex life to another woman," said Gilda, "then it's all up for grabs."

"A therapist doesn't count as another woman," said Annette.

"You reckon not?"

"I don't think he's sleeping with her," said Annette.

"But it's occurred to you?"

"Yes," said Annette, "of course. But she's much too holy, much too prissy. And Spicer would keep her existence secret if he was. Wouldn't he?"

"You reckon?" asked Gilda.

"I just don't know," said Annette. "If she was, she wouldn't have had the nerve to ask to see me. She'd be too guilty."

"In the name of healing, people do extraordinary things," said Gilda. "Perhaps she wanted to take a look at the opposition. And therapists don't feel guilt. They justify everything."

"Anyway she'd be struck off," said Annette. "It wouldn't be ethical."

"Struck off from what?" asked Gilda. "Some association which formed itself last year? Which invented its own ethics the week before last?"

"Gilda, what's the matter with you? You sound really upset."

"Steve's joined a group called Fathers as Equal Parents."

"They have a card up on the board at the Clinic. What's the matter with it? I wish Spicer joined things like that."

"He wants me to have the baby the Leboyer way, in water, and I don't want to—I'd be frightened the baby would drown—and I say to Steve, surely what I want goes, but he says no, why should it if he's going to be an equal parent, so we're arguing all the time."

"Oh, Gilda, I'm sorry. I was relying on you to be happy, so I could be unhappy at you."

"Well," said Gilda, "it's not as hard as all that, and at least I'm not married to a monster."

"Spicer isn't a monster," said Annette. "He's Spicer, my beloved husband; it's just he's in therapy and the therapist's got it in for me."

"Is he seeing her today?" asked Gilda. "How often do you think he sees her?"

"I don't know. He said four times a week while the crisis lasts. But perhaps the crisis is over? At least this morning he left the house happy and friendly. I can hardly walk, but he's okay."

"Well," said Gilda, "we all have our ways of fighting back. I must go now. I'm meeting Steve for lunch."

"*I* have Mr. Horrocks on the phone for you," said Wendy. It was three o'clock. Annette had her feet up on the sofa. "Or I will have in a moment. He's just signing some papers in the other office. Could you try persuading him to let us have our coffee machine back? It made dreadful coffee but at least it was coffee. Now he keeps trying to get us to drink herbal teas. Mr. Horrocks can do as he likes, but why should he impose his views on us? If we want to kill ourselves with caffeine that's our business, not his. Here he is."

"Hello, Annette," said Spicer.

"Hello, Spicer," said Annette. "Wendy sounds very lively."

"We're all in a good mood today," said Spicer. "What are you doing?"

"I have my feet up on the sofa. I'm sewing proper name-tags on all Jason's sports gear. It keeps going astray at school."

"I love thinking of you sitting there at home, being domestic. I thought we could go and see a show tonight. Kids and all—"

"Oh, Spicer, how wonderful!"

"I've had Wendy check it out. We can get tickets for *Buddy*."

"But that's rock and roll. You'll hate it."

"The kids will love it. That's the main thing. I can't impose my tastes on others all the time."

"Does that mean you'll give the staff back their coffee machine?"

"Probably. It's only gone for cleaning. But it does them good to live in suspense a little. Keeps them on their toes."

"I see," said Annette.

"How are you feeling, sweetheart?" asked Spicer, settling in to talk.

"I'm just fine, Spicer."

"I knew you would be. I'm glad we got all that out of our systems. We're going to make a go of things, aren't we, Annette."

"Of course, Spicer. I never doubted it."

"Dr. Rhea has been a great help to me. It upset me when you got so paranoid about her. It made me feel you didn't really love me."

"I do love you, Spicer."

"Dr. Rhea really liked you, Annette. She says, if it helps to get you back in balance, and I can handle it, then I can postpone treatment for a time, until after the baby's born. But you would need to go back now for regular weekly treatment with Dr. Herman: one or other of us has to be working towards equilibrium."

"But I thought Dr. Herman was away?"

"He came back unexpectedly. Rhea can make the appointment."

"The trouble is, Spicer, I think it was seeing Dr. Herman which so upset my equilibrium."

"Rhea thinks it will be difficult for you to go through the parturition process unless you come to terms with your own tendency to sexual fantasy. That was quite an episode to which you subjected us all."

"Yes, I know. I'm sorry. Did you see Dr. Rhea this morning?"

"Yes," said Spicer.

"Did you tell her about last night?"

"Annette, don't begin again. Please."

"I'm sorry, Spicer," said Annette.

"So, what do you say about Dr. Herman?" asked Spicer.

"I would rather wait to see him until after the baby's born, Spicer. But I promise to see him after."

"Okay," said Spicer. "It's a deal. We'll both give the thera-

TROUBLE ✳ 117

S wants to take a break from therapy

pists a rest. Just you and me; the mountain and the tree. It's an early show tonight. We'll be back by nine. I'll bring back some champagne. Shall we have one of our special suppers, to celebrate?"

"What are we celebrating, Spicer?"

"Oh God, darling, everything."

"My book?"

"Annette, don't provoke."

"Sorry, sorry. We'll leave the book out of it. An accidental outcrop on the mountain, not true female creativity: not proper soil for the tree."

"You're learning, my sweetheart. I really liked your analogy to Samson and Delilah. It quite turned me on. I think Wendy's coming back. We'll have to stop now. Tell you what, Annette—"

"What, Spicer?"

"Steak would be going too far, but we could have lamb cutlets for supper."

"Red meat, Spicer! How wicked—how wonderful—"

"Bye, my sweetheart," said Spicer.

"*I*s that you, Annette?"

"Yes. Who's that?"

"It's Marion. You know, Ernie's Marion. That's how people know me, I don't understand why. Perhaps it's because I'm so much younger than him. No one takes me seriously. I have a crystal which is supposed to help with that kind of thing. A rose-quartz crystal. It increases self-esteem."

"Does it really?"

Marion calls A. & tells her to be careful

"It's meant to, but you're supposed to leave crystals overnight in running water in the full moon if they're really going to work, and whenever I remember the full moon's always been and gone. I used to wash them in the little lead fountain in Queen Elizabeth's Rose Garden, but because there's an official drought they've had to shut it down, and I don't think tap water works. Anyway, my self-esteem isn't up to much at the moment."

"I'm really sorry, Marion."

"That's not why I'm calling, though. It's just I was doing your tarot cards and they came up with all these frightful things. First the Tower—all that red and black, with all those bodies falling from it; then that awful card with the man lying flat on his front with seven swords skewering him through; and then I turned up Death, though everyone says that really means life—I can't think why. So I just thought I'd call and say please be careful, Annette: stepping out into traffic, that kind of thing. None of it means anything: just do be careful."

"Marion, why on earth were you doing my tarot cards?"

"Well, Ernie and I had a row, and he told me he'd had affairs with all his lady authors under forty and I asked if that included you and he said yes, and after that he denied it, so I didn't know what to think. You're supposed to be able to find out the truth from the cards, so I consulted them. One has a right to the truth."

"I certainly haven't had an affair with Ernie, Marion," said Annette, "nor would I ever. I'm happily married to Spicer."

"Spicer comes and talks to me sometimes, Annette."

"Does he?" asked Annette. "What do you mean, talks?"

"Just talk, Annette. He knows I get lonely, and the office is just round the corner from us. And Ernie is away so often—off with all his lady authors under forty, for all I know—and Spicer and you have your troubles, and he needs to talk about them. Everyone has to have someone to talk to. But I do get kind of worried sometimes in case you'd mind. Women should stick together. I feel better, already. There's nothing in it. I love *Lucifette Fallen*. What a brilliant title. Ernie gave me a proof copy to read. Is it really about your family life? Your mother and father? It must have been really grueling. Poor you. I'm always sorry for the children in this kind of thing."

"Aren't we all," said Annette.

"I gave the book to this friend of mine," said Marion. "An astrologer, to see what she thought of it. She did this review for *New Astrology*. I'll send it on to you."

"Dr. Rhea Marks?"

"Yes. How did you know? God, she's brilliant. She has proper medical qualifications along with everything else."

"And then *The Oprah Winfrey Show* picked it up," said Annette.

"Did they? That's wonderful!" said Marion. "So you're going to be a TV star! No wonder we're all so jealous. Things just fall into your lap."

"Marion, it was through you that Spicer got to see Dr. Marks?"

"It was me who recommended her, yes," said Marion.

"Does Spicer still come round to talk to you, Marion?" asked Annette.

"Not since he started seeing Dr. Marks. I rather wish I hadn't mentioned her," said Marion.

"So now you're doing the cards and wishing me a road accident," said Annette.

"How could you say anything so awful, Annette?" said Marion. "It isn't like that at all. It was only the once with Spicer; after that it was just talk. I've just felt so guilty: it will never happen again, I promise. I love Ernie with all my heart; I just wish he had more soul, he was open, you know? And I'm sure Spicer loves you, Annette. He kept saying so. He said you had sexual problems. It was hard for him. I just wanted to help. It'll never happen again."

"Okay, Marion, okay," said Annette. "What's past is past. Spicer and I are starting again; we've all been through a bad patch. Thank you for calling. Really."

"Only do be careful," said Marion, "stepping into the road. Those cards were really dreadful. And don't be angry with me, Annette. I can't bear it."

Annette banged down the phone.

"*O*n our sides is nice, really nice," said Spicer. "Worth being pregnant for. Why didn't we do this before, you missionary you? But turn over on your face now. That's right. I didn't use Vaseline the other night; I should have. Perhaps I was angry. Yes, perhaps I was. I wanted to hurt. I don't know. I love you. I've given up everything for you, Annette. When I say I love you, your insides do such wonderful things. Bring your knees further up now, so I can move up easily from there to here. That's it: what an easy slippage it is, meant by the Maker. You're not comfy, I can tell. If I take the pillow from under your face and put it below your breasts above your bump . . . ? Keep your head on the side, so you can breathe—there, that's glorious for me—is it comfy for you?"

"Yes, Spicer. You seem to know such a lot about doing it

like this. Is this what Marion taught you? Spicer, please don't go!
I only asked—I thought you'd find it exciting, thinking of her as
if she were here too. Isn't this how your mind works? Where are
you going? Don't leave me like this now. It's so humiliating.
Spicer? It's not even as if you can't. You can but you won't.
Spicer?"

"*T*his is appalling," said Gilda.

"After that Spicer just went to the spare room. I cried all
night. I heard him leave at about six in the morning."

"You can't go on like this," said Gilda. "You'll have to go to
your mother's."

"That's defeat," said Annette. "That's going back to where
you were before you began. It's just so up and down with Spicer
and me at the moment."

"You can say that again," said Gilda. "But drifting down-
wards all the time. The major drift is to rock bottom, Annette."

"I don't want to think that," said Annette. "Don't say it. It
isn't true. Yesterday we all went to a show. The kids loved it. So
did I. Spicer pretended to, for our sakes. We were just a normal,
happy family, on an outing. For twelve whole hours I was so happy,
Gilda. I was so confident. Not even Marion calling and saying what
she did could really shake me."

"Spicer and Marion! I still can't believe it."

"It was only the once," said Annette.

"Oh yes?"

"Spicer does end up in bed sometimes with other women if
he's had too much to drink or taken too much coke," said Annette.

"I don't like it but I have to accept it. It doesn't mean anything: it's me he loves."

"Oh yes," said Gilda.

"It's because I'm so bad at sex," said Annette. "It's a kind of disability. You can't blame Spicer. Sex just doesn't come naturally to me, the way it does to other women. I say the wrong thing or do the wrong thing at the wrong moment and spoil everything. You don't mind anything Steve does to you, do you?"

"Steve isn't Spicer. Steve wants me to be happy," said Gilda. "He doesn't care what I do or say or when. It makes no difference. And he's given in about Leboyer."

"I'm so glad," said Annette. "I'm dreadful. All I do is talk about myself. That's another thing Spicer has to put up with. I'm so self-centered."

"I'd talk about myself if I were you," said Gilda.

"I can't let go in bed, I expect that's the trouble," said Annette. "I can't stop thinking. I keep wondering if the cat's been put out or what's for breakfast."

"Then perhaps it's Spicer who isn't very good at it."

"No, it's me," said Annette. "I can't blame Spicer. Sex makes my mind active. All the energy flies into my head. I hardly ever have orgasms. There, I've told you. I'm so upset, Gilda."

"I know," said Gilda. "I can tell."

"I was trying to play it Spicer's way," wept Annette. "Or I wouldn't have even mentioned Marion. How was I to know he'd react like that? Only six words—'Is this what Marion taught you?'—and your whole life falls to pieces."

"I reckon Spicer's playing games with you, Annette," said Gilda. "He's nice for a bit just in order to be nasty. He does it on purpose. He reads you. He presses a button. He knows how you'll react and he does it deliberately."

"But why should he, Gilda?" asked Annette.

"Because he's a sadist," said Gilda. "It's how he gets his kicks. And you're a masochist. Or you wouldn't put up with it. As for Marion, she's perfectly capable of making the whole thing up just to upset you."

"Why should she do that?" asked Annette.

"I don't know, Annette," said Gilda. "Perhaps Marion's found out about you and Ernie and is getting her own back."

"Oh God," said Annette.

"There! Caught you!" said Gilda. "I knew I was right about you and Ernie. Why did you deny it in the first place? I'm your friend. It was that time Spicer was at the Bordeaux Wine Feste, wasn't it? Did you get herpes?"

"No, I did not. That's just a disgusting rumor. Industrial espionage probably, put about by other publishers who hate him making money and not being a gentleman. Please, please, keep it to yourself, Gilda. So Spicer could have thought it was just me being paranoid again, by mentioning Marion? That's why he acted the way he did?"

"It's perfectly possible, but how would I know?"

"Poor Spicer," said Annette.

"I wouldn't go as far as that, Annette. Just divorce the bastard."

"But I love him."

"I have to go now," said Gilda. "Steve's got the engine running. He sends his love, by the way. Bye, Annette. Look after yourself. Call me tomorrow. I worry about you."

"Bye, Gilda. Thanks."

"Spicer," said Annette.

"Wendy," said Spicer to his secretary, but so that Annette could hear, "I did ask you not to put calls through to the office. It's too bad. Annette, I'm really very busy. Please, please, just leave me alone for once."

"But, Spicer, I have to talk."

"Annette," said Spicer, "I am trying to keep this business afloat. We are in a recession. Try to help, not hinder."

"I can't bear it when you leave in the morning without saying goodbye."

"Why don't you go and stay with your mother for a while?"

"You know I mentioned Marion last night," said Annette, "and it seemed to upset you so much?"

"I have no idea what you're talking about, Annette," said Spicer.

"It's just that Marion rang me up—"

"For God's sake," said Spicer. "I'm so busy, and here comes the hysteria again. Obsessive sexual jealousy. I'll be late tonight."

"Why?"

"Don't crowd me, Annette," said Spicer. "As it happens, I'm seeing Dr. Rhea after work. She found time for me. I wish I didn't have to see her. But since you refuse to see Dr. Herman, I have no choice. The tensions get too great: I can't cope with you without help."

"I didn't say I wouldn't see Dr. Herman," said Annette. "I just wanted to wait until after the baby was born."

"For all I know, you've invented this baby," said Spicer. "It's a hysterical pregnancy which gives you an excuse and an outlet for your hostility to men and your destructiveness towards yourself."

"But the baby showed up on the scan, Spicer," said Annette. "How can it be a hysterical pregnancy? Perhaps you didn't want it to be a girl, perhaps that's it?"

"Annette," said Spicer, "I am way beyond worrying about this baby's gender, I just worry for all our sanity. You ought to think seriously about going to stay with your mother."

"How could I? What about the children?"

"Jason and Susan? They're hardly children any more," said Spicer. "They've had to grow up too fast. I can get someone to come in a couple of hours a day after school easily enough, to fill in the time before I get back. They're not accustomed to much mothering, God knows. The pizza-and-video generation. Prime candidates. Now this next one turns up for another round of punishment."

"Oh, Spicer—" said Annette.

"What?"

"You sound so cold," said Annette, "and hateful."

"Oh, Annette," said Spicer, "you do so little to warm me up, and the hate flows from you, not from me. Is this all for Wendy's benefit?"

"Of course not."

"Because I have a new telephone system, and from now on calls on this number come over the speaker in Wendy's room and are recorded."

"Why didn't you tell me? Don't you have a private number?"

"I don't think I can trust you with it, Annette," said Spicer. "Not with you in the mood you are."

Hate him!

"*H*ello, child," said Annette's mother, Judy.

"Why, hello, Mum," said Annette. "How are things with you?"

"Just fine, sweetheart," said Judy. "And you?"

"Just fine, Mum," said Annette.

"Now, don't say that, Annette," said Judy. "I know they're not, because dear Spicer rang and he said things were definitely not right with you. He is so concerned. I'd worry much less about you if you would only tell me what was really going on, instead of pretending everything's okay when it isn't."

"What was Spicer concerned about?"

"Don't sound like that, Annette," said Judy. "You're lucky to have a husband who cares. So many don't. Spicer asked me to talk to you: apparently he's having some kind of therapy and you've developed an obsessional aversion to whoever it is he goes to see. Is this so?"

"You could see it like that," said Annette.

"Because it's not very helpful of you, dear," said Judy. "Not that I'm in favor of shrinks—they do encourage introspection so —but if Spicer wants to be in the swing of things I suppose he should be allowed. I don't see why you should object. It only causes trouble."

"It's all a bit complicated, Mum," said Annette.

"But you're all right? In yourself?"

"Yes, of course," said Annette.

"Because Spicer seemed to think you wanted to come and stay with me and Dad for a while."

"It might be a little difficult to arrange," said Annette.

"That's what I told Spicer," said Judy. "I don't think it's a good idea at all; you can't just leave Susan and Jason on their own, and you need to be near the hospital."

"Yes, I know," said Annette.

"I don't really know what Spicer was thinking of, suggesting it," said Judy. "Men are so impractical. They seem to think women just have to wave a wand and it's done. Your father and I lead very quiet lives; you know how he likes his routine. I must warn you, Annette, it is simply not a good idea for a wife to leave a husband alone if she can help it. Spicer's bound to get into trouble. He is a very sexy man."

"Yes, he is, Mum," said Annette. "You're quite right."

"And a good man is hard to find," said Judy. "Annette—"

"Yes, Mum?"

"Did Spicer actually get round to putting the house in your joint names, dear?"

"I don't think so," said Annette. "I'd have known, wouldn't I? I'd have had to have signed something?"

"Because he was going to do that as security for the loan your father gave him," said Judy. "This whole family is so vague and trusting. And Spicer hasn't made any repayments lately and your father doesn't like to press him, it's so unfamily, and he rather wondered if you'd bring the matter up with Spicer. You married him after all, and it was because of you your father made the loan, and though the whole world seems to rejoice when interest rates go down, I'm sure your father and I don't. It's what we live off. And a whole chunk of capital is tied up in Spicer's business."

"I'm sure it's all okay, Mum," said Annette. "Spicer knows what he's doing."

"That's what worries me," said Judy. "Men do tend to. Annette, I don't like saying this, but, whatever you do, don't leave the matrimonial home."

"Why would I want to do a thing like that?" asked Annette.

"Because I feel uneasy, Annette," said Judy. "Why does Spicer want you out of the way? Has he found someone else? Is that what the matter is? Men do get very odd when their wives are pregnant."

"Don't ill-wish me, Mother," said Annette.

"That's a perfectly horrible thing to say, Annette," said her mother.

"Please, don't you get upset, Mum," said Annette. "It didn't mean anything. I was joking."

"I lie awake worrying about you, and all I get in return is this kind of insult. Of course I'm not ill-wishing you. How can you think such a thing?"

"Sorry, sorry, sorry," said Annette. Her headache had returned.

"*O*live Green speaking. How can I help you?"

"I'd like to make an appointment to see Dr. Winspit, please," asked Annette, on the phone to the surgery.

"Who's speaking?"

"Mrs. Horrocks. Annette Horrocks."

"In future," said the receptionist, "please try and contact the appointment desk before nine A.M."

"I thought that was just for house calls," said Annette.

"Not any more," said Olive Green. "By nine A.M. we've usually filled our books for the day. We run a busy and efficient service here, Mrs. Horrocks."

"I don't doubt it," said Annette. "I just need to come in and see Dr. Winspit now."

"Now? Dr. Winspit is fully booked until next Friday afternoon. He's very busy."

"Jesus Christ!" said Annette.

"There is no need to be abusive," said Olive Green.

"I wasn't," said Annette. "I'm sorry."

"According to our computer records, you've missed three Maternity Clinic appointments without explanation," said Olive Green. "So I am unable to fix an appointment anyway, unless you send a formal letter of request."

"That's insane," said Annette.

"I don't like your attitude, Mrs. Horrocks," said Olive Green, "and I don't make the rules. But what's the point of making appointments for you if you don't mean to keep them?"

"I don't want to get into an argument with you," said Annette, "and I'm sorry I've upset you somehow, but I'm very pregnant and I don't think I'm at all well and I need to see someone today."

"If it's an emergency," said the receptionist, "we suggest you go to Casualty at the Royal Free Hospital. Otherwise your best plan is to attend tomorrow's antenatal class at the Clinic. You can't not turn up week after week and then demand special attention from the doctor just on whim."

"I'm not demanding," said Annette. "It's not a whim. I just need to see a doctor, for fuck's sake."

"Please try not to be so aggressive," said Olive Green.

"Why? Will it go on my notes?" asked Annette.

"It already has," said Olive Green. "Swearing always does. We have to put up with a lot, but we don't have to put up with this." And she put the phone down.

"*It's* been a dreadful day, Gilda. Spicer was so horrible on the phone I could have died; my mother ill-wished me; and when I tried to get an appointment with the doctor it just ended up with me having a row with this person on the appointment desk."

"That will be Olive Green," said Gilda. "She's always like that. You have to creep and crawl and beg for help before she relents and lets you see someone. Then she's the one dispensing charity: it's the only way she has of being kind. Why do you want to see a doctor?"

"I just get headaches all the time," said Annette.

"Personally, I blame Spicer," said Gilda.

"I expect it has a lot to do with it," said Annette. "He's had a new phone system put in, so if I ring him the calls are public. You've no idea how hurtful that is."

"You shouldn't be hurt," said Gilda. "He's just got one of the new systems that record everything automatically."

"How do you know that?" asked Annette.

"Steve told me," said Gilda.

"I see," said Annette.

"No need to say 'I see' in that tone of voice," said Gilda. "Are you feeling okay? Spicer told Steve you were insane, suffering from a paranoid episode. I told Steve there was nothing insane about it: the proper response to Spicer is paranoia. Do you want me to come round? I'm rather top-heavy but I will."

"No. I'm okay," said Annette. "Susan's cooking us supper. Jason's sulking in his room because I made him throw away a marijuana plant he was growing on his windowsill. At this very minute Spicer's seeing Dr. Rhea."

"I thought you said he'd given up seeing her," said Gilda.

"He's changed his mind," said Annette. "He says he can't cope with me without help from her."

"That figures," said Gilda. "It's how you train dogs. You're quixotic. They never know what to expect next, a kick or a pat, so they end up fawning and licking every boot that comes along."

"But I haven't given in about *Oprah Winfrey*," said Annette. "I won't. And that's what it's all about, I'm sure. Or most of it."

"You look for one thing in a marriage going wrong," said Gilda, "you look for another: you can never quite be sure. If I were you, I'd go and see this Dr. Rhea Marks on your own and just tell her to leave Spicer alone. She's spoiling your marriage and damaging your health."

"I'm frightened of her," said Annette. "I only have to think about her and I get a headache."

"Or issue Spicer an ultimatum," said Gilda. " 'Her or me.' "

"Ultimatums are dangerous," said Annette. "Supposing he chooses her? No, I just have to sit it out until the baby's born. My mother's always saying men behave in a peculiar way when their wives are pregnant."

"That's because your father had an affair when she was pregnant with you," said Gilda.

"Fancy you remembering that, Gilda!" said Annette. "I'm touched. You're a really good friend to me."

"I want to be, Annette," said Gilda. "I'm trying to tie up loose ends before giving birth. Look, there's something I have to say to you. About Spicer."

"What?" asked Annette.

"It was a long time ago," said Gilda.

"I don't want to hear this," said Annette.

"I think you ought to know. It was when he was having this thing with Marion," said Gilda.

"You knew about that?" asked Annette.

"Yes," said Gilda.

"Then why didn't you tell me?"

"Because it's so difficult. You know that perfectly well," said Gilda. "And anyway, I had my suspicions about you and Ernie Gromback, and I thought Spicer was probably just evening things up a little. It was just all too complicated. And Spicer's so charming, and you and I weren't such good friends at the time."

"Please just tell me, Gilda," said Annette. "I don't want to hear your excuses. What happened?"

"Nothing happened," said Gilda.

"Liar," said Annette.

"It didn't," said Gilda. "I promise. Spicer just wanted me to make up a threesome with him and Marion."

"I can't believe that! Was he drunk, or on drugs, or what?"

"It was only a phone call, Annette," said Gilda. "I don't know Spicer well enough ever to tell if he's on anything."

"And where was I?" asked Annette.

"I think your father was ill," said Gilda.

"And did you?" asked Annette. "A threesome? Oh, Gilda!"

"Of course I didn't. I was with Steve by then anyway," said Gilda.

"But why should he think you would?" asked Annette. "Why should he call you?"

"Because Marion told Spicer about her and me ending up in bed together after some stupid drunken party. I'd had so much of this and that, I couldn't tell male from female, and things happened that shouldn't have. Marion's like that. Anything for kicks. Of course she's into celibacy now, or says she is, for Ernie's benefit."

"Oh God, I don't want to know any of this," said Annette. "I just want to have some kind of decent home to bring my baby into."

"I feel better now I've told you," said Gilda. "Please don't say anything to Steve."

"I just want to forget the whole thing. If you said no, who do you think said yes? Eleanor Watts?"

"It isn't beyond the bounds of probability," said Gilda. "Just because she looks like a horse doesn't mean she doesn't enjoy an orgy. Annette, it was years ago and we were all a lot younger. I'll come round tomorrow and we'll talk more, shall we? Spicer does love you, Annette. He just has a lot of sexual energy but he's not very good at sex so he has to experiment," said Gilda. "I'm only speculating. And anyway, according to Steve, Spicer's trying to reform. That's why he's been seeing this therapist: for your sake."

"Is that what Spicer told Steve, or what Steve thinks for himself?" asked Annette. "Or what you're all just saying to make me feel better?"

"What Spicer told Steve," said Gilda. "Spicer wants to make a go of the marriage: he's trying to settle down sexually. I didn't know how much you knew about what Spicer gets up to. Now I know about you and Ernie Gromback, I reckon there's no point in you not knowing everything I know. Some marriages depend upon fidelity; some don't. Mine and Steve's does. Yours and Spicer's doesn't."

"It does so," said Annette.

"You took Marion quite calmly," said Gilda. "I'd have gone mad."

"I just feel so depressed," said Annette. "I'm going to bed. Susan's making cheeseburgers. I can't face them. She slices the onion really thick."

"Spicer."

"What is it, Annette? I'm reading. I thought you'd gone to bed."

"I went to bed early," said Annette. "At eight o'clock. What time did you get in?"

"Around midnight," said Spicer.

"I didn't put any fruit out for you. I'm sorry. There's some in the fridge I bought specially. Shall I fetch it?"

"That's okay, Annette. I ate out."

"It isn't very warm in here," said Annette. "You've opened the windows."

"This temperature suits me," said Spicer. "You keep the house hotter than I really like."

"Isn't it too dark to read? You're using candles."

"Candles are natural, Annette," said Spicer. "Electricity is cold and harsh."

"What are you reading?" asked Annette.

"A book called *Healers of Olympus. Theotherapy: The Magic of the Gods. Symbols and Practice.* You wouldn't be interested."

"Did Dr. Rhea give it to you?" asked Annette.

"Please, Annette, go back to bed, go to sleep," said Spicer. "I'm not doing you any harm. I'm just sitting in my study and reading by candlelight. I wish you very well. I'll sleep in the spare room so as not to disturb you."

"*I* was coming round this morning, Annette," said Gilda on the phone, "but there's a new washer-dryer being delivered. Steve bought it for a surprise. Now I've got to wait in for the man."

"That's okay. Have you heard of Theotherapy, Gilda?"

"I can't say I have, Annette."

"It's archetypal psychology," said Annette. "Jungian."

"You've already left me behind," said Gilda.

"Symbols are primitive analogues that speak to the unconscious," said Annette. "I've been reading this book. Actually it's rather more complicated than that. To quote Carl Gustav Jung himself, they're also ideas corresponding to the highest intuition produced by consciousness. Archetypes get to us all, Gilda. They're what we know without knowing."

"Is it Spicer's book?" asked Gilda.

"Yes," said Annette. "He said he'd sleep in the spare room, but he didn't. He read till about five, when he slipped in beside me. He was very cold. I think he just wanted to get warm. I was sorry for him. I don't know why. He says if my reactions are screwy it's because I have the moon in Aquarius. He seemed inclined to forgive me for my existence. Poor Spicer. I wish he were happier. A threesome with you and Marion and him won't make him happy: I can see it might relieve some inner pain, but how horrible to have the pain in the first place."

"The threesome didn't happen, Annette," said Gilda. "Believe me."

"I believe you, Gilda," said Annette. "I feel quite calm this morning. I think probably I'm good and he's bad. But at least he's trying to be good. I stretched out my hand and touched him. You know how men will be in bed, careful not to touch you but wanting your warmth?"

"I can't say I do, Annette," said Gilda. "I don't know men like that."

"Lucky old you," said Annette. "In the early days we'd lie entwined, facing each other; I'd have my knee between his legs. That hardly ever happens now. Of course, I've always had to wait for him to make sexual overtures to me; he's always had to initiate lovemaking. If I make the first move he'll turn over and go to sleep, or turn on the light and start reading, so I've learned not to. But last night I just touched him because I was so sorry for him. He winced. He just shrank away from me. It was worse than if he had hit me."

"You don't have to tell me all this, Annette," said Gilda.

"I'm sorry, Gilda," said Annette. "It's too personal, isn't it, sorrow? Even more personal than threesomes. Let's get back to Theotherapy. Oh, look, it's inscribed inside the front cover: 'To Spicer—a special gift, from Dr. Rhea Marks.' "

"Are you crying, Annette?"

"No. I feel quite calm," said Annette.

"It could have said 'To darling Spicer with love from Rhea,' " said Gilda.

"Quite so," said Annette. "It's the 'special' I don't like. There's a pencil mark down the side of page eighty-one. Spicer never marks books. He hates the children doing it, or me. So we've learned not to. I expect Dr. Rhea did the marking. He wouldn't think to reproach her. The passage marked is about the goddess Hera, Gilda. Otherwise Juno. I suppose the first is Greek, the second Roman. It says: 'Attributes: Fatal softness, gullibility, dependence: ill treatment by husband: shame, embarrassment, bickering: scheming; meddling: intrigue: lying: insane jealousy: use of sex as a weapon. . . .' Gilda, what's going on? A little further on it says: 'Therapies, bathing in moonlight, running water, wearing of bangles, bracelets and anklets.' I am suddenly so sleepy, Gilda, I am just going to lie down and sleep. I can't go on talking."

"I wish I could help more, Annette."

"We used to be happy, Spicer and me," said Annette. "Really happy. But he seems not even to remember that any more. It's as if someone were stealing all our good past: replacing it with something dreary and dreadful. But how can that be? I have to go to sleep."

"*A*nnette, darling, you took ages to answer the phone."

"I was asleep, Spicer."

"Sleep is the best thing for you," said Spicer. "You've been looking so tired! Good news. The British Rail deal has come through at last. All signed and sealed. Horrocks Wine Imports is out of the woods."

"I didn't know Horrocks Wine Imports were in the woods," said Annette.

"I didn't like to worry you with it, darling," said Spicer. "It's all been touch and go, financially, over the last couple of months. If I've been behaving out of character, that's all it's been. I've been under a strain."

"Spicer, I wish you'd told me," said Annette. "I thought I was causing the strain, but all the time it was only business worries! How wonderful—"

" 'Only business worries' is a rather mild way of describing near-bankruptcy, Annette," said Spicer. "You've no idea how close to ruin we were. How it distressed me, the thought of letting the family down: you, Susan, Jason, the baby, all of you!"

"You would only have let us down in a material sense, Spicer," said Annette. "We wouldn't have thought you loved us any less. You have been behaving rather strangely, Spicer."

"In what way, strange?" asked Spicer. "I'm sorry you see it like that!"

"I don't see it any way, I'm just so pleased to have you back," said Annette. "Your voice is altogether different—"

"The BR contract means me spending quite a few months in France each year," said Spicer. "I'll have to go over in January, February. I'm sorry about that. The baby will be so new I'll hate to miss a day. My loss. Shall we go out to lunch to celebrate? One o'clock? Can you make it?"

"I've let myself get into such a mess," said Annette.

"Stick your hair under the tap," said Spicer.

"My eyes are swollen—" said Annette.

"Why? Does pregnancy do that?" asked Spicer.

"Seems to," said Annette.

"We'll have champagne and lobster," said Spicer.

"I'm not sure about lobster," said Annette. "Salmon would be good."

"You can't not like lobster all of a sudden," said Spicer.

"My digestion's a bit queasy," said Annette. "But it's only temporary."

"I should hope so," said Spicer. "You're my lobster-and-champagne girl. Don't let new motherhood change you too much. So it's meet me for lunch, sweetheart, and put all our troubles behind us and start again."

"Oh, Spicer! Oh, darling!"

being nice now – Spicer got BR contract

"*G*ilda, it's Annette. Gilda, everything's explained. Spicer nearly went bankrupt. That's why he's been so dreadful. He'll give up therapy now, I know he will. It's only when the material world fails that the spiritual one seems so exciting."

"Annette," said Gilda. "I can't bear to hear you sounding so happy."

"Why?"

"Because it's too sudden," said Gilda.

"We're having a celebration lunch, Gilda. Just him and me. Everything's just fine. I'm sorry to have been such a pain. I have to go. I can't find the hairdryer anywhere."

"*H*appy birthday, Annette!"

"Happy birthday!"

"Many happy returns of the day—"

"Here's to you, Annette!"

"Many happy whatsits."

"Why, Spicer! And Ernie and Marion—and Eleanor and Humphrey! Good heavens, it's my birthday! I'd quite forgotten!"

"Trust Annette to forget her own birthday!"

"Champagne, Annette? We opened it," said Spicer. "You are rather late. I said one. It's one-twenty—"

"Spicer, I'm sorry. It's just when you say one it's always one-thirty—" said Annette, "so in my head I was going to be early. . . ."

"It's party time again! My beautiful wife. Isn't she lovely, isn't she perfect, in spite of her bump!" said Spicer. "In spite of

Annette's birthday surprise

140 ✳ FAY WELDON

her being the vaguest person in the world. Forgetting her own birthday!"

"Because of her bump," said Eleanor, "not in spite of. It's not the neatest bump in the world, it's true. It is kind of all-pervasive. Round the back as well as in the front."

"I'd marry Annette tomorrow if I wasn't married already," said Humphrey. "I love every single bumpy bit of her."

"That's only because to live with Annette is to live in the Crescent," said Eleanor, "and that is your major ambition in life. You say it's mine but everyone knows it's yours."

"Hump would have to move me out first," said Spicer. "And if I ever move out of that house it will be feet first, so I'm afraid we're talking about murder."

"I did your tarot cards again this morning, Annette," said Marion. "Here's the computer printout. Happy birthday! You can get a tarot program now. It chooses your cards at random. Jungian synchronicity. You should read the great Carl Gustav's intro to the *I Ching*. All part of the flow, the ebb and the flow. Isn't that so, Spicer? Your cards were brilliant, Annette. Death upside down. That means new life, new hope, rebirth."

"And I've got Annette a couple more chat shows," said Ernie, "and a *Guardian* interview. It looks as if this book of hers is going to make quite a splash, even without the *Oprah Winfrey* intervention!"

"I may not be feeling up to any of it," said Annette. "I'll let you know."

"Annette will decidedly not be feeling up to it," said Spicer. "Here comes the lobster thermidor. I ordered for everyone, inasmuch as it's a working weekday: we've all got to get back to work, except of course the birthday girl, who can sleep all day and often does. We have so very much to celebrate, Annette and myself:

haven't we, darling? Here are my birthday gifts to you, Annette, with all my very, very, very, very, very special love. One present for every 'very.' Annette, the love of Spicer's life. The only one."

"Thank you, Spicer," said Annette. "That was a really lovely speech."

"Start opening your presents now," said Spicer. "Nothing messier than lobster thermidor when the claw crackers start cracking."

"What pretty little packages," said Marion. "What can they be? Five little flat circles, so prettily wrapped! Are those mandalas on the paper?"

"Mandalas, Marion?" asked Ernie. "The things you know. Marion is into the occult. She's had a pyramid made above her bed to focus the energy, but it's the energy of dreams that concerns her, nothing else."

"Sex is a waste of time, Ernie," said Marion. "It stands between a soul and its dreams."

"Bangles, bracelets, and of solid gold, Spicer? You are so extravagant—" said Eleanor, "and only recently you were talking bin-ends and desperation."

"I went down to Bond Street this morning and bought them," said Spicer. "Between one meeting and the next. I wanted something very special for Annette, on this very special day."

"But what's the gold chain for, Spicer?" asked Eleanor.

"It's an anklet chain," said Marion. "So pretty!"

"Spicer, how glamorous, how thoughtful, just what I want. I simply love the bracelets," said Annette, "but the anklet will have to wait till after the baby. My ankles are so puffy! Look at them! I couldn't bend down to get it on, let alone take it off, but I can put the bracelets on now. Just!"

"Baby wrists," said Spicer. "I love them. Let me put them on. Not too tight?"

"Just nicely firm," said Annette.

"Now you look positively Indian!" said Marion. "Properly docile. Not wild-eyed and academic at all. Ernie, will you buy me some bracelets?"

"No, I will not," said Ernie. "I'll give you some anti–New Age books to make you think."

"I'll jangle wherever I go," said Annette, "from now on. And wherever I go I'll think of you, Spicer. Thank you, my darling husband. I am so happy."

"Eat up your lobster," said Spicer.

"*G*ilda?"

"Hi, Annette," said Gilda. "I'm in the bath. Can you hear splashing? I have a phone in the bathroom now. Steve bought it for me, so you and I could talk more comfortably. Steve worries about you. So now I can lie in the warm water, which always relaxes me, and watch my tummy rippling, and call Steve if I go into labor. Ooh, there it goes! Hump, bump, and gone again. A foot or an elbow. Some people can tell which: I never can. The Clinic says he'll be on time. You didn't go to antenatal class again. I like being pregnant: I never thought I would. Being helpless is so sensuous. I don't look forward to the birth one bit. I'm quite sure I'm going to die. How was the kiss-and-make-up lunch?"

"I told Spicer I didn't want lobster but he just went ahead and ordered it."

"I expect he just forgot."

"Yes," said Annette. "I expect so. But now I have indigestion. And it wasn't tête-à-tête at all. There were other people."

"Spicer's sociable by nature," said Gilda. "We all know that."

"Why didn't he ask you and Steve? He asked everyone else."

"I've no idea," said Gilda, after a little pause. "Do you think I've offended him in some way?"

"It's easy to do," said Annette. "Quite often nowadays it happens all by itself. It was my birthday and he gave me gold bracelets."

"Oh my God, I forgot your birthday!" cried Gilda. "I'm so sorry, Annette."

"I forgot it too," said Annette, "what with one thing and another."

"That is just terrible!"

"Spicer remembered," said Annette. "That was something. But I wish he hadn't given me the bracelets."

"Sometimes I feel quite sorry for Spicer," said Gilda. "Not often, just sometimes. It does seem difficult for him to do anything right. It sounds a really nice present to me."

"If you remember," said Annette, "the therapy for the goddess Hera is bangles, bracelets and anklets. Turn to the relevant page and there's another passage marked by Dr. Rhea in the book on Theotherapy: it says Hera is endowed with all the positive characteristics of a good wife and mother, but is at the same time so prone to feelings of jealousy that she is prepared to sacrifice everything she believes in—even her own life, if need be—in an attempt to establish what she believes to be her own rights. Consequently, her married life tends to be dogged by ever-growing crisis."

"So?" asked Gilda.

"So, Gilda," said Annette, "having got nowhere with horoscopes, Dr. Rhea is now attacking me with Theotherapy. She's just near enough the truth to do me down in Spicer's eyes. I'm not an unreasonably jealous person, am I?"

"Not considering the way Spicer behaves, no," said Gilda.

"But she will somehow persuade Spicer I am," said Annette. "She's resetting his tuning, as people do with radio sets. So all he hears is what she says he'll hear. But why is she doing this to me? He's not going to stop seeing her, not if he went out this morning and bought me bangles, bracelets and anklets. The bracelets are really tight round my wrist. The skin is already rubbing. It's the curse of Dr. Rhea Marks and I'm walking round with it on my body."

"I think you'd better go and see her, Annette," said Gilda. "Not just for your sake, but for Susan and Jason and the baby too. You are getting really obsessive."

"Yes, I know," said Annette. "I will. Now I've washed my hair, I feel stronger."

"By all means come and chat to me, Mrs. Horrocks," said Dr. Rhea on the phone. "Just you, or Spicer too?"

"Just me," said Annette. "If you're going to call Spicer 'Spicer' perhaps you'd better call me 'Annette.' "

"Well, no, Mrs. Horrocks. Spicer is my patient, and we believe in a degree of informality in treatment. You are the spouse, and formality is in order. These are the ethics of the situation. You are an interested but not primarily involved party to the counselor/client relationship."

"I'm his wife," said Annette.

"I am very well aware of that, Mrs. Horrocks," said Dr. Rhea. "Shall we say five on Friday week?"

"I would rather come and see you today," said Annette.

"Oh dear," said Dr. Rhea. "As bad as that?"

"It would just be more convenient today," said Annette.

"As it happens, I do have a cancellation," said Dr. Rhea. "Five today."

"Thank you."

"Not any earlier, Mrs. Horrocks," said Dr. Rhea. "We still have the builders in, and my husband is using his consulting room, so there is no waiting room available. I'm sure you understand. I'm sorry."

"I get the message," said Annette.

"No message is intended," said Dr. Rhea. "I am simply stating that we have the builders in."

"Five o'clock, then, Dr. Marks," said Annette.

"I look forward to it," said Dr. Rhea Marks.

"Perhaps you would answer one or two questions, Dr. Rhea," said Annette.

"I would be happy to," said Dr. Rhea, "so long as the answers don't breach the confidentiality which exists between Spicer and myself."

"But he's my husband," said Annette.

"You keep saying that. Spouses don't own one another. He is your husband. Very well. He is my patient. Likewise, very well. I am sorry you have seen fit to discontinue your treatment with my husband. It would have been very helpful to you, and indeed to Spicer, if you'd gone on with it. Spicer has had a lot to cope with lately."

"I know," said Annette. "So have I."

"Perhaps you don't realize to what extent Spicer is in crisis," said Dr. Rhea, "or how your own matrimonial jealousies exacerbate the situation, and exactly how important it is for you to see Dr. Herman. I do suggest twice a week, at least."

"Well, I'm not going to," said Annette, "and that's that. I don't have money to throw away. And what situation are you talking about?"

"Both Lilith and Saturn eat their children," said Dr. Rhea. "Now, I put that very bluntly, in terms of the archetype, but I think you are intelligent enough to understand. In Spicer a malefic Saturn struggles to assert himself. It's unwise to underestimate Saturn."

"I'll try not to," said Annette.

"The pull of Saturn is into deadness, inertia, and unconsciousness. Into depression, in fact."

"Spicer isn't depressed. He's funny, clever, lively—or was till he came to see you."

"You protest too much, my dear," said Dr. Rhea. "In any case we are talking about a creative depression, which contains within its core unbridled life energy, but which can be stultified if the shadow-side remains unrecognized. Then we have all the ingredients for a human tragedy."

"I think I'd rather you called me 'Mrs. Horrocks' than 'my dear,' " said Annette.

"It's quite natural for you to be angry with me," said Dr. Rhea. "Believe me, I understand and sympathize, but it doesn't alter the situation. The work against nature, against the endless mechanical cycle of reincarnation, is necessary work against Saturn and towards creativity. Every effort Spicer makes to escape his habitual nature, his conditioning, environment, habits, duties, parents, spouse, is an effort to escape the devouring jaws of Saturn. And I, as his therapist, am duty-bound to help him. It is a perilous venture for both of us."

"So you are helping him escape me?" asked Annette. "His spouse? Is that what you mean? I quite certainly heard you say that."

"Only insofar as you represent Lilith," said Dr. Rhea. "And inevitably you must."

"And who the fuck is this Lilith," inquired Annette, "they all keep talking about?"

"Lilith is the Black Gall; she is under the rulership of Saturn; she is the melancholy of the deepest realm of death, poverty, darkness, tears, complaints, and hunger. She is the screech owl. The destructive force that works against the flow of harmony that should exist between men and women."

"Oh, thanks," said Annette.

"I don't want to feel I am wasting my time here," said Dr. Rhea.

"I'm sorry," said Annette. "Please go on."

"Spicer stands on the brink of a very great journey," said Dr. Rhea. "He is a very special person—a profound artist—destined for spiritual greatness. Only Saturn and Lilith hold him back from his appointed task. Once he's free of these principles, once he has faced and incorporated his shadow-self—I have never met one so strong, Mrs. Horrocks—Spicer will shake free from the material world. He will cut the ties that bind. You understand what in your culture you describe as someone who is a mystic, I take it?"

"It's your culture as well, Dr. Rhea, but tell me more."

"The Buddha, in the blunt Christian term, is a mystic. A great spiritual leader. The Buddha left wife and family behind when he had grown out of them, could see beyond them, and set off on his mission in the world."

"And that's what Spicer's going to do?" asked Annette. "If you have your way? If I don't see your husband and somehow stop it? Be a Buddha?"

"It's nothing to do with what I want," said Dr. Rhea. "It's there in Spicer's chart. I am just the instrument of his liberation from the material world."

"I hope you can stand up and say this in a court of law," said Annette. "It may well end up there."

"I think basic Jungian thought is now well accepted in most courts," said Dr. Rhea. "Certainly the counselors and social workers are acquainted with the language of the archetype: many are trained in astrology too. The AAP is affiliated to the ATCCT."

"What's that?"

"The Association for the Training of Court Counselors and Therapists."

"You have wormed yourself in everywhere with all your nuttiness," said Annette. "And seem to be dragging the whole world along with you. You'll be ducking witches next: pricking people to find out if they're child abusers."

"Interesting that you should say that," said Dr. Rhea. "That child abuse is what comes to your mind."

"What you're really saying to me," said Annette, "is that if I don't have therapy from your husband you'll break up my marriage. You're blackmailing me."

"Poor Spicer," said Dr. Rhea. "I thought he exaggerated, but he doesn't. Lilith is very, very strong in you. But Spicer is strong too. He's breaking free."

"Spicer took me out to lunch yesterday," said Annette. "We had lobster and champagne. He didn't seem all that spiritual to me. I think he lays a lot of it on for your benefit. It's how he entertains himself."

"I think he only took a little of the fish, Mrs. Horrocks, and sipped the champagne, to keep you in countenance. Strange you forgot your own birthday. Or perhaps you wanted to. Fight against fate all you want, Mrs. Horrocks, be as rude to me as you like— really it makes no difference. The spiritual change has begun in Spicer and will continue in spite of all your efforts to hold him back. You'll have noticed the change in his diet. His body now rejects red meat, alcohol, craves natural foods. It's a sure sign of spirituality. You'll find stops and starts in Spicer's progress. Of course you will. He'll suffer from what I like to call the hot flushes of the soul. His sexuality may become suddenly more intense, alternating with periods of abstinence, melancholy. He will turn himself back for a time into a family man, or someone preoccupied with business, but the process towards oneness, once begun, is inexorable. Spicer is leaving you, Mrs. Horrocks, and the material world."

"Dr. Rhea," said Annette, "I'm sorry if I've spoken out of turn at all. As you say, it's natural for me to be angry. This all comes as rather a shock. But please, for my sake, the family's sake, could you stop encouraging Spicer in all this? Not flatter him by talking about his spirituality, his creativity? He's just a wine merchant, with a wife and two children and a baby on the way: no one special, just himself, which has always been good enough for me, and him. The consequences of his breaking up the home are so terrible for so many people. Couldn't you somehow include all them in the area of your responsibility? Because we're all going to suffer terribly if Spicer goes on like this. Please search your conscience, to see if you can't find a way within it not to break up this marriage. Not tell lies to Spicer, not as strong as that—just stay quiet about his spiritual destiny, as you see it?"

Dr. Marks thought for a little.

"In all conscience," she said, "I can't. My responsibility is to my patient, not to his family and associates. As I say, these are the ethics of my profession. Your husband approached me for help of his own free will, and I must give it to him. That, and only that, is my duty."

"Even if helping him actively makes so many people unhappy?"

"In my experience families adjust very quickly," said Dr. Rhea. "Sometimes material details can be a problem, but in this case they're minor. I have encouraged Spicer to talk to you about them, but I'm afraid he keeps putting it off. The Lilith in you is so quickly aroused. I think Spicer finds it quite frightening: you frequently alarm him, Mrs. Horrocks, with what he sees as sexual insatiability."

"What about my baby, who according to you must do without a father?"

"Every child has a father," said Dr. Rhea. "I'm sorry you seem so out of sympathy with your husband. Don't you care about his welfare at all? I don't think you've ever grasped how ill he was until he came to see me: how unhappy his childhood was."

"We all have unhappy childhoods. So what? Didn't you?"

Annette saw Dr. Rhea Marks' face flicker: the colorless lashes lowered over the pale, prominent eyes.

"I was the child of an unsupported mother," said Dr. Rhea Marks.

"Is this your plan for all newborn babies?" said Annette. "That, like you, they'll end up with no father?"

"Try not to be so excitable," said Dr. Rhea. "It's bad for the baby. I understand your ambivalence towards your coming child but try to control it."

"Do your patients often set out on this journey of theirs," asked Annette, "and leave their spouses behind?"

"Quite often, Mrs. Horrocks, yes," said Dr. Rhea.

"That doesn't seem strange to you?"

"Not at all," said Dr. Rhea. "Men who stand on the brink of spiritual revelation do naturally gravitate towards me. We like to call it synchronicity."

"You don't put it into their heads?" asked Annette. "This leaving of spouses? You don't have your own agenda, hidden or otherwise?"

"This is bizarre," said Dr. Rhea Marks. She rose from her chair and went to the window and contemplated the trees. The legs that emerged from the long skirt were slim and her ankles were pretty.

"And perhaps your plan for all pregnant women," said Annette, "is that they'll end up alone, and repeat your mother's story? You're not so much helping the men as attacking the women, and have found an ideal way of doing it. Power-mad, like the teachers and the doctors. Now the therapists too. I think you just want other women to end up lonely."

"We don't talk about loneliness," said Dr. Rhea, smugly. "We prefer to talk about aloneness."

"I bet you do," said Annette. "But you're all right, aren't you? You're safe enough. Not much chance of your old man going on a spiritual journey. He's too busy palpating breasts, the disgusting old pervert, and sticking his cock into his female patients, and you collude. You even procure. I expect he prefers them pregnant."

A pissed i tells Rhea
abt. Dr. Herman

Dr. Marks picked up the internal phone and dialed. "Herman, could you come in a minute? I have Mrs. Horrocks in my surgery. She's being abusive."

Rhea calling her husband

"Gilda, thank God you waited," said Annette. "Get me away from here quickly. I can't get the seat belt on; I'm sorry. Is there some way you can turn the alarm off? Hang on, I'll try and move the seat forward. No, that's hopeless. I can't fold myself in half any more. You have such a neat little bump: I'm just overall, all-purpose vast. No, I'm okay. Really. Not even particularly upset; I expect that will come later. I was in there with her for ages, wasn't I? It felt like it. Things were shapeless; what she said was random; the conversation was without form: like me, pregnant all over the place. What she's about to give birth to is some great lump of evil. It doesn't mean Dr. Rhea's necessarily bad: she may just be rather stupid and likes to have power, and has found a way of using it; I suppose that could add up to evil. But, no, I don't think so. Evil is something which attached from outside: you can't use it as a description; it's a thing in itself and she's going to give birth to it. Did you know that Rhea was Saturn's wife? I wonder if she was born that; more likely it was Doris Legge. Can't you turn that alarm off? Take out a fuse or something, Gilda. Wedge a match in there. Bloody Volvos, always doing things you don't want for your own good: if it's not the lights, it's the fasten-seat-belt buzz. Thanks, that's better. No, I don't want coffee. Let's go straight home. Those lights were red, Gilda. God, you're an awful driver. It's just as well we're in a Volvo, the four of us. Gilda and baby Henry, Annette and baby Gillian. These bangles are beginning to cut into

A telling G abt. Rhea

my wrist. My hands have got so puffy. Do you think they'd cut bangles off at the fire station? Shall we go there? Rhea Marks has entered into this marriage as a third party. She's halfway between a mistress and a voyeur. Perhaps Spicer just has this appetite for threesomes. Spicer and me and baby makes three. I was never absolutely certain I wanted this baby; Spicer and Aileen plus Jason never made it. You start off anti the first wife, don't you? You think she didn't understand him; you think she was cold, heartless, stupid, faithless—she must have been. In the end you see she was just another woman, trying to cope.

"I hit Rhea Marks on the chest. She told me Spicer was leaving me to go on a spiritual journey; she told me there were just a few material details left to clear up. God knows what Spicer's told her: they chat twin souls, I suppose, and mutual creativity. She's just the kind of woman who longs to write a novel. She always had the last word: you know how therapists do. If you're angry, they say they understand your anger; if you do anything at all, they tell you to stop acting out. I found myself saying dreadful things to her. I accused her of procuring, God knows what. When Herman came in, I hit her. I pummeled her chest; she said, 'Stop acting out, you are no longer a child'; and he came from behind me and said, 'Daddy's here—stop hitting Mommy,' and put his arms round me and pulled me away, and his fingers dug into my breasts for longer than he need have, and he just held me at a distance from her, and she smiled at me sweetly and forgivingly. I'd have a fuller, happier life once Spicer was gone, she said; I was now a media personality and a successful writer, and I must stand on my own feet; I wasn't the woman Spicer had married: people's life paths sometimes split and went in different ways, and some more guff about Lilith and Saturn. So I swore and spat a bit more, and they turned me out, and thank God you were still waiting in the car."

"Annette?" said Gilda.

"Yes, Gilda?"

"Do you really want to go to the fire station to get the bracelets off?"

"Yes, I do," said Annette. "They hurt like hell."

"I'm not sure you handled the session very well," said Gilda.

"Why not?" asked Annette. "Why shouldn't I call her names? And him. They're filth."

"Because you don't want them telling Spicer about Ernie Gromback, et cetera, do you?"

"I'd just deny it," said Annette. "Look at these weals coming up on my wrist. Not just are the bangles cutting into the flesh, I'm sensitive to the metal. Spicer probably got them from her and they've been soaking in some magic potion. Her husband's piss, probably. Or hers. I bet they're into Golden Showers."

"Calm down, Annette. This can't be good for the baby. Shouldn't I take you to Spicer?"

"No. The fire station. At once."

"I just don't like the feel of this," said Gilda. "Not at all. You don't want people like the Markses as enemies."

"They're not much cop as friends," said Annette. "What do I care? What can they do?"

"You remember what I said about Spicer asking me to join him and Marion?" said Gilda.

"Yes, I do, Gilda," said Annette.

"I'll swear there was a fire station somewhere down here," said Gilda. "Where's it gone? Well, I did."

"Oh, did you," said Annette.

"Don't sound so dull and drear, darling," said Gilda. "It was a long time ago. Spicer and I, well, sometimes when you were out, or at a party when you were in the kitchen, we'd have a quickie under the coats; it just got to be a habit. Actually, Annette, it was always a quickie, because that's how Spicer is. I hate the way you think you're so bad in bed, Annette, because actually it's Spicer. He has no natural instinct for sex. If you lie there thinking about what's for breakfast, it's because he's trying to remember the sex manual. It was Spicer and me asked Marion in: not Spicer and Marion asking me. When Steve and I got together, that was the end of it: and by that time Spicer had got more interested in Marion than in me. That's the problem with threesomes: they end up with a different twosome. So that was the end between me and Spicer. I won't say I was hurt, but I took offense."

"They've closed the fire station," said Annette. "Look, it's a garden center now. Perhaps it's just as well or I'd have asked them to cut my throat."

"*M*rs. Horrocks?"

"Yes? Who's that?"

"I'm sorry, have I disturbed you?"

"No. I'm just a bit sleepy. A friend gave me some stuff to take called Easy Night. I took rather a lot. Who am I talking to?"

"I'm so sorry, didn't I say? This is Amelia Hardy of *The Oprah Winfrey Show*. I'm the researcher. I wondered if we could have a brief conversation about tomorrow?"

"Tomorrow? I thought it was months ahead."

"We did write to you."

"I haven't been opening all my letters lately."

"That's your privilege as a creative artist," said Amelia Hardy. "Never mind, tomorrow it is, your publisher okayed it, and we're all set up and ready to go, if I can just have this brief conversation with you first."

"Actually, could I call you back in half an hour?" asked Annette. "I'll call you at—what's the time now, three-fifteen? In the afternoon. At four o'clock precisely. Will you be there?"

"Yes, of course," said Amelia Hardy. "I'll wait for your call."

"Just fine! I expect the Easy Night will have worn off a little by then," Annette said.

"Shall we make it four-thirty? I take Easy Night sometimes myself. I swear by it, but it is quite strong."

"*W*endy, can I speak to Spicer? It's urgent."

"He's in a meeting, Mrs. Horrocks."

"Can you get him out of it?"

"I don't think I'd better try. The meeting's with British Rail," said Wendy. "You know we have this great big deal going through: it's really saved our bacon. I've got Jason and Susan here. Susan, do you want to talk to Mum?"

"Hi, Mum!"

"What are you doing in the office?" asked Annette. "I thought you were both upstairs in your rooms."

"Dad's taking us to a puppet show in Islington," said Susan. "Jason wanted to go to London Dungeon and I wanted to go to the zoo, but Dad said scenes of torture were unsuitable and the zoo was an abomination, so there's only puppets left. If we'd known, we'd have stayed home."

"Why didn't you tell me?"

"We tried to but you were asleep," said Susan. "Dad just rang and said, hi, let's go, so we went."

"Why are you calling him Dad all of a sudden, not Spicer?"

"He says he wants me to. It makes us feel like more of a family. But I keep forgetting. Spicer—I mean Dad—said it would get us out from under your feet, give you time to rest if you needed rest. Was that okay? It didn't seem right leaving you, but you were so fast asleep. You looked so pretty and peaceful. You hadn't been crying or anything?"

"No."

"I wondered," said Susan. "I suppose when you're pregnant you're meant to get puffy all over. You looked like a kind of mushroom."

"Thank you, Susan," said Annette. "I reckon I'm okay. What sort of puppet theater?"

"I don't know," said Susan. "Rainbow Childline something or other. I'm not looking forward to it. It'll be meant for much younger kids: it will be full of tree spirits and stuff; understanding each other, and what to do when your parents start touching you up. Jason will make puking sounds all the way through. But it's always nice going out with Dad. Doesn't often happen."

"We all went to *Buddy* the other day," said Annette.

"Buddy Holly's Stone Age," observed Susan. "We're more back into Angry Medieval, Sounds of the Suburbs stuff. But it was a nice try. Thanks, parent."

"Can I speak to Jason?" asked Annette.

"Probably not," said Susan. "He's trying out the graphics on Wendy's PC."

Spicer wants Susan to call him "Dad" now

"Give him my love."

"He sends it back," said Susan. "You don't have to worry, Mum. Jason isn't withdrawn. He just likes computers. Why, hi, Dr. Marks. Dad's still busy with British Rail, but he shouldn't be a minute. Bye, Mum, must go now."

Dr. Rhea in S* office

"*W*endy!"

"Yes, Mrs. Horrocks."

"Who exactly have you got in your office?"

"Susan, Jason, and this other lady who's just come in," said Wendy, sotto voce. "I haven't seen her before. She looks harmless enough."

"I want to speak to her," said Annette.

"Are you sure you want to?" asked Wendy. "You sound a bit strange. Hang on, I'll go through to the other office."

"Are you there, Mrs. Horrocks?"

"Yes, I am, Wendy."

"I've been a bit worried," said Wendy, "because I think it's the woman he keeps speaking to on the phone, and meeting for lunch, and what with you being pregnant it doesn't seem fair: and now, if he's taking the kids out mid-afternoon, and he actually canceled a meeting, and she's turned up in person—well, I don't like it, Mrs. Horrocks. I know it's none of my business, but you've always been really nice to me. I'm sure there's nothing to it: she looks really quiet and perfectly sweet and very serious, and she's a doctor, so she must be responsible. Your kids are yawning already, but even so— Here comes Mr. Horrocks, out of his meeting. Mr. Horrocks, please speak to Mrs. Horrocks. No, don't make faces at me, do it now."

"Hi, Annette—"

"Hello, Spicer," said Annette. "So, you're taking the kids for an outing?"

"You were too fast asleep to even answer the phone."

"And Dr. Rhea Marks is going too?"

"My, what a lot you seem to know, sitting up there in the safety of Bella Crescent. Yes, Annette, Dr. Rhea Marks is coming with us. She wants to observe the children a little: see if there are signs of precocious behavior, that kind of thing. We thought just an ordinary family outing would be a good background for it."

"I don't understand," said Annette.

"Let's face it," said Spicer. "You have become rather seriously disturbed, Annette. The Markses practically had to get the police today, to have you removed from their offices. You were violent. You really can't go on behaving like that. But I don't want to talk about it on the phone. I for one don't want the kids to overhear."

"So you, Dr. Rhea Marks, and the children are going to the theater together," said Annette, "leaving me behind at home— that's what it amounts to?"

"You are such a child, Annette," said Spicer. "You don't seem to understand the seriousness of your own situation. Dr. Herman Marks thinks it's unwise for you to be alone with the children too much. In his judgment, your fantasy life is too strong to be ignored; it might slip, might already have slipped, over into real life, particularly in relation to Jason, who's your stepchild. Annette, none of this is your fault; don't think I blame you. But

Jason's obsession with video games and X-rated films just isn't natural. I have to protect the children."

"By leaving them?" asked Annette. "Dr. Rhea Marks says you plan to leave us to pursue your spiritual journey, so what is this sudden concern for the children? It sounds rather hypocritical to me."

"You have obviously misinterpreted what Dr. Rhea said," said Spicer. "It's part of the negative pattern. You're having a very difficult pregnancy, which means that we all are. Most certainly I see the way ahead to the light, but I could hardly leave my family in the state it is: I love you, Annette, in spite of everything. What kind of man would I be if I just abandoned you? Not much cop on the wheel of life. I'd fall right off, right through to the cockroaches. Laughing?"

"Trying to," said Annette.

"Take another slug of Easy Night. Gilda rang me. She was really worried about you. Go back to sleep, sweetheart. See you later. We'll bring back fish and chips."

"And Dr. Rhea Marks? Will she come over too for fish and chips?"

"I shouldn't think so," said Spicer. "You've terrified her out of her wits. Annette, I'm not exactly looking forward to Rainbow Childline Theater. Don't make matters even worse than you've made them already."

"Sorry, Spicer. Is this call being broadcast through the office?"

"Yes," said Spicer, "come to think of it. But you're a media personality. It shouldn't worry you."

her calls are broadcasted through office

"Mrs. Horrocks?"

"Yes?"

"This is *The Oprah Winfrey Show*. Amelia speaking."

"Oh, hi."

"We mean to record tomorrow and hold over and screen for our New Year show. We like to do things live, but even Oprah has to have a holiday sometimes. Can I just say how much I loved *Lucifette Fallen*? Of course, the timing is good for you—Ernie Gromback tells me he's scheduled publication to fit in with our transmission. Isn't he a charmer?"

"Oh yes," said Annette.

"We're building the program around the domestic quarrel," said Amelia. "We figure God and Lucifer had the first one: brilliant of you to have seen that Lucifer was female. After that it was Jupiter and Juno. What can the rest of us poor mortals do in the face of the archetype? We have our pet psychotherapist to help us see through the dark to the light. That's the bit we'd like you to read from *Lucifette Fallen*: on page eight of the proof copy. I must say your publisher whizzed it around to us. The para beginning 'Where darkness becomes light'—down to 'What can a child do but repeat the experience?' And then sit next to Oprah and chat a bit about your own experiences and what drove you to write the novel."

"I'm sorry—I've lost you. I'm still a bit sleepy—"

"You are very central to the show, Mrs. Horrocks," said Amelia. "Have you had experience with TV before?"

"No," said Annette.

"Welcome to the real world," said Amelia.

"*G*ilda, hi. What is going on here? I'm not taking any of that stuff of yours ever again. I'm only just beginning to wake up. First there was you saying you had an affair with Spicer—I must have dreamt that. Then there was the thing about Spicer taking the kids out with Dr. Rhea Marks—that's completely unbelievable. And then there was this conversation about archetypes and *Lucifette Fallen* with a TV company. It can't be true. TV is the antithesis of the archetype. What's the time, Gilda? I feel too languid to get up and look at the clock."

"It's nine-twenty-one," said Gilda, "in the evening. Steve and I have just had supper and are settling in to watch TV. Careful what you say. He's in the next room. He likes me to watch the news with him."

"Nine-twenty-one? In the evening? Then where are Spicer and the kids?"

"Probably still out with Dr. Rhea Marks," said Gilda.

"Are you trying to tell me," asked Annette, "that those conversations actually happened?"

"Yes," said Gilda. "Well, the one with me certainly did."

"And you used to go to bed with Spicer?"

"It wasn't often the bed, it was usually the sofa," said Gilda.

"The sofa I'm lying on now?" asked Annette.

"You've had it covered since," said Gilda. "I was glad when you did. It made me feel better. Shall we just forget that and get on to what's important?"

"You and Spicer are both fairly important to me, Gilda," said Annette.

"I trusted you with the information in order to help you," said Gilda. "I don't want you letting Spicer know you know, because

A waking late from "Drozy Night" medicine ∞

Spicer can be vindictive. He might tell Steve, and Steve will go on and on about me not being open with him, and then I'll have to say it's all Spicer's fantasy, and honestly I haven't the energy for any of this at the moment, Annette, I'm going to give birth any minute, so just shut up, okay?"

"Okay," said Annette. "It's not what I want everyone to know either."

"Now, what does worry me is if Spicer said to you the things you say he did, then something not very nice is going on. You are being told that if you don't back off about Dr. Herman Marks assaulting you they'll start accusing you of child abuse, and they're the therapists, and they'll win."

"That's absurd," said Annette. "Why should they do a thing like that?"

"Think about it," said Gilda. "It happens a lot these days. And be glad there seems to be some kind of bargain being struck. They could just charge in there and get your kids taken away."

"How could they possibly do a thing like that, without proof, without evidence? You're being bizarre," said Annette.

"If I were you," said Gilda, "I'd shut up and be sweet as pie about the pair of them until the baby is born, and just hope they fade out of Spicer's life. The AJAP trains the counselors who train the social workers, and if they say child abuse, you've had it. If Jason so much as looks up Susan's skirt, that's it."

"Sometimes Jason helps me with the ironing," said Annette. "He irons Susan's knickers, because I can't see the point in ironing them. Jason says I just screw them up: he doesn't like it."

"Well, there you are. Condemned already. Unnaturally sexually precocious, and 'screw' is a pun, isn't it."

"That's ridiculous."

"Think about it," said Gilda. "Okay, Steve, I'm coming."

"Sweet as pie," said Annette. "That's me. Don't worry."

"Hi, Mum!"

"Hi, Susan. Hi, Jason. How was the show?"

"Spooky," said Susan. "I don't want to know about all that stuff. I'm sick of having it rammed down my throat."

"What do they think we are?" said Jason. "Children?"

"Where's Dad?"

"He dropped us off and took Dr. Rhea home and said he'd get fish and chips on the way back."

"Did you like Dr. Rhea?"

"She was okay," said Susan. "But she kept asking questions and pretending she wasn't."

"She smiles all the time," said Jason, "but she isn't really. Who is she, anyway?"

"A friend of Daddy's," said Annette.

"What does he want friends for?" asked Susan. "He's got you. What sort of doctor is she, anyway?"

"A head doctor," said Annette.

"Why? Is one of us mad?" asked Susan. "It's probably Dad, taking us to a show like that."

"She made us drink caffeine-free Coke," said Jason. "She can go and take a leap at herself."

"*A*nnette?"

"Hello, Spicer."

"You always take so long getting to the phone," said Spicer. "I nearly gave up. I'm speaking from a call box. Look, all the fish-and-chip places in London seem to be closed. And I promised the children."

"Don't worry," said Annette. "They'll survive. They can have an omelette. They're very tired anyway. They loved the show, Spicer. And they really liked Dr. Marks."

"Good," said Spicer. "I just can't understand your antagonism to her. Or all this stuff about her unfortunate husband. It makes things really difficult for me."

"I feel more settled in my head now, Spicer," said Annette. "The rush of hormones when you're pregnant can do all kinds of things. It says in my *Before the Birth* book that in the later stages of pregnancy women sometimes get very sexy; they even find themselves reading pornography."

"Good God, do they really?"

"Yes," said Annette. "So I expect it was just that kind of energy gone sour: I kind of imagined things that just weren't happening. I'm ever so sorry, Spicer," said Annette.

"I might ask you to put that in writing when I come home," said Spicer.

"Which bit, Spicer?" asked Annette. "About it not happening or about being sorry?"

"Either or both, darling," said Spicer. "Or none at all, so long as it's all clear in our heads. Actually, Rhea can be a bit of a pain: all this stuff about transitional crisis. Anyway, I'm on my way home, fish-and-chip-less. Shall I buy some champagne?"

"I thought you were off alcohol?"

"Well, you can go too far, can't you? And champagne's different," said Spicer. "It doesn't count."

"Brilliant!" said Annette. "Did Rhea think the kids were okay?"

"Tell you when I get back," said Spicer. "Shall I bring you an interesting video?"

"What sort of video?"

"A later-stage-of-pregnancy video."

"Oh, Spicer! How exciting. You are in a good mood. Come home quickly. You'll find me sweet as pie."

"Spicer," said Annette. "The price tag's still on the bottle. A hundred and twenty pounds. It's insane."

The children had gone to bed. The fire was lit.

"Don't wet-blanket, Annette," said Spicer. "So's our telephone bill insane. You talk too much to Gilda."

"Sorry," said Annette.

"What do you find to talk to her about?"

"Just babies," said Annette. "Childbirth. Washing machines. Domestic detail."

"And, Annette—"

"What, Spicer?"

"You're married to a wine merchant."

"I know that, darling," said Annette. "And a very successful one."

"To a wine merchant," said Spicer, "all bottles are cheap at the price. A hundred and twenty pounds is not insane."

Spicer in good mood - coming home w/ champagne

"Sorry, Spicer," said Annette. "I'm the one who's insane."

"Funny one," said Spicer forgivingly.

"It's lovely having you here beside me in such a good mood," said Annette.

"I have been worried," said Spicer. "To be frank. Anxious, even."

"About money, you mean?"

"No, about you and what peculiar things were going on in your head, and whether it was okay to leave you with the kids," said Spicer. "That's why I wanted Rhea to see them."

"I see," said Annette.

"I've been doing my best," said Spicer. "Family outings and so forth. But you've been really distracted."

"In what way has it shown itself, darling?" asked Annette.

"How long since you cooked a proper meal?" asked Spicer. "You don't eat dinner any more."

"That doesn't mean the kids have to be doomed to frozen TV chicken platters," said Spicer. "But, according to Rhea, the kids are just fine."

"I'm so glad she thought so," said Annette. "I really trust her judgment. A warning shot over the bows does no one any harm."

"Rhea's very well qualified," said Spicer. "A wise woman, in both the Jungian and the worldly sense. Highly respected in her profession. Her word goes in a court of law. Not many laughs, though, on an afternoon out. I really missed you, Annette. And the play was dire. Embarrassing."

"I'm sorry you didn't enjoy it," said Annette.

"Life can't be all wine and roses," said Spicer.

"There's the soul as well," agreed Annette.

"There's a time and place for the soul," said Spicer. "Shall I put on the video?"

"Anything you say, darling. Anything that makes you happy."

"That makes *us* happy," said Spicer.

"That makes us happy," repeated Annette.

"Ernie Gromback called this morning," said Spicer. "He couldn't raise you at home. He seemed to think you were doing *The Oprah Winfrey Show.* I told him you weren't, you didn't want to be gawped at by the whole world."

"I wouldn't dream of doing *The Oprah Winfrey Show*," said Annette. "They're bound to worm things out into the open one would rather keep to oneself. Family's more important than fame. Fame's vulgar."

"Annette, you haven't even finished one glass. I've had three."

"I'm not saying it's acid; champagne can't be acid at a hundred and twenty pounds the bottle," said Annette. "It's just that being pregnant makes me exceptionally prone to indigestion."

"Killjoy!" said Spicer.

"Actually, Spicer," said Annette, "they do say these days pregnant women shouldn't drink alcohol. I worry."

"Who's they? Old wives and young doctors and people who are trying to drive wine merchants out of business? Don't tell me you've joined the enemy!"

"Of course I haven't, Spicer," said Annette.

"Then drink up. It will help you enjoy the film. Champagne's hardly alcohol anyway."

"Yes, Spicer," said Annette, sipping away, smiling away.

"Dr. Marks agrees with me the whole nation is descending into a frenzy of negation," said Spicer, "in which Bacchus is the first to get it in the neck. We have to fight back. But let's talk a little less, watch a little more. Lean your head into my shoulder: let me put my arm round you. I'm always here to look after you."

"I know that, Spicer."

"Why are you shutting your eyes?" asked Spicer. "This is a good bit."

"I expect it is," said Annette, "but I don't think I want to look at it."

"Prude!" said Spicer. "Perhaps Dr. Herman Marks was right about you. Perhaps you need treatment more urgently than any of us realize?"

"I've opened my eyes," said Annette. "I'm just fine."

"I'll put it on pause so you can tell what's going on," said Spicer.

"Thank you, Spicer," said Annette. "That's very thoughtful of you. Doesn't it hurt? Two men at the same time like that?"

"That's a silly question."

"I'm sorry. I thought you wanted my comments."

"God, Annette, you are hopeless. In answer to your question, not if she relaxes, not if she enjoys it, no, it doesn't hurt."

"But I suppose, if it does hurt just a little bit," said Annette, "she enjoys it a bit more."

"Yes. Exactly. Everyone does," said Spicer.

"Well, I'm really glad for the human race," said Annette, "that it's evolved the way it has."

"Next you'll be saying the one behind her reminds you of Dr. Herman Marks," observed Spicer.

"He's not in the least like Dr. Herman Marks," said Annette.

"I was only joking," said Spicer. "Why do you have to take

everything so seriously? You're sure the kids are asleep? We wouldn't want them to come in and find us watching this."

"No, we certainly wouldn't."

"You in later pregnancy and liking porno all of a sudden."

"I didn't say that exactly, Spicer," said Annette.

"I certainly heard you say it," said Spicer.

"Well, if you heard it, I said it," said Annette. "I have no excuses to offer. It's perfectly clear that anything I say about Herman Marks was just me making trouble."

"But why should you have wanted to make trouble?" asked Spicer.

"I was jealous about you seeing so much of Dr. Rhea Marks," said Annette.

"At last you admit it!" said Spicer.

"I want to make it up to you now, Spicer," said Annette. "To show how sorry I am. Jealousy is a truly pathetic emotion."

"I've had enough of pause," said Spicer. "Let's put it on play."

"It's quite on-turning," said Annette. "You can't help it in the end."

"Thank God for that," said Spicer. "You're becoming human at last. See how the woman's enjoying it? Even more than the men? She's not faking. You can tell. You just relax. At least there's only one of me. That should suit you."

"Couldn't we go upstairs? Do we have to do it on the sofa?"

"Oh, for God's sake, Annette!"

"Sorry, Spicer," said Annette. "We'll stay here."

"You are so inhibited," said Spicer. "But perhaps that's why I love you. I as Zeus the seducer/lover/divine, you as Danaë."

"Just call me sweet-as-pie," said Annette, "and I'll answer to it."

"Those bracelets are practically sinking into your arm. You can't have got fatter since yesterday."

"Water retention," said Annette.

"Don't be proud of being unglamorous," said Spicer. "Don't the bracelets hurt?"

"Yes," said Annette.

"I quite like the thought of that," said Spicer. "Turn over."

"Dr. Rhea told me you were leaving me," said Annette.

"I'm beginning to think Dr. Rhea's nuts," said Spicer.

"But did you tell her that?"

"I tell her all kinds of things she wants to hear," said Spicer. "From dreams I make up to scenarios about my future. None of them necessarily true."

"But why do you say what she wants to hear if it's so disloyal to me?"

"Because I'm easily bored," said Spicer. "And she drones on and I like to get her to change the subject, or at least the archetype."

"But why do you go to her in the first place? If it's boring."

"Because I'm in a transitional crisis, because I need to liberate my Perseus from my Polydectes, and slay Medusa, the poisonous feminine, or, look at it another way, cast off Medusa and escape Lilith; or simply be the tree, the trunk, the pillar, the stake, the antinatural which penetrates the cleft hill. Does that hurt?"

"Yes."

"It's meant to," said Spicer. "Just a bit. Isn't this good?"

"Yes," said Annette. "Just call me Tweetie-pie. Each to their own myth. Personally, I choose Disney."

"*A*nnette?"

"Hello, Mum."

"Did you speak to Spicer about your father's money?"

"No, I didn't," said Annette. "Spicer has had business worries. They're over now. I'm sure the repayments will start flowing any minute. Don't worry about it."

"Don't you know anything about Spicer's business affairs?"

"Not much, actually. Look, Mum, I've got a headache: please, can't this wait?"

"I don't think so, Annette," said Judy. "I was awake all night worrying. Spicer's such a charmer, but do we really know him?"

"Probably not, Mum," said Annette. "Men are always full of surprises. Wives can be married to bigamists and not know it till both families meet up at the funeral. Rapists and serial killers likewise."

"I'm not suggesting Spicer is a bigamist, a rapist, or a serial killer, Annette," said Judy. "Don't misrepresent me. I'm very fond of Spicer. I have to be. He's going to be the father of one of my grandchildren. I want everything to go well for you both. You can always come and stay with me, Annette. You know that. This is always your home."

"Thanks, Mum," said Annette. "But things are looking okay. Just fine."

"I'm glad to hear that, Annette, because something's just occurred to me. You remember yours and Spicer's wedding?"

"Of course I do," said Annette.

"It wasn't a legal ceremony, was it? You were going to have that later. Did you?"

Mother reminds A that marriage isn't legal

"It was a wonderful wedding party. A marquee in the garden: all those roses, and songs."

"It was all very charming, Annette, but it wasn't legal. Your divorce hadn't come through."

"A scrap of paper," said Annette.

"Your voice has gone very quiet."

"You're right, Mum. I don't think Spicer ever did put the house in joint ownership, and we didn't actually get to the Registry Office. They're such dismal places. Births, deaths, marriages all lumped together, and you have to book up so far ahead, and either Spicer or me were always busy, and it just kind of drifted off into 'One day we'll get round to it.' But it's okay, Mum. It doesn't make any difference. I'm a common-law wife."

"There's no such thing, Annette. A woman has some legal rights once there's a baby of the unwed union, but none at all if there isn't. She has just the same status as a friend who's happened to live in all those years, and enjoyed the perks while she was at it."

"But I am having a baby, Mum, so there's no worry."

"I don't mean to upset you, puss," said Judy, "but you do need reminding of practicalities sometimes. Your father's been looking it all up."

"Dad hates Spicer, Mum," said Annette. "Of course he's been looking it up."

"He doesn't hate Spicer," said Judy. "Not at all. He finds him as charming as I do. We're just both the worrying kind. You are our only daughter. Now, don't get upset and start lashing out at us because we're in the way. I'm going to put the phone down now, puss, so you can get a hold of yourself."

"I'm perfectly in control of myself, Mum," said Annette.

"Goodbye, Annette," said Judy. "Love to Spicer. And I mean that. And look after yourself."

"Goodbye, Mum."

"*A*nnette, are you okay?" asked Gilda. "There was another child-abuse case on the news last night. I sometimes wonder what my own father was like. He died when I was three. If you don't remember it, is it there in your psyche, traumatizing you forever? Or do you have to remember it for it to damage you? The things they never tell you; it's worse than AIDS. Annette, are you there?"

"I'm here, Gilda."

"Annette, I spent most of the morning on my hands and knees scrubbing the kitchen floor," said Gilda. "Scrubbing! Does that mean I'm going to have this baby any minute now?"

"Probably," said Annette. "It's the nest-building instinct. You make things clean."

"I hate being taken over like this," said Gilda. "I'm terrified. Supposing I split?"

"You do split," said Annette. "They sew you up afterwards. Or else they cut you open neatly before you begin."

"They don't say that at the Clinic, or did I miss it? It's all about holding your birth partner's hand."

"That's why I don't go much to the Clinic. I don't want to hold my birth partner's hand, I want gas-and-air and an epidural and a nurse I've never met who's never heard of an archetype."

"What's the matter?" asked Gilda.

"Do you remember when Spicer and I got married?"

"Yes."

"Well, we didn't," Annette said.

"It was a wonderful wedding," said Gilda. "A marquee and champagne and a band. But none of us got asked to the ceremony itself, I do remember that. We felt demoted to second-class friends. I went right off you, and that was the real reason I had that stupid thing with Spicer. I keep trying to think of reasons. I feel so bad about it, Annette. I'm superstitious. If I have a clear conscience, I'll have an easy birth. So I keep confessing to everyone. It's insane. I know it's insane but I can't help it."

"There was a hold-up to my divorce decree, but Spicer and I had done all the organizing, so we went ahead with the reception anyway. And then we just never got round to getting married. It didn't seem to matter."

"Get married now," said Gilda. "Suggest it to Spicer. How can you get divorced if you're not married?"

"Now seems a little edgy, Gilda," said Annette. "Though I'm being as sweet as pie, I really am. And it's working. He's running down Dr. Rhea himself: I don't have to do it."

"Oh God, Annette, is it worth it?" asked Gilda. "I'm getting false contractions. They don't hurt; my belly just goes hard as a board. I rather like it. Do you think men feel like this when they have an erection? Purposeful and out of control at the same time?"

"I expect so," said Annette. "I wonder if Spicer realizes about the house and us not being married?"

"Of course he does, darling," said Gilda. "He's a very successful businessman."

"Not all that successful," said Annette. "If it wasn't for British Rail we'd be bankrupt; poor Spicer was just about to put everything in my name."

"Who told you that? Spicer? Steve says he has so much salted away it's unbelievable," Gilda said. "Annette, I can't talk any longer, I'm going to lie in the bath."

"Don't do that," said Annette, "because if the waters break you might not notice."

"*A*nnette?"

"Who is it?"

"It's me. It's Ernie. Where are you? Why did you take so long answering?"

"I went back to bed," said Annette. "I was tired."

"But you're okay? I worry about you."

"Thank you, Ernie. I just didn't get much sleep last night, one way and another. And I had to grope for the phone. Somewhere on the floor in the bedclothes. I'm sorry."

"It sounds a wild scene," said Ernie Gromback.

"It was rather."

"Should you be doing this kind of thing?" asked Ernie Gromback. "You being so pregnant?"

"I'm told it's natural," said Annette. "And if it's natural it must be good, or else the patriarchal spirit will triumph, and Eve will be wrenched once more out of Adam's rib."

"You're rambling, Annette."

"Am I? Sorry."

"You sound like Marion on a bad day," said Ernie Gromback. "I want to run off with you and look after you."

"What do you need, Ernie? Why did you call?"

"Don't be like that, Annette," said Ernie Gromback. "It's

eleven o'clock: you're meant to be at my office seeing the *Oprah Winfrey* researcher at half past, you're recording this afternoon and you're not even out of bed."

"I didn't know we had a meeting," said Annette.

"Didn't Spicer give you the message last night?"

"He must have forgotten," said Annette. "We got rather tied up. Ernie, I'm not going to do *Oprah Winfrey*."

"Why not? Because Spicer doesn't want you to?"

"I suppose so," said Annette.

"You can't let him do this to you," said her publisher.

"There seems to be rather a lot at stake," said Annette. "More than you'd imagine."

"What I need like a hole in the head," said Ernie, "is a first novelist in a time of recession turning down *The Oprah Winfrey Show*. Do you want my entire business to go down the drain?"

"If it's my marriage, or what passes for my marriage, or your business," said Annette, "I'd rather it was your business down the drain. I need the roof over my head."

"Do you have a marriage there worth saving?" asked Ernie.

"It's not just me," said Annette. "It's Susan, Jason, my parents, our friends, the house, the garden, everything. I have to have time to think."

"You've been brainwashed," said Ernie Gromback. "The man's a monster."

"He's the man I love," said Annette. "You just say that because you want me to do *Oprah Winfrey* and make money for you."

"It's money for you," said Ernie Gromback. "Fiction is your way to independence. That's why Spicer doesn't pass on messages."

"I'm so tired, Ernie, and I keep getting pains," said Annette. "I expect it's indigestion. I drank too much champagne last night."

"Who gave you champagne in your condition?"

"Spicer says champagne doesn't count as alcohol," said Annette. "It wasn't too much in ordinary terms, Ernie, just too much because I'm pregnant."

"And Spicer doesn't think of that."

"He used to," said Annette. "But he doesn't any more. Perhaps it's because the wine trade is in such a bad way. You know what men are."

"I'm a man too," said Ernie. "I wouldn't delude myself. I'd know how to look after you. I know a lot of things. I know Spicer didn't give you my message. I know Spicer has been seeing a lot of Marion. I know it's hopeless to try and do business with friends. When Spicer gave me your manuscript I should have run a mile. Get your clothes on and come down here at once, or Spicer will have won."

"But I'm so tired," said Annette.

"Of course you are," said Ernie. "Spicer made you tired."

"It wasn't calculated, Ernie," said Annette.

"No? When did Spicer ever not calculate anything? I'm coming round to fetch you. I'm going to bring you back to my office, where you can put your feet up. Then you go on to the studio. What are you going to wear?"

"I haven't got anything to wear."

"Borrow something from someone," said Ernie Gromback. "Spicer gave me that manuscript because he expected me to turn it down. It wasn't my kind of book. He knew that."

"Then why didn't you?"

"Because it was really good."

"*G*ilda."

"Hello, Annette," said Gilda. "I feel okay again. A false alarm. I did have a bath. Now I'm busy decorating the crib. Steve's home: he bought all these ghastly things from a car-boot sale. White satin ribbons and stuff."

"Have you got anything I can wear for *The Oprah Winfrey Show*?"

"What sort of thing did you have in mind?" asked Gilda. "Spicer's going to be furious."

"Too bad," said Annette. "Anyway, Spicer won't know. I'll be home by seven, before Spicer gets back. He has an appointment with Dr. Rhea at six-thirty. The last one, he says. I was right to do a Tweetie-pie, it really worked. Disney wins against Mount Olympus. Spicer and me are on course, truly on course. I just want to be on *The Oprah Winfrey Show*. They're not screening it till January, when Spicer will be in France. He'll never even see it."

"I do have that blue sort of spotted shift," said Gilda. "Armani."

"Shows too much arm," said Annette.

"Wear it with a jacket," said Gilda. "What about your hair?"

"I'll do it under the shower now," said Annette.

"Someone's bound to tell Spicer," said Gilda. "You won't get away with it."

"Oh, shut up," said Annette. "There's no possible way I can know what to do for the best, so I'll do what I want."

"Good thinking," said Gilda. "What the hell."

"What the hell, Gilda, what the hell. In my mother's good days she used to quote Don Marquis. He wrote an epistolary work called *Archy and Mehitabel*. Archy was a cockroach, Mehitabel was a cat. They typed each other letters on the office typewriter; they couldn't manage the upper case. Mehitabel used to sign off: 'what the hell, archy, what the hell.' So that's what I'm signing off to you, Gilda: what the hell, gilda, what the hell. And Tweetie-pie wasn't Disney. It was Warner Brothers."

"*D*o you know where you are?"

"I think so. Who are you?"

"I'm Dr. McGregor, casualty officer. Who are you?"

"I don't know you," said Annette. "You have really nice straight teeth."

"Thank you. Try and understand what I'm saying."

"Why can't I?"

"You're still feeling the effect of the anesthetic. Now, what is your name?"

"Annette."

"That's a very pretty name," said Dr. McGregor. "Could we have a second one? And an address? Even the luxury of a next-of-kin?"

"What's it got to do with you?" asked Annette.

"We like to know these things," said Dr. McGregor. "You are in hospital, Annette. You collapsed in a taxi you'd picked up in the street. You didn't have a handbag with you. Just some loose change in your pocket. So you're a mystery to us."

"That's not my fault. I couldn't find my bag and I was in a hurry."

"Good. If you can remember that, can you tell us your second name?"

"Shan't."

"Where are you? Can you remember that?"

"In hospital."

"Good girl. We're admitting you. We're waiting for a bed in GYN."

"That's nice," said Annette.

"We need to find your husband."

"Do I have one?" asked Annette.

"We had to cut off a wedding ring when you were under the anesthetic. And some bangles. I hope you don't mind. There was a nasty mess beneath them."

"I wish I could remember more," said Annette.

"Don't worry. It will come back. You're very thin, but well dressed. Designer clothes, nurse said. We don't see many of those."

"Thin? I'm enormous," said Annette. "Vast like a mountain, like a cleft hill, like Lilith, like Medusa; I'm about to flood the world."

"Oh Christ, she's gone again," said Dr. McGregor. "It may not be just the anesthetic. She may be disturbed."

"She's in some kind of therapy," said the nurse. "We were doing that archetype stuff in Bereavement Counseling. I'm new in this hospital. What's the deal on fetus disposal? Incinerator?"

"At this stage? Coffins, memorial service, and counseling," said Dr. McGregor. "We do things properly here."

"You mean my baby's dead?" asked Annette.

"Don't try and sit up," said Dr. McGregor. "You'll find it difficult for a couple of days. You had an emergency cesarean. You were hemorrhaging. A flamboyant toxemia: you're lucky to be alive. Why did no one pick it up? This is what our entire antenatal service exists for. The baby didn't make it. We couldn't pick up a fetal heartbeat. I'm sorry. She had probably been dead for a couple of days. This is no way to break this kind of thing to anyone. That was why I needed to find your husband. You do have a husband?"

"Listen, and you hear your own heartbeat. Listen hard enough, and it'll tell you the story of your life. Whether it's comedy or tragedy depends only upon where you stop, at a good bit or a bad bit. But the heart doesn't let you stop," said Annette onto the tape machine Dr. McGregor had given her. "It just goes on and on, carrying its owner along with it, past the definite conclusion its owner longs to have. My resentment at this is nothing to do with suicidal inclinations: just the desire for proper endings and understandings, proper tyings-up, in real life as well as fiction. Not that you care about my mind, Dr. McGregor; your area is my body. One of the rules of writing feature films, or so Ernie Gromback told me, is that, if everything's looking just fine three-fifths of the way through, the next two-fifths must be devoted to making everything go sour. If all is black and sad three-fifths in, thereafter you move relentlessly towards your happy ending. If I could see losing the baby as three-fifths of the way in, I could then look forward to happiness. Or was the three-fifths point when Wendy startled me with 'Oh, born in November, a little Scorpio, a little stinger'? And the five-fifths when the new casualty nurse said, 'What's the deal on fetus disposal'? It felt like five-fifths at the time but the heart goes on beating, and before you know you're carried on into some other film, quite possibly three-fifths of the way through and sitting up and paying attention again, wondering what's going to happen next. The plural of 'fetus' ought actually to be 'feti,' but catch a nurse, anyone, knowing that, let alone acting upon it. People in hospitals have more sense than to be sticklers. She came up and apologized later. She'd thought I was unconscious, but I'd just had my eyes closed."

"You could try contacting your friends on the telephone," said Dr. McGregor. "I'm no therapist, but shouldn't you be sticking to the point? I'm a busy man."

"Just give me another tape," said Annette. "You are under no obligation to listen. Indeed, I hope you won't. I don't want to speak to my friends. I can't be sure who they are, not even Gilda. And I don't feel like saying, 'I'm just fine.' Not yet. But it's true that from spending so much time on the phone I have become accustomed to understanding my own life through my ears: so I need the tape. Call it aural predilection if you like, and it may well have to do with overhearing the rows between my mother and my father as a child—listening through doors, working out patterns. I used the patterns in *Lucifette Fallen*, a novel I wrote, Dr. McGregor. A stupid and pretentious title for a rather neat, too controlled, short novel. But you are obviously too busy to listen to all that."

"The girl from *Oprah Winfrey* was furious when she heard I was in hospital," observed Annette to her tape recorder, "and had lost my baby. 'Now what am I going to do?' she said. 'Annette Horrocks, pregnant, was to be the center of the show. And I've had to come all the way into town for nothing.' Ernie Gromback wrote to tell me about it: Ernie seems to be the only person left in the world able and willing to write a letter. I've had no visitors. It's not their fault, I know, but it doesn't stop me feeling deserted.

If I have visitors, if anyone from the outside world comes near, my blood pressure zooms up. Dr. McGregor's getting it under control, Staff Nurse says: they drip various drugs plus antibiotics into my arm. As well as toxemia, I had septicemia, its source of origin, where the skin had broken beneath one of the bracelets. The nurses bring me three-times-daily messages from Spicer: of the I'm-thinking-of-you,-darling, get-better-soon kind, but they somehow lack conviction. I can't quite feel Spicer's real, though I send loving messages out again. Poor Spicer: his baby too, his idea becoming my flesh. It's just hard to feel poor Spicer.

"I had a Bereavement Counseling session: a young woman called Anya told me the sense that Spicer wasn't real could only be a function of the drugs I was being given. Such medicines poisoned the mind, she said: she disapproved of them. She described herself as a holistic healer. When the drugs stopped, she told me, I'd bring Spicer to life again, and have proper sympathy with him. She made me visualize a flight of white marble stairs and at the top a place where I had been happy. She held my hand and persuaded me to climb, in my mind, a step at a time towards this goal. I obliged, though I felt embarrassed. It was unfortunate that the place at the top was a McDonald's: Anya thought I was mocking her when I said so; I wasn't. I just remembered taking Susan and Jason out to the cinema one day, and we ended up at McDonald's, and we were all, for some reason, pleasantly and simply content, stealing each other's French fries. In my 'visualization,' as she called it, the man behind the counter was large, strong, and surrounded by a brilliant white light: he had a face which looked as if it had been hewn out of a piece of wood. I imagined I was seeing Jesus, but I didn't tell Anya that: I didn't know her well, but enough to tell she wouldn't want Jesus described as a fast-food counter-hand. It was my vision, not hers, anyway, and, the paramedics being under instruction not to excite me, when I mentioned McDonald's she smiled stiffly and brought the session to a rather sudden end, which I'm sure she wasn't meant to. She left me with instructions to visualize a mandala—which I gathered looks rather like a pie chart with four divisions in different colors, representing intuition, intellect, sensation, and emotion. The trick is, apparently, to get the colors evenly balanced in your mind, and hold them there for two minutes. Then you become less 'stressed.' I did try. Really. I don't want to be a mocker. Spicer hates mockers. Cynicism, he once told me, is sneering at your own soul. I don't want to do that."

"If you don't mind," said Dr. McGregor, "since we are under instruction to work with nonorthodox healers when practicable, to save the cost of expensive drugs, we'll give hypnotherapy a go. A pleasant young man has just joined the team. His name is Peter. I will send him along to you."

"Hypnotism!" said Annette, and the bleepers on her blood-pressure monitor began to sound. He switched them off.

"Well?" asked Dr. McGregor on his rounds the next day. "What happened? It didn't go too well, I hear."

"Listen to it on the tape," said Annette, turning her head into the pillow, "if you're really interested and not just being polite. It's all there."

Dr. McGregor took the tape away.

*   *   *

"This Peter, this person from the fringes, was slight and sweet and had soft thick wavy hair, nut-brown, and a baby face. It was, as I feared, Peter, Peter Pan, Pan the Goat God. Rhea had got into my head. So I expected him to bring out a pipe and start playing it to me, and found myself looking down to see if he had cloven hooves. He didn't: he had brown shoes, rather worn but much polished. So perhaps he was a Peter Pan after all. He told me that if I would allow myself to be put in a light hypnotic trance he would locate the psychological trauma which, according to him, was sending the blood pounding so through my veins and keeping my blood pressure high. This account of my condition seemed to me to beg many questions. I asked him if he had any medical training and he said no: but he'd studied psychology at college and found he 'had a knack for hypnotism.' Even the most orthodox practitioners had begun to view many forms of illness as internalized behavioral problems—which had always been obvious so far as facial tics, stammers, addictions, and so forth were concerned —and hypnotherapy was proving a useful, inexpensive, effective, and nontoxic form of treatment in many cases: in particular the lowering of blood pressure. I then asked him what he would do with the psychological trauma once he located it in me, and he said, if appropriate, he would re-lay the memory so it ceased to be traumatic.

" 'Tell me more, Peter,' I said, 'tell me more,' thinking of the way Spicer now recalled the matter of the bacon sandwiches, and he replied that actually, though the re-laying of memory was considered okay in the States, it was still seen as unethical in Europe.

I was fortunate that the hospital I was in had a management team imported from the U.S., and, so long as a treatment worked, didn't bother too much with the detail of how or why it worked. How, I asked, did he do this locating?

"A traumatic memory, Peter said, could be located by regressing the patient—a victim of, say, child abuse—to the period of its occurrence, recalling the episode in its fresh form, and retuning it, as it were, persuading the child/adult that the fear, self-loathing, and sense of guilt experienced were inappropriate, and by bolstering accompanying feelings of affection, response, and gratitude, even creating them if necessary. The memory, dusted down and polished up, would then be re-laid in the adult mind as something that could be coped with—still unpleasant, perhaps, but no longer traumatic. A whole range of behavioral problems could quickly and cheaply be dispersed by re-lay hypnotherapy.

"I only report what Peter Pan told me, though I can't quite believe it. An isolated instance, perhaps, but you surely couldn't wipe away an entire childhood's wretchedness by simply persuading the victim to forget it? Surely memory would re-emerge through its coating of forgetfulness? Old stains beneath new wallpaper? I asked him if you could re-lay pleasant memories with nasty ones, turn a pleasant seaside outing into a horrid one, a good sexual experience into something oppressive and smothering—by restructuring a past, turn a wife against a husband, a husband against a wife—and he said oh yes, he assumed so, but who would bother?

*   *   *

" 'Does this apply to everyone?' I asked. 'Can everyone be hypnotized?' And he said, one in a hundred perhaps not, and so you could get any women into bed with you, bar the one in a hundred, by persuading her that you were the most attractive man in the world, and Peter Pan said, well, yes, most women, eighty in a hundred. But he, though he admitted he had been tempted, would never do anything like that. Common wisdom held that you couldn't get anyone to do anything under hypnosis that went against their conscience, because they would snap out of the trance at once. But with a little ingenuity any hypnotist could alter the perspective in which that conscience worked—the mildest person would take an ax to a door if told a child was dying behind it, the most honest would rob a bank if persuaded a nation would perish otherwise. A truly loyal wife could find herself in a situation in which disloyalty was the only appropriate answer: if the hypnotherapist is the Chief of Police, say, and the husband about to be put to torture, then what can the wife do but oblige the Chief of Police to keep the husband safe?

" 'I think,' I said, 'I'm the one in a hundred,' and he asked me to fasten my hands together above my head and told me I couldn't separate them, but I could and did, and he laughed and said I was indeed the one in a hundred, but he'd enjoyed our chat. The blood-pressure machine began to put out warning bleeps; Nurse McKenzie, who has red hair and freckles, and reminds me of Wendy, asked him to leave. Nurse McKenzie sat beside me for a while and told me of a newly married friend of hers who went to a hypnotherapist to be cured of overeating and ended up having sex on the sofa with him and being charged double, which post-hypnotic suggestion made her pay without argument. On the other hand, her friend had lost weight and didn't regret any of it. Whatever knockout drops they've added to my drip are beginning to take effect. I'm drifting off again."

"Well, hypnotherapy didn't work," said Dr. McGregor, visiting Annette in the Special Care Unit, to which she had been moved. "I had a quick listen to the tape. I don't think Peter will stay on the team for long. Obviously the sleazy end of alternative medicine."

"How can you have a quick listen to a tape?" asked Annette. "You either listen or you don't. I have another one here for you to ignore." Dr. McGregor took it away.

"I try not to think about Dr. Rhea or Dr. Herman Marks, because my blood pressure goes sky-high if I do. Thieves, murderers, perverts, devourers of babies! Destroyers of true love. Lilith and Saturn. In mythology Rhea is Saturn's wife. In Spicer's book on Theotherapy—Spicer sent it to me here in hospital, unasked: what can this mean?—the title page with Rhea's dedication written in was missing, but a few more passages had been marked. These were the ones relating to the goddess Rhea. If I keep an eye on the blood-pressure monitor I can sometimes direct my will and organize my mind—I can't describe it in any other way—to keep the level steady. But I can't, alas, focus in this way and read at the same time. Perhaps that's the reason I read so little? I risk glances at the pages from time to time.

*   *   *

" 'Overeagerness to promulgate divine mysteries,' I read, 'of the goddess Rhea. Shamanism, the grandmotherly guardian of much secret love: the woman who smothers those around her with an excess of love. The less love she gets the more she gives. Her problems are severest around midwinter.' Good. We're moving into the cold, dark months. 'Before Hellenic masculinization—by which we mean the imposition of the Greek gods upon the earlier pagan ones—Rhea was the Universal Great Mother Goddess and ruled supreme, needing no protective consort.' She can manage well enough without Saturn, in other words. Just my luck to fall foul of the Great Mother Goddess Cow. Other people's husbands end up with ordinary therapists. Perhaps what Spicer was doing to me with the tree and the cleft-hill business was nothing other than Hellenic masculinization? The rendering male of the female. Eleanor Watts wouldn't want to move into Bella Crescent if she understood how the archetypes roared up and down it, sucking us all in, whirling us around with their almighty backdraft.

"Still my blood pressure won't go down. It's been worse since Peter's visit. I might die of a stroke, they carefully don't say. I've been moved into an SC Unit, Special Care, but not yet IC, Intensive Care.

"Gilda has had her baby, in the maternity ward, below this one. A healthy baby boy; both are doing fine. Gilda came to stand in the ward doorway this morning and wave at me. She was wearing a bright-blue wrap which, together with her red hair, by virtue of some reflected halo effect, made her shimmer within a mauve aura. Blue and red make mauve, or is it purple? Gilda didn't have her baby with her. I was sorry not to have a glimpse of him. Gilda was being tactful. But really she didn't need to be. Her baby was a little bit mine, as mine had been a little bit hers, and I was proud for her. So it's okay. Really. There was never a friend as good as Gilda in the whole history of the world, and if anyone's to have a baby when I don't, it had better be her."

"I think Mrs. Horrocks can be moved to Light Care," said Dr. McGregor. "She seems to be much improved. Now, how do we account for that?"

"I'll leave you a tape to explain it," said Annette, "though you won't believe it."

"This afternoon I got really tired of the drips and tubes and being wired up and couldn't stand the business of screens and bedpans for a single minute longer, and when the nurses were elsewhere I plucked off terminals, cuffs, leads, and unhooked drips and got out of bed and went to the ward bathroom. I was very weak, and almost sorry for my poor little feet—they were quite translucent against the white-tiled floor. I remembered my feet as having been firm, strong, and solid. Well, everything changes. I stood beneath the shower and let the water run over my hair, my face, my shoulders, breasts, and too flat stomach, the thin loins. There wasn't a towel, so I had to go back to my bed still dripping. Nurses McKenzie and Smiley dried me down—their instructions not to excite me warring with their natural desire to kick my ankles hard—and got me back into bed and rewired me. The blood-pressure cuff round my forearm went into its automatic tightening phase: the diagnostic readouts settled at pulse rate seventy, and BP one twenty over eighty. Perfect. Nurse McKenzie dealt the screen a sharp blow with a ruler: the numbers quivered but stayed steady. Nurse Smiley switched off the whole machine and switched it on again, which sometimes did the trick. The cuff took another reading. Pulse seventy-five, BP one twenty-five over eighty-five. The extra fives were no doubt the product of my reaction to what I could only describe as McKenzie and Smiley's condition of doubt. Staff Nurse came to admire; then Sister. It was twelve hours before the Registrar turned up, but hospitals are so full of bad news there's not much time for the good. In a couple of days I can go home.

"Thus it became apparent to me that running water—described in Spicer's book on Theotherapy as being the best cure for Hera's problems, along with moonlight, bracelets, and bangles—had done its bit, though the bracelets and bangles, being false gifts, poisoned offerings, had all but killed me. All it took was a shower. Why I had so resisted being Hera—typified by slyness, softness, gullibility, shame, embarrassment, jealousy, use of sex as weapon, and so forth—I couldn't imagine. If we're all just a mixture of adjectives, one representative goddess is as good as another, so long as Saturn's ravenous wife, Rhea, doesn't have her hand in it. Which of course she had.

"I'm now downgraded from Special Care to Light Care, where all they do is feed me up, and I'm allowed to make phone calls, except the phone is out of order. 'What's the name of this ward?' I ask a nurse, reporting the fault. 'Olympus,' she says. 'We're part-funded in here by the sports firm. We have to rely in this hospital on business sponsors.'

"I can all but see Pegasus, trapped in Medusa's sick body for so long, bursting through from the end of my bed, breaking free, spreading his white wings in the sky above Mount Olympus, dissolving into nothingness, bearing my soul away for safe-keeping.

"Spicer. Real again."

"Two visitors to see you," said Nurse McKenzie, who was also being allowed a rest in Light Care. "If you're okay with these two, we'll let the others in."

"Hi, Mum," said Susan.

"Hi, Annette," said Jason.

"We're sorry about the baby," said Susan. "When are you coming out?"

"Probably about a week," said Annette. "How've you been?"

"It's been okay," said Susan. "But Gran won't let us have our meals in our rooms."

"And Granddad takes us out to find fossils in cliffs," said Jason, "which is boring."

"And we have to get a taxi to school," said Susan, "and people see."

"Though we get him to drop us on the corner so they don't," said Jason.

"And I haven't had a pizza for five weeks, since you came in here," said Susan.

"And the games disc on my computer's corrupted and

Gran says she can't afford a new one," said Jason. "So I've nothing to do."

"Do you mean to say," said Annette, "you haven't been at home? Spicer hasn't been looking after you? You've been at my mum's?"

"Spicer hasn't been very well either," said Susan. "There's some kind of trouble at the office. He says he may have to go bankrupt. Something to do with British Rail."

"I've set the bleeper warning at one sixty over one ten," said Nurse McKenzie. "If you get to that the kids will have to leave. Try not to upset your mother more than you have to."

"I'm not upsetting her," said Susan. "She's our mother. We're bringing her up to date. And Jason can't upset her, because he's concentrating on his Game Boy."

"I'm up to level six," said Jason.

"Did Spicer say when he'd be in to see me?" asked Annette.

"He's coming this evening," said Susan. "He said to send his love. They'll only let in two visitors at a time, so he said we should come first."

"How does he seem?" asked Annette.

"Just the same," said Susan. "Are you two getting divorced?"

"Of course not," said Annette. "Why should we?"

"Perhaps you ought to," said Susan. "You look quite different in here. Much younger. Your face had got a funny sort of fixed expression on it, as if you were expecting someone to hit you all the time."

"Don't be silly," said Annette.

"Gran's got it in for Spicer too," said Susan. "She says he owes her a lot of money. She goes on and on about it. I wish they'd let you out of here so you could get home and sort things out."

"It isn't very nice at Gran's," said Jason.

"I thought you were too busy with your Game Boy to listen," said Susan. "If I say anything to you, you tell me you can't hear. So why is it different now, all of a sudden?"

"I hear all kinds of things you don't know about," said Jason. "Life at Bella Crescent is just one long primal scene. Shit, now I've blown it. Back to level five."

"You'd better go now, kids," said Nurse McKenzie. "Your mother's bleeper's going. If this is what the children do, what's going to happen when the husband arrives?"

"*H*ello, darling," said Spicer.

"Oh, Spicer," said Annette. "It's been so long! I've missed you so. Our poor baby—I'm so sorry."

"It wasn't your fault," said Spicer. "The sooner you're out of here the better."

"They say I should stay another couple of days."

"It's probably the hospital itself that's making you ill," said Spicer. "If the taxi driver hadn't brought you in, but taken you home, none of this might have happened."

"I don't think it was quite like that, Spicer," said Annette.

"What do any of us know?" asked Spicer. "Only what the doctors see fit to tell us. But what's done is done. Now we pick up the pieces."

"Susan said there was trouble at work," said Annette.

"Don't worry your head," said Spicer. "Just a hiccough. You look really pretty, Annette. Perfectly healthy. Glowing, in fact."

"It's because I'm so happy to see you," said Annette.

"Why don't you discharge yourself?" asked Spicer. "Come home now?"

"They've been so good to me here, I don't like to do that," said Annette.

"You don't want to come home to me?"

"Of course I do, Spicer."

"Dr. Herman said you would probably quickly develop a dependency on the hospital, the authority figure: the substitute father. It seems to be in danger of happening," observed Spicer.

"I just don't want to get ill again, Spicer," said Annette.

"All the more reason to get out of here and into therapy as quickly as possible," Spicer said.

"Therapy follows you to hospital, Spicer; you've no idea," said Annette. "It sweeps over you: a great tidal wave of it."

"Not much has changed, Annette," said Spicer. "You can't avoid the smart retort. Your book has had a few prepublication reviews. Everyone says how smart it is, you'll be glad to hear."

"I think the doctor was hoping to discuss things with you, Spicer, before I went home."

"We have our own doctor," said Spicer.

"Dr. Rhea? Still Dr. Rhea?" asked Annette.

"Of course," said Spicer. "She's a great support. You and I need to talk about your reaction to her. It's of course projection. It's to do with your affair with Ernie Gromback. I understand, Annette. There's no need to deny it. I was upset at the time but I'm over that. Enforced monogamy is absurd. And you're a child, so far as your sexuality is concerned. Dr. Herman says this is the problem with the sexually abused child: maturity is seldom reached."

"And he told Dr. Rhea and she told you," said Annette. "So much for them. They're rubbish."

"Shall we avoid the gossip," said Spicer, "and get back to important matters? Who cares who fucked who one dark night? I certainly don't. Your anger with your mother is finally explicable. She failed to protect you from your father—"

"My father did not abuse me," said Annette. "I am not angry with my mother."

"While you continue to block out the truth, you will continue to make my life a misery," Spicer said.

"If you truly think that about my father," said Annette, "why have you sent my daughter and your own son to live with him?"

"Shall we get back to Ernie Gromback et cetera, Annette?" asked Spicer. "Your casual infidelities? I think you should have told me, but perhaps you were too ashamed? At least my relationship with Marion was not an act of degradation, but based on common interest and a shared spirituality. I wish you could have chosen someone less physically unattractive than Gromback. But I suppose that's part of the syndrome."

"I think perhaps you'd better leave," said Nurse McKenzie. "I've seen Mrs. Horrocks in all kinds of states, but not hyperventilating and in tears. She's lost her baby: she needs comforting, not whatever it is you're doing, Mr. Horrocks."

"She didn't lose *her* baby, she lost *our* baby," said Spicer. "She didn't even lose it: she threw it away. You don't understand how disturbed my wife is. Or indeed how powerful. She didn't have to take an instrument to herself, as she's done many a time in the past: she simply had to will the poor creature's destruction. Dr. Rhea predicted it, Annette. She told me your ambivalence towards Gillian, a girl child, would affect the fetus, and in all probability lead to stillbirth. It's been the source of so much distress: the Lilith in you so strong. Lilith Annette, destroyer of man's virility, sapper of male strength, strangler of babies."

"I'll fetch Security," said Nurse McKenzie. "The man's mad. And truly nasty."

"No," said Annette. "I'm discharging myself. Stop the bleepers, set me free of all these wires."

"*G*ilda?"

"Annette? Where are you speaking from? The hospital?"

"No," said Annette. "I discharged myself."

"Where are you?"

"I'm at home, locked in my bedroom," said Annette.

"Is the key on the inside," asked Gilda, "or the outside?"

"The inside," said Annette. "Spicer drove me home. I came straight in, ran upstairs, into this room, and locked the door. He banged a bit and then went away."

"That's all right," said Gilda. "Well, it's better. Not exactly good, though. How do you feel?"

"Okay," Annette said. "In fact, I'm fine."

"What happened?" asked Gilda.

"Spicer wanted me to discharge myself, so I did," said Annette.

"He's irresponsible," said Gilda. "He's a monster, but what's new?"

"I know that now," said Annette. "I called his bluff, that's all. Spicer knows about Ernie Gromback."

"Oh God," said Gilda. "Well, it was bound to happen. So

much for confidentiality. Marion has left Ernie Gromback. She said he was too worldly for her. Where's Spicer now?"

"I don't know," said Annette. "It's terribly quiet out there. What do I do now?"

"Wait for the enemy powers to gather," said Gilda. "I'm sure they will."

"How's the baby?" asked Annette.

"Divine," said Gilda, "but I won't say so if it upsets you."

"It doesn't upset me," said Annette. "It cheers me up no end."

"How long do you think he's known about Ernie Gromback?"

"Probably from the day I told Herman Marks," said Annette. "God, I was naïve."

"Steve says Spicer is what the Americans call a mind-fucker," said Gilda. "Hang on, I have to fetch the baby. . . . You still there, Annette?"

"Yes," said Annette. "Of course I am. You are my only contact with the real world. What's that gurgling noise?"

"It's the baby feeding," said Gilda. "I'm lying on the bed. Do you mind?"

"No," said Annette. "I've just found something under Spicer's pillow that's really interesting."

"What?" asked Gilda.

"I'll tell you when I understand it better," said Annette. "I'm glad you're feeding the baby yourself. I thought perhaps you wouldn't. They added something yet more to my drip to dry up my milk. I should have gone to the Clinic, though. I do blame myself for that, terribly."

"There were lots of people around you," said Gilda, "certainly me, who should have got you there. While everyone was thinking about the state of other people's heads, the body was in trouble. I blame the therapists."

"God, how I blame the therapists!" said Annette. "I can hear the front door. It's Spicer and someone coming back. I'll ring you later, Gilda. All is becoming clear."

"Annette," said Spicer, "I've brought Dr. Rhea and Dr. Herman to reason with you. Why don't you open the door so we can talk?"

"No," said Annette.

"Please," said Spicer.

"I'm not leaving this house, Spicer. You are. Go and live with your friends the Drs. Marks."

"It's my house," said Spicer, "and you have no claim on it. We are not legally married. So anything I let you have is out of my goodwill. You had better make sure you keep it. I suggest you open the door."

"Okay," said Annette. "First round to you."

"There's no need to get so upset," said Spicer. "I spoke what was in my head rather brutally, I do admit that, but at least it's out and we can work on it. I was very upset about the loss of the baby."

"Hello, Dr. Rhea," said Annette. "How are things?"

"This is a very distressing situation," said Dr. Rhea.

"Hello, Dr. Herman," said Annette. "How's the wanking?"

"We are recording this," said Dr. Herman, "so be careful."

"Second round to you," said Annette. "But I do have a trump card."

"What's that?" asked Spicer.

"Never you mind," said Annette. "Carry on with your observations."

"You would do better to return to your parents' home," said Dr. Herman, "at least for a time, and come to terms with your childhood trauma. There is a great inner peace resultant from eventual reconciliation with the damaging parent."

"This is my home," said Annette. "I'm not leaving it. Spicer is."

"It's my home in law," said Spicer.

"We'll see what a court has to say about that," said Annette.

"It's not as if we had any children together," said Spicer.

"You saw to that, Mrs. Horrocks," said Dr. Rhea, "I am sorry to say. Refusing medical and psychological care while pregnant! In the U.S. women get put in prison for that. The right of the fetus predominates."

"That law is not here yet," said Annette, "though I can see it coming."

"You're not even my wife," said Spicer. "You're just a mistress. You sponged off me for years."

"Spicer doesn't love you," said Dr. Rhea. "It's a long time since he loved you."

"He did love me," said Annette. "Why did he want us to have a baby if he didn't love me? He loved me until you put it into his head that he didn't."

"What is this word 'love'?" said Dr. Rhea. "I don't understand its meaning."

"It's the best part of a person," said Annette. "Take it away and the worst is left. All I have of Spicer now is the worst; all there's left of him is dregs. You two dismantled him in six months. That's all it took. Nothing to do with therapy, with healing. You wanted his body, his soul, his money, his house. I was in the way, and, unfortunately for you, the one in a hundred. So you got Spicer to get rid of me, to drive me out."

"You're insane," said Spicer. "Paranoid. But, then, you always were."

"Dr. Rhea is a hypnotherapist," said Annette. "That's what AHTM means. The Association of Hypnotherapists in Medicine."

"So?" said Spicer.

"As well as therapist, healer, counselor, astrologer, homeopath, she is a hypnotist. She is in every part of you. She has your soul."

"At last our Annette believes in the soul," said Spicer. "That's something achieved."

"All they've left of you is dregs, husband," said Annette. "But it doesn't devalue what went before. Even if you don't remember it, I do."

"You always adored me," said Spicer, "that's true enough, but I always rather despised you. I needed someone to look after Jason, so I took you on. I should have known it was a mistake."

"You believe that because Dr. Rhea and Dr. Herman made you believe it, not because it's true. We're together because we fell in love."

"Ah, such romantic fantasy!" breathed Dr. Herman. "Such Englishness!"

"Let her wear herself out," said Dr. Rhea. "She soon will."

"Spicer," said Annette, "they've made you forget all the good memories of you and me together; they've taken them out, re-laid them, re-placed them. They even got to the bacon sandwiches. You can't even have those as a pleasant memory, in case you remember you loved me."

"What are you raving about? Bacon sandwiches? Pork's disgusting," said Spicer.

"When you think of our time together, Spicer," said Annette, "you associate it with trouble, boredom, and the need to escape. You even believe I render you impotent."

"You do," said Spicer.

"Where once you thought of your Annette, you now think of Lilith, who is dangerous and destructive. Spicer, you couldn't even remember having met Dr. Herman, though of course you had. God knows what else they wanted you for. Well, I do know, but never mind that."

"What are you raving about?" asked Spicer. "Just get out of my house. You have no right here. Take your personal possessions and go: stop persecuting me."

"I've given you up, Spicer," said Annette. "I could call in my friend Peter Pan and have your memories relocated and re-laid properly and truthfully, but I don't like you any more, let alone love you. I don't believe anyone can make a human being talk and behave the way you do to me, unless there's a large slice of that human being that wants to. Dr. Rhea can set up whatever scenario she likes in your mind—the reasons other than sheer forgetfulness that you didn't put half the house in my name, the reasons other than idleness that we never got properly married— it makes no difference. There is every excuse for you, but I don't accept them. I want to be free of you."

"When you're finally out of here," said Spicer, "Dr. Rhea and Dr. Herman are to set up their surgery in this house. There's no room for you, or the kids."

"I thought as much," said Annette. "The Drs. Marks' Hampstead house is leased to them by the AJAP, the Association of Jungian and Allied Psychotherapists, or the British Psychodrama Association, or the Association of Sexual and Marital Therapists, or whatever comparatively respectable association you care to name, and the Drs. Marks have been struck off and turned out, quite rightly, so they think they'll try further down the hill, where there's quite a shortage of therapists and a gap in the market to fill, and ours is a nice house, isn't it? Or was. We were happy here, Spicer, you and me, but you won't remember that."

"What a fantasist she is," said Dr. Herman. "You know she made the most extraordinary sexual advances to me?"

"Poor thing," said Dr. Rhea. "She has been abusing her children. The boy more or less told me so."

"You'd better get out, Annette," said Spicer, "or things will turn really sour for you. Dr. Rhea and Dr. Herman are good people; you are a very nasty piece of work."

"Spicer," said Annette, "I would like you to look at this Polaroid photograph I found beneath the pillow of our marital bed."

"Why should I?" asked Spicer. "What trickery is this?"

"It is a photograph," said Annette, "of you, Dr. Rhea, and Dr. Herman engaged in sexual intercourse in this very room. Triolism. Dr. Rhea in the middle. Do you have any memory of this? Look closely, Spicer. You can see the faces quite clearly."

"I don't understand," said Spicer. "What is this? Oh dear God!"

"It is a photograph," said Dr. Rhea, "my dear Spicer, of you and me standing in Highgate Cemetery, next to the bust of poor old Karl Marx."

"So it is," said Spicer. "You have a very sick mind, Annette, full of the most distressing sexual fantasy. Now, please, just leave, before we throw you out. You are such rubbish, such a soulless person. Here today, gone tomorrow. There is no place for you here. You have always made me profoundly unhappy."

"Oh well," said Annette. "I suppose I had better go. I just wanted to be sure I understood the situation properly. Saturn and his loathsome wife, their lease expired on Mount Olympus, taking refuge where they can, spreading destruction and the end of love wherever they set foot."

"I understand your anger," said Dr. Rhea. "It is perfectly natural. When relationships break down, it is the unfortunate therapist who always gets the blame."

"Gilda?"

"Oh God, Annette, is that you? We've been so worried!"

"What about?"

"It's been more than three weeks! No one's heard from you. Where are you?"

"I told Spicer where I was. I called him. I left a phone number. I'm sure I did."

"Well, he didn't tell us. All he said was that you'd walked out on him and the kids, and gone off with Ernie Gromback, and he didn't know where you were. We called Ernie and he sounded really surprised and said he hadn't heard from you either; he wished to God he had. So we called Spicer back and Spicer said he'd been trying to save your face, you'd left him because he was in financial difficulties and ill, and perhaps you were with your mother. Are you okay, Annette?"

"I was until you started telling me this, Gilda."

"Shall I stop? Is it very painful?"

"It's okay. You can go on."

"Your voice sounds quite strong, so I will. You need to know. I got through to your mother, who said she had the kids but she had no idea where you were. Spicer had told her you'd aborted the baby to go off with a lover, and though your mother didn't believe that, your father was inclined to. You'd better get in touch with your parents, Annette. They sounded rather miffed. Well, I suppose they would, if the kids have just been dumped on them. Spicer told your mum and dad he was too ill to have them back; his doctors had advised him to sell up his business. The stress was too great, what with you killing his baby and then walking out on him. I got Steve to call Spicer, but all Spicer said was that you'd been having an affair with Ernie Gromback all these years, and that's why poor Marion had walked out on Ernie. Spicer said you were the destructive goddess Kali and then he hung up. Are you okay?"

"Not as okay as I was five minutes ago, Gilda."

"Of course I don't believe any of it, Annette."

"Good. I'll try not to. But it's hard. I believed everything Spicer said for so many years! If husbands say dreadful things about you, why should they be lying? If you've shared a bed for so long and been close and companionable and in and out of each other, wouldn't the other know?"

"I guess they just sometimes turn, Annette. And, the closer they've been, the more they want to damage you in other people's eyes, to justify the turning."

"But why should Spicer want to hurt me? Wasn't losing the baby enough? I haven't hurt him. I'm just trying to hang on in here, Gilda, and survive."

"Where are you, Annette?"

"Never mind. I thought I was getting better, but I'm not. I must go and pick some more flowers."

"Pick flowers? Like Ophelia? You can't, it's winter," said Gilda.

"Winter rosemary grows round here. It must be, or else it's

magic. Rosemary for remembrance. The whole place is scented. I hadn't realized it flowered. Blue and tiny flowers, and very pretty. I put them round the shrine."

"What shrine are you talking about, Annette? Are you in some kind of religious center?"

"Good heavens, no. I have a photograph as a talisman, that's all, in my bedroom. I've built a shrine around it. I surround it with flowers. I worship it as objective truth."

"What sort of photograph, Annette?"

"I'm pretty sure it isn't of Karl Marx's grave."

"Do you have someone with you, Annette? You're not on your own?"

"I'm not with Ernie Gromback. I'd notice a thing like that."

"Are you in your right mind, Annette? Are you in some kind of nuthouse?"

"No. I'm just staying with friends till I feel better."

"But you're okay? I hope I haven't upset you."

"It comes in waves. This kind of conversation makes my head sink and sink, right under the water, so I guess I'll stop now. I'm not as strong as I thought."

"Annette, tell me where you are, please don't just hang up—"

"Oh God, Steve, that was Annette and she just hung up and didn't leave a number. Yes, I suppose I was tactless. But that's what Spicer's saying about her. The trouble is, Steve, she loves him. Supposing she decides to go back to him? She needs to know the truth. She needs to know what a bastard he is."

* * *

". "Can I speak to Spicer, please, Wendy. This is Gilda Ellis. Annette's friend."

"Is Mrs. Horrocks okay, Mrs. Ellis? I worry for her. I know I shouldn't, what she did was unforgivable, but she was always so nice to me. Secretaries and wives don't necessarily get on. She made a real effort, and I liked to think it worked well between us."

"What is Mrs. Horrocks meant to have done, Wendy?"

"Terminating a fetus at that late stage! I'm a pro-lifer. A dreadful thing to do! She'd even given the poor little girl a name. Gillian. Mr. Horrocks has been so upset about it. Mrs. Horrocks put her career before her family, before everything. Apparently she couldn't bear to be seen pregnant on a TV screen: she said it was bad for business. And we're all to lose our jobs, and no redundancy money because of the bankruptcy. Mr. Horrocks doesn't seem to know what he's doing any more, now that Mrs. Horrocks has walked out on him. What a time to choose! We've got this great big order: why is he declaring bankruptcy? Strange, isn't it. Everything seems so normal and happy, and then one day it all just shatters to bits. It almost makes you believe in astrology. Some kind of transit in the heavens—stars getting too close for comfort—all you can do is sit it out and try to do the right thing, and hope it passes without dragging you with it. But I can't chatter on like this. I'll put you through."

ironic

"Hello, Spicer."

"Is that you, Gilda? I'm very busy."

"Spicer, I heard from Annette. I forgot to get her number. She said you had it."

"I don't know what kind of sick game you and she are playing now, Gilda, but, whatever it is, it won't work. The truth is out now. You were in on her affair with Ernie Gromback. Must have been quite a turn-on for the pair of you, sniggering at me from the corners of rooms. Forever whispering and giggling, running up telephone bills, the pair of you, for me to pay. Mr. Stupid! Mr. Cuckold, the universal provider. What does Annette want from me now? Money? Tell her from me I don't pay women who murder unborn children and sexually molest the others—"

"Spicer—"

But Spicer put the phone down.

"Gilda?"

"Annette, before you say a thing, please give me your phone number."

"I will later. It's okay, I'm better now. I won't hang up."

"Where are you?"

"Does it matter?"

"Describe the room you're in," said Gilda.

"It's in Yorkshire, I think. It's a square room with white-washed walls, and the telephone's fixed to the wall. It's an old-fashioned one with a dial. It takes forever for the dial to rattle back after every number. I'm standing at the window looking at some moors and some gray stone walls. I can count twelve sheep. Did you know most grazing animals have to eat for twenty-two hours out of twenty-four to get enough nourishment to survive? I'm really glad I'm not a sheep."

"So am I, Annette."

"If you, as a human, eat slices of sheep," said Annette, "you can get your daily nutritional requirements in about ten minutes, because they've done all that work and all that focusing. If you're a vegetarian it can take a whole half an hour munching away: you're getting the value of mere photosynthesis. There's a three-piece suite here with big yellow flowers on it, and an Axminster carpet in purple and red, and a blue-spotted lampshade. Nothing goes very well together, but I'm not complaining. If I stretch the telephone cord I can sit on the arm of the chair, just about. There! It's really good to be on line again, as it were. Things are looking up."

"Why do you only think you're in Yorkshire? How come you don't know?"

"Because I reckon I'm two hundred and eight miles more or less north of Watford, which would be about Yorkshire, wouldn't it?"

"I could look it up in an atlas if you wanted, Annette."

"You don't have to humor me, Gilda. I'm not insane. I have been, I think. And I had this nasty wound in my neck, but it's healing now. At any rate, Henry and Buttercup say it is. It's round the side, so it's really difficult to see in a mirror. It certainly feels better."

"Who are Henry and Buttercup, Annette?"

"They're the ones I'm staying with. The ones who picked me out of the ditch."

"A ditch, Annette? What were you doing in a ditch?"

"Crawling about. What one does in ditches. Henry and Buttercup are quite old. He must be eighty-five, she's ninety-something; quite a bit older than him. I don't think these gaps in ages matter much, do you? He has more rheumatism than she does. I don't think she was christened Buttercup, but that's what

everyone calls her. Not that everyone is very numerous round here.
I'm talking about the postman, the doctor, the milkman, and the
man who came to dip the sheep. Sheep have to be dipped annually
for scabies by law, but the stuff the Ministry give you to dip them
in can really poison you if you so much as breathe the fumes in.
Henry says the Ministry care more about sheep than they do about
people, but a department has to do what a department has to do.
Henry is a very uncondemning person. He sees people as on the
whole helpless in the face of circumstances. They need to be forgiven, even Spicer."

"That seems to be going a bit far. You were telling me about
the ditch, Annette. Is it on an A road or a B road?"

"You're trying to find out where I am, aren't you, Gilda?"

"Yes, I am, Annette."

"If I just give you a telephone number, will you stop?"

"Yes, Annette."

"It's on the B 3210, and the telephone number is 0886
435281. Okay? Have you got a pen?"

"Steve just handed me one."

"Steve's not listening in on the extension, Gilda?"

"No, he's not, Annette."

"I believe you, because you're my friend, even though you
did sleep with Spicer. So Steve had better not be on the extension,
had he, or you'll be in trouble. It's better when I talk to you than
when I just think about you."

"Don't brood, Annette. I've said and said I'm sorry. And Steve
knows."

"As I say, it comes in waves. I can feel one coming on now.
It's a pit in the stomach."

"Tell me more about the ditch. Please."

"I'm using Henry and Buttercup's phone. They can't afford luxuries, and I haven't any money. Perhaps you'd better call me back?"

But when Gilda called the number Annette had given her, all she got was a computerized voice saying she had dialed a nonexistent number.

A gave her wrong #

"Spicer, are you in there?" Steve called through the letter box of the Horrockses' house in Bella Crescent, since no one had answered his knocking and his ringing. "I know you are, because you just opened the door to Marion. She got out of the taxi ahead of me, and pretended not to see me. We need Annette's number, nothing more. Give it to us and we'll go away and leave you in peace."

"What makes you think I have Annette's number?" asked Spicer cheerfully, opening his study window, sitting on the sill. He wore an Indian-cotton dressing gown, striped red and yellow.

"Annette says she gave it to you."

"Annette is a liar," said Spicer. "Hadn't you heard about her secret affair with Ernie Gromback? It's been going on for years. What did Annette care about what she was doing to poor Marion? She's ruthless. I suited Annette while I was well and could oblige her, physically and financially, but now I'm ill and bankrupt and have to sell the house, she's just buggered off. Marion comes round to nurse me. That's all there is to her and me. We're not exactly a number. Christ, someone has to be nice to me after all I've been through."

"You look quite well to me, Spicer."

"That's the high blood pressure—it produces a flush. I'm told I could have a stroke at any moment."

"Don't you worry at all about Annette, Spicer?"

"Worry about Annette? As well worry about a piranha fish. She dropped that baby without turning a hair. Dropped it dead, of course, as suited her purposes."

"Gilda speaks to Annette on the phone. She says Annette doesn't sound too good," said Steve.

"Don't be taken in by Annette," said Spicer. "She had the nerve to call me the other day, pretending to be in tears, begging me to have her back. I didn't believe a word of it. Gilda had put her up to something, I could tell."

"Spicer, I don't think you're in your right mind."

"Never been more in it, old chap," said Spicer from his windowsill. "They're two of a kind, Annette and Gilda, a monstrous conspiracy of women. Take my advice, Steve—get rid of Gilda the first opportunity you've got. She's foisted that baby on you. I could tell you things about Gilda which would surprise you, a nice fella like you."

"I expect you could, Spicer. On a more realistic level, have you actually sold this house?"

"Are you spying for Annette? What's going on here? I'm not a material person. I'm not interested in money. I'm not selling this house. I am giving it away by deed of gift, before the official receivers get their filthy hands on it."

"So who are you giving it to, Spicer? Not Annette, I take it?"

"Are you joking? Give it to the woman who drove my poor wife out of her own house, rendered my son, Jason, a virtual orphan, and then took sexual and emotional advantage of him? Why should I give her my house? No, I'm making it over to a couple of people I trust. Not many of those around."

*   *   *

"Then he slammed the window shut," said Steve to Gilda, "and as he moved away his dressing gown fell open and I'll swear he had an enormous erection."

"Don't tell me," said Gilda, "or my milk will dry up. Was Marion in the room with him?"

"I have no idea," said Steve. "My feeling is he just gets off on abusing Annette."

"I suppose that could be a tribute to his love for her," said Gilda, cautiously, "which will emerge again when this mental illness, or whatever it is, has passed over the pair of them. Because he must be mad, mustn't he?"

"For a nasty piece of work read mad," said Steve. "For mad read a nasty piece of work. Who knows?"

"Life's easier to bear," observed Gilda, "if you can write off a sector of the populace as mad: that is, not pertaining to the race of the proper people, the nice, kind ones. Then you don't have to think any more about any possible resemblance between you and them. You're sane, they're mad. Finis."

They fell silent.

"Perhaps Spicer's right about Annette," observed Steve in due course. "Perhaps Spicer is to be pitied more than Annette."

"I don't think so," said Gilda. The baby cried in the next room. Steve went to fetch him, and Gilda unbuttoned her blouse, and they sat close together while she fed him, as if by so doing they could keep the world out.

"Hi, Gilda."

"Annette, you gave me a wrong number. I tried to ring back but it was unobtainable."

"What number did you try?"

"0886 435281."

"You must have written it down wrong. I told you 0846. Have you got that?"

"Yes."

"You can test it if you like, when I ring off."

"I don't trust you. I'd rather you gave me your address, so Steve and I can come and fetch you."

"I don't think I can quite cope with that yet. Anyway, where would I go? I don't have a home any more. Spicer's hijacked it."

"You can stay with us. Or you could just walk back in, and say, Hi, Spicer, I'm back home. If anyone's going to leave, you are. Or, Hi, Spicer, why don't we set up home together again?"

"It just doesn't feel as if I could do that, Gilda. If you're rejected by a man, your instinct is to stay in the gutter: you're disallowed the home. Besides, Marion's there. And I have no legal rights."

"I think perhaps you ought to get back in there, Annette. Spicer seems to be giving the house away."

"Don't tell me. To the therapists, just to hurt me more."

"I suppose so, Annette. To a couple of people he trusts, he says. At the very least, you need to get your stuff out of it."

"But there's almost nothing in the house that's mine, apart from some clothes. I've lost a couple of stone, so I reckon they'd look really weird on me now. Spicer bought the car and the stereo and stuff like that: my earnings paid for holidays and food and loo paper, and it was always me who filled up the tank. So I've nothing to show at all for those years, not even by way of possessions. I don't like talking about it, Gilda. It makes my neck start hurting again."

"What's the matter with your neck?" asked Gilda.

"I cut it on a bit of metal when I fell into the ditch."

"This ditch. How did you get into it?"

"It's a kind of black pit, not just a simple ditch, Gilda. It takes forever to get out of it. The sides are slippery. There's mud and blood everywhere. I always knew there was bound to be a gap; but in my head I'd sanitized it into The Gap—you know, the chain store, all the clothes neat, clean, folded, and properly catalogued, and the same wherever you are in the world, not in the least like the gap really is."

"What are you talking about, Annette?"

"Do you think Spicer's seeing Marion, Gilda?"

"Yes, I think he is."

"Sleeping in my bed, casting her disgusting tarot cards on my dining table, cooking at my stove, using up my soap, her hand on Spicer's cock; she's so stupid, Gilda, why does he prefer her to me?"

"Perhaps that's why, Annette. Because she's stupid. Or to get back at Ernie Gromback. I have no idea. Forget it, forget him, or else just walk back in."

"He's forgotten me. He's blocked me out. And the Marks team—the Grouchos and the Harpos, the Lenins or the Stalins, now the therapists, what's the difference?—will own the house and set up surgery, and all the freaks and nutters in the world will walk up my steps and ring my bell and take off their clothes and cavort in my rooms, and Herman's hands will palpate two thousand breasts and Rhea's soft voice will destroy a thousand marriages, and the negative archetypes will swoop and whistle and scream down the Crescent, and bow the trees down, because I'm not there to ward them off. You know Spicer and I conceived

Gillian in the back garden? We made love under the racing moon, before we had any idea how damaging the transits of the moon could be, when he loved me as much as I loved him."

"Stop it, Annette. You're upsetting yourself."

"I am not upsetting myself. It is being done to me. Head over heels down into the pit again, slipped through the gap, the waves breaking over me again. I'm going to have to go now, Gilda. Do be careful of the gap. You know how the guards call out on certain stations of the London Underground, 'Mind the gap! Mind the gap!' What can this possibly be, this 'gap'? foreigners wonder, looking round for some little scuttling thing you're supposed to look after. When what's meant is 'Notice the space between the straight line of the carriage and the curve of the platform and don't slip down it.' The true gap is the space between the world as it ought to be, and the world as it is; between what you think love and marriage and babies are going to be and what it turns out to be, and its proper name is Disappointment. Anyone can fall into it, Gilda. It's horrible down here. Bloody and pulsating; mean, spiteful, and full of hate; grabbing and sucking down and grasping. Disappointment is the mother of all nasty emotions. You want the world to be perfect and it isn't. It drives you to terrible deeds. You can't see properly down here, because your eyes are misty. You think it's tears have done it and feel sorry for yourself, but it isn't; your vision is cloudy because you're growing a cataract of rage, a kind of second eyelid. The white skin across the eye cats reveal to you when they're sick. You never knew it was there: you just stroked the shiny fur and trusted and hoped for the best, but all the time the cat's worms were traveling to its brain, and by the time you notice it's too late to help. It's having fits."

"Can't we come and fetch you, Annette?"

"No. Once you're in the black pit you've got to get out of it yourself. There's a route somewhere. I'll find it somehow. You've got to blink away the rage so you can see clearly: the trouble is, the rage is the only way you know how to survive. And you keep stumbling over wreckage. I keep thinking I've found the way out, and I even get my hands on the edge to pull myself out, but there's Spicer's great black boots, tramping and stamping and kicking me down into the pit again. He circles it forever. I'm falling, Gilda, even as I speak. He's such a shit, isn't he?"

"Yes."

"Not worth loving. No special relationship, ever. Just him laughing at me behind my back, mocking me, wondering how to get rid of me. If I learn to despise him, will I stop loving him? Is that the way?"

"I don't know, Annette."

"The pompous shit, the sleazeball, the Man with No Eyes. I'll practice and see. I'm going now, Gilda. Goodbye. Buttercup's just come in."

"Gilda?"

"Hello, Ernie."

"I can't stand this not knowing," said Ernie Gromback. "Someone has to find Annette. My PR people are going crazy. Now she's not available, all the media big guns want her for their shows. I can't hold up publication forever. Besides which, I'm worried about her. What a bastard Spicer is. The only good thing to be said about him is he's taken Marion off my hands just in time for her Macrobiotic Vegan phase. All she'll eat then is grapes and brown rice. I want all the clues you have, Gilda."

"Two hundred and eight miles north-ish of Watford, twelve sheep, a moor, rosemary, a dial telephone, a shepherd with a breathing problem owing to ingesting Ministry chemicals, a bedroom with a shrine to a photograph in it, a front room which sounds peculiarly horrible, and an elderly pair called Henry and Buttercup. That's it."

"I'll get my people on to it."

"Oh, Ernie, you sound so rich, effective, and powerful."

"Are you mocking me, Gilda?"

"No, I'm not, Ernie."

"Why would Annette be so certain of the exact mileage, when she's so vague about everything else?"

"I kind of don't want to ask her that, Ernie."

"Why not?"

"I don't know. I'm afraid of the answer."

"Can you accept a reverse-charge call, please, from a call box?"

"Where's the call box?"

"Yorkshire."

"Okay, okay. Put her through."

"Gilda?"

"Hi, Annette. How are things?"

"Better. I was telling you about this ditch."

"The black pit of the soul. I'm having a real problem with my milk, thanks to you."

"I'm sorry. I've forgotten all that old stuff. I'm back in the real world. It was just a perfectly ordinary ditch and I was just very lucky Henry and Buttercup happened to pass by in their old Ford Prefect. Or I might have been there all night and died from loss of blood and/or hypothermia. That's what the doctor said. Though I don't know. I was half out of the ditch when their lights caught me, something shapeless and struggling in the mud. Brave of them to stop. One of their headlights goes off at an angle, like someone with a cast in their eye; otherwise I wouldn't have been seen. They picked me up, washed me down, stitched me up, and here I am, cold-turkeying on Spicer, tied to the mast to stop me going back to burn the house down, cut out the crotch of his trousers, scratch the side of his car with a coin, get the Markses three months in prison under Section Four of the Vagrancy Act— using a fortune-telling device, namely a horoscope, to discompose one of Her Majesty's subjects, and that's what you can get, three months—tar and feather Marion, all the things I knew would help me out of the pit, only Henry and Buttercup tell me it's another false exit, all I'll see silhouetted when I look up to the sun will be Spicer's boots, Spicer's smiling face. They're right."

"You're still not really better. You said you'd lost two stone. That's a worry. You must be almost not there."

"I can't think why. We live on chops, potatoes, and lardy cake."

"How horrible."

"It helps break the pattern."

"You're not on drugs, Annette?"

"I'm addicted to Spicer; that's why Henry and Buttercup tied me to the mast. I am hooked on my own punishment."

"Punishment for what, Annette?"

"For being a victim. Blame the sinned-against for the sin, blame the victim for the crime. See how Spicer blames me! Dear Spicer, please forgive me for the hurt you have done me. Dear Spicer, forgive me for the death of the baby you killed. Spicer, cruel master, let me lick your boots, let me fawn upon you; take me back; if I can't have your kindness, let me have your cruelty."

"Annette, that is disgusting."

"I know. I am entropied, degraded. Did my father really believe I aborted the baby? Went off with a lover? Or was that just what my mother said he believed?"

"Your mother said it."

"Then we can discountenance it. She has never forgiven him for his affairs. Neither have I. If he wanted anyone but her, why didn't he have me? Did you speak to the children?"

"No."

"Please do. Tell them to hang on in there. Say I'll be in touch very shortly."

"Okay. You are getting better, Annette. I can hear it in your voice. How's the pit?"

"The shit and the mud and the block seem to be drying out. It would make good fertilizer. But I still can't find the path out. Any number of false starts, but you keep slipping back and you know Spicer's roaming up there anyway. Shall I tell you how I got to be in here?"

"Yes, please, Annette."

"Well. I got out of hospital and went home and found the photograph of the Drs. Marx and Spicer naked and doing God-knows-what to each other—in the name of therapy, no doubt—and got thrown out. I had the evidence of my own eyes but it still wasn't good enough. I started walking north. I don't know why, except the further north you get in this hemisphere the colder it gets, so it seemed a fitting direction. All kinds of people stopped to offer lifts, so I accepted them. Why not? None of them were going far, that was the problem. A woman gave me her jumper, a man gave me sandwiches. Two young people tried to take me to a doctor. I suppose I looked very strange. I shivered a lot. I got as far as the big service station at Watford, where I took the initiative and started hitching. I probably should have just let what happened, happen. A lorry driver picked me up. He was young and good-looking and had tattoos on his arm. They were brown and bare and muscly. It was kind of domestic in the cab. A rug on the seat; some artificial flowers in a silver vase he'd won in a raffle; a photograph of his mother's cat stuck in the rearview mirror. He said he'd take me as far as I wanted if I'd have sex with him once every fifty miles, that was his fee for lady hitchhikers. I said yes, okay."

"Annette!"

"Well, why not? He was very warm and soft to the touch. I can't explain it. Spicer was always so contained and somehow chilly, even in performance. Straight trade seemed better to me. We got fifty miles and stopped in a lay-by, and another fifty, and another and another, and then he wanted to again after only another five miles, and I said that wasn't in the deal and began to get angry. Why was he so definite if he was going to go back on it? It was dark by then. He left the main road and went off into the countryside, bump, bump along tiny roads, in a temper, and I got frightened, which was stupid, because what could he do which he hadn't done already—but I was passionate in defense of the deal. It is the only way I can describe it. It seemed a matter of life and death to me that he should stick to the bargain, and to him that the sex should be more than the bargain."

"What a disgusting person," said Gilda.

"No, Gilda, you don't understand. He wanted me to love him, not just to use him, and he was disappointed."

"You are out of your mind. Well, what's new?" said Gilda, bitterly.

"There's such a wonderful smell of rosemary up here. I can see for miles and miles, through the squares of glass in this telephone box. The sky's like the kind of color wash they make children do in Rudolph Steiner schools, but latticed. Watercolors on wet paper. Susan went to a Steiner school once, till she got so bored I took her out. 'Rosemary and rue keep seeming and savour all winter long.' Something like that. That's just after 'Exeunt pursued by bear' in *The Winter's Tale*. Jason was in that. He was very good. Even Spicer said so."

"English oil of rosemary is infinitely superior to the stuff you get from France or Spain," said Gilda, "because of the colder climate, but we never bother to produce it here. Quite a marketing problem for the EEC. You worked on a program with me, Annette. Don't you remember?"

"Just about. But it isn't the green-leaved rosemary that grows round here, the stuff you use to get the oil, it's the silver-and-gold kind, with little blue flowers, that just grows. Anne of Cleves wore a wreath of it at her wedding. Was she one of the wives who was beheaded or one of the ones who survived?"

"I'd have to look it up, Annette."

"Don't bother. Anyway, here we were, this truck driver and I, fighting, and he just opened the cab door and pushed me out, all the way down to the ground, and I rolled into this muddy ditch. It was raining. He got out and looked at me down in my ditch and said I was lucky he hadn't raped me and strangled me, and drove off. I didn't think I was particularly lucky; I daresay that was what I'd wanted. So there I was in this ditch, exhausted and without my knickers, which can chill you down a lot, and it was raining, and my neck was hurting and bleeding. I found later there was this great cut in it. I had to have a tetanus jab. He shouldn't have left me there, should he? Do you think he was worse than Spicer, or better?"

"Annette," said Gilda, "truck drivers are expected to be brutes. Terrible things happen to girls on the road. That's why good girls don't hitch. But Spicer is meant to be civilized, and you are his wife. Spicer is worse than the truck drivers."

"But I might have been fighting him in some way I didn't understand and he did, so what he did was reasonable?"

"No."

"Thank you, Gilda. And I don't suppose they're exactly in competition for worst place, anyway. One must just be grateful for not being raped or murdered, physically or spiritually. I'll have to go soon. There's someone wanting to use this phone box. How extraordinary! It's so isolated up here. Moors to the right of you, moors to the left of you, just this footpath and this phone box in the middle of nowhere, and the smell of rosemary. I couldn't resist calling you. I hope you don't mind me reversing the charges. I thought we could talk forever. And now there's someone else here. Another person. A man. He doesn't seem threatening. I can go on a little, I guess. I'll turn my head and pretend I haven't seen him. Where was I? Another photograph. In the paper the other day. An old atrocity picture, dating back to the forties. The newspaper reprinted it, with apologies to their readers' sensitivities, in an attempt to explain contemporary times in Yugoslavia. You don't want to look, you have to. This photograph was of a young man, alive and well and handsome, except he is being held down by three other young men, looking perfectly cheerful, and a fourth is sawing through his neck with an ordinary wood saw. He's trying to keep his head in its proper position and there's a look of total surprise on his face—he's taken aback—"

"Please don't, Annette—"

"I only mention it because Henry and Buttercup observed that people get so civilized they don't dare do that kind of thing to you physically, they'll do it to you mentally. We're all Serbs and Croats and Bosnians at heart. Spicer's been sawing through the inside of my head, not the outside, that's all. People like to do to each other the most gruesome thing they can possibly think of. Sawing people's heads off is quite funny, in its way. Separating the conscious, aware part from the automatically twitching part. There! That's the way to do it, that's final, that's the end of disappointment. Do you a good turn. Spicer hurts me. I twitch. Get to the spinal column, and he can put a stop to all that and feel good again. Only Spicer didn't quite manage. I'd laid my head on the block but I got it out in time. Hardly his fault at all. My neck's healed. Are you crying?"

"Yes. I thought you were out of the pit. You're not."

"You don't have to get out of it, Gilda. There isn't any route out. You just clean it up a bit, grow a few flowers, and ask everyone in. Gilda, he's tapping on the glass, he's getting really angry. I have to go. Oh dear God, it's Ernie. What is Ernie Gromback doing out there in a suit and tie and shiny shoes? He looks absurd."

"*E*rnie," said Annette.

"What is it, my dear?" said Ernie.

"Shall we just drive down Bella Crescent, past the house?"

"Are you sure you want to?" asked Ernie.

"Yes, please," said Annette. "Tell you what, I'll shut my eyes till we're there, then I'll open them for a second, take in what I see, close them again, and you drive like hell out of there."

"We're going to pick up Susan and Jason from school," said Ernie. "We don't have much time to spare."

"You just don't want me to see Spicer again, in case I fancy him," said Annette. "Fall back under his spell."

"You are so right," said Ernie Gromback.

"Don't worry about it," said Annette. "It was in another country, and the Spicer I knew is dead. A simulacrum walks around in his place. How can you love a simulacrum?"

"A pity about the property, though," said Ernie. "To be cheated out of it like that."

"Never mind," said Annette, "I could put it all into a novel."

"Nobody would believe it," said Ernie. "Don't even think of it."

"I've changed my mind," said Annette. "Let's go straight to the school. I don't want to drive down Bella Crescent, after all. I know what I would see. The house in a kind of seedy disrepair; its porch somehow shrunk in stature; the steps crumbling; two plates outside the door, with a fresh set of bogus initials on them. Spicer looking out of a top window—a kind of poodle for their pleasure—and Marion too, perhaps. The windows will be foggy from a haze of incense, marijuana, and the quality of the minds within. There will be a trail of trusting people to the door, looking for someone to believe in, anyone: so what if families split and, in the name of love and peace, malice abounds? You wouldn't want to see that, and neither would I. It might put my blood pressure up, and that would be bad for our baby. I reckon we'd better forswear the experience, keep what belongs to the past in the past."

"I reckon so too," said Ernie Gromback, and turned the car, and they went to pick up the children.

*   *   *

"Ernie," said Annette, as they parked the car outside the school gates. "Do me a favor?"

"Anything," said Ernie.

"Take a look at the photograph."

"What, again?"

"Please," said Annette. "Do you see a bust of Karl Marx in it?"

"No," said Ernie. "I don't."

"That's okay, then," said Annette.

"Put it away, in case the children see it," said Ernie. "Let's try for a little respectability round here. Thank God it's a Polaroid, and already fading."

FOR THE BEST IN PAPERBACKS, LOOK FOR THE

In every corner of the world, on every subject under the sun, Penguin represents quality and variety—the very best in publishing today.

For complete information about books available from Penguin—including Pelicans, Puffins, Peregrines, and Penguin Classics—and how to order them, write to us at the appropriate address below. Please note that for copyright reasons the selection of books varies from country to country.

In the United Kingdom: For a complete list of books available from Penguin in the U.K., please write to *Dept E.P., Penguin Books Ltd, Harmondsworth, Middlesex, UB7 0DA.*

In the United States: For a complete list of books available from Penguin in the U.S., please write to *Consumer Sales, Penguin USA, P.O. Box 999— Dept. 17109, Bergenfield, New Jersey 07621-0120.* VISA and MasterCard holders call 1-800-253-6476 to order all Penguin titles.

In Canada: For a complete list of books available from Penguin in Canada, please write to *Penguin Books Canada Ltd, 10 Alcorn Avenue, Suite 300, Toronto, Ontario, Canada M4V 3B2.*

In Australia: For a complete list of books available from Penguin in Australia, please write to the *Marketing Department, Penguin Books Ltd, P.O. Box 257, Ringwood, Victoria 3134.*

In New Zealand: For a complete list of books available from Penguin in New Zealand, please write to the *Marketing Department, Penguin Books (NZ) Ltd, Private Bag, Takapuna, Auckland 9.*

In India: For a complete list of books available from Penguin, please write to *Penguin Overseas Ltd, 706 Eros Apartments, 56 Nehru Place, New Delhi, 110019.*

In Holland: For a complete list of books available from Penguin in Holland, please write to *Penguin Books Nederland B.V., Postbus 195, NL-1380AD Weesp, Netherlands.*

In Germany: For a complete list of books available from Penguin, please write to *Penguin Books Ltd, Friedrichstrasse 10-12, D-6000 Frankfurt Main 1, Federal Republic of Germany.*

In Spain: For a complete list of books available from Penguin in Spain, please write to *Longman, Penguin España, Calle San Nicolas 15, E-28013 Madrid, Spain.*

In Japan: For a complete list of books available from Penguin in Japan, please write to *Longman Penguin Japan Co Ltd, Yamaguchi Building, 2-12-9 Kanda Jimbocho, Chiyoda-Ku, Tokyo 101, Japan.*

FOR THE BEST LITERATURE, LOOK FOR THE

☐ **THE BOOK AND THE BROTHERHOOD**
Iris Murdoch

Many years ago Gerard Hernshaw and his friends banded together to finance a political and philosophical book by a monomaniacal Marxist genius. Now opinions have changed, and support for the book comes at the price of moral indignation; the resulting disagreements lead to passion, hatred, a duel, murder, and a suicide pact.   *602 pages   ISBN: 0-14-010470-4*

☐ **GRAVITY'S RAINBOW**
Thomas Pynchon

Thomas Pynchon's classic antihero is Tyrone Slothrop, an American lieutenant in London whose body anticipates German rocket launchings. Surely one of the most important works of fiction produced in the twentieth century, *Gravity's Rainbow* is a complex and awesome novel in the great tradition of James Joyce's *Ulysses*.   *768 pages   ISBN: 0-14-010661-8*

☐ **FIFTH BUSINESS**
Robertson Davies

The first novel in the celebrated "Deptford Trilogy," which also includes *The Manticore* and *World of Wonders*, *Fifth Business* stands alone as the story of a rational man who discovers that the marvelous is only another aspect of the real.   *266 pages   ISBN: 0-14-004387-X*

☐ **WHITE NOISE**
Don DeLillo

Jack Gladney, a professor of Hitler Studies in Middle America, and his fourth wife, Babette, navigate the usual rocky passages of family life in the television age. Then, their lives are threatened by an "airborne toxic event"—a more urgent and menacing version of the "white noise" of transmissions that typically engulfs them.   *326 pages   ISBN: 0-14-007702-2*

You can find all these books at your local bookstore, or use this handy coupon for ordering:

Penguin Books By Mail
Dept. BA Box 999
Bergenfield, NJ 07621-0999

Please send me the above title(s). I am enclosing _____
(please add sales tax if appropriate and $1.50 to cover postage and handling). Send check or money order—no CODs. Please allow four weeks for shipping. We cannot ship to post office boxes or addresses outside the USA. *Prices subject to change without notice.*

Ms./Mrs./Mr. _____

Address _____

City/State _____ Zip _____

☐ A SPORT OF NATURE
Nadine Gordimer

Hillela, Nadine Gordimer's "sport of nature," is seductive and intuitively gifted at life. Casting herself adrift from her family at seventeen, she lives among political exiles on an East African beach, marries a black revolutionary, and ultimately plays a heroic role in the overthrow of apartheid.

354 pages   ISBN: 0-14-008470-3

☐ THE COUNTERLIFE
Philip Roth

By far Philip Roth's most radical work of fiction, *The Counterlife* is a book of conflicting perspectives and points of view about people living out dreams of renewal and escape. Illuminating these lives is the skeptical, enveloping intelligence of the novelist Nathan Zuckerman, who calculates the price and examines the results of his characters' struggles for a change of personal fortune.

372 pages   ISBN: 0-14-009769-4

☐ THE MONKEY'S WRENCH
Primo Levi

Through the mesmerizing tales told by two characters—one, a construction worker/philosopher who has built towers and bridges in India and Alaska; the other, a writer/chemist, rigger of words and molecules—Primo Levi celebrates the joys of work and the art of storytelling.

174 pages   ISBN: 0-14-010357-0

☐ IRONWEED
William Kennedy

"Riding up the winding road of Saint Agnes Cemetery in the back of the rattling old truck, Francis Phelan became aware that the dead, even more than the living, settled down in neighborhoods." So begins William Kennedy's Pulitzer-Prize winning novel about an ex-ballplayer, part-time gravedigger, and full-time drunk, whose return to the haunts of his youth arouses the ghosts of his past and present.

228 pages   ISBN: 0-14-007020-6

☐ THE COMEDIANS
Graham Greene

Set in Haiti under Duvalier's dictatorship, *The Comedians* is a story about the committed and the uncommitted. Actors with no control over their destiny, they play their parts in the foreground; experience love affairs rather than love; have enthusiasms but not faith; and if they die, they die like Mr. Jones, by accident.

288 pages   ISBN: 0-14-002766-1

FOR THE BEST LITERATURE, LOOK FOR THE Ⓟ

Mrs A
Mark
Todd

PENGUIN BOOKS

THE RECONSTRUCTION

Claudia Casper has been writing short stories and screenplays for ten years. She lives in Vancouver with her husband and two young sons. *The Reconstruction* is her first novel.

Claudia Casper

THE
RECONSTRUCTION

Penguin Books

PENGUIN BOOKS

Penguin Books Canada Ltd, 10 Alcorn Avenue, Toronto, Ontario,
Canada M4V 3B2
Penguin Books Ltd, 27 Wrights Lane, London W8 5TZ, England
Penguin Books USA Inc., 375 Hudson Street, New York,
New York 10014, U.S.A.
Penguin Books Australia Ltd, Ringwood, Victoria, Australia
Penguin Books (NZ) Ltd, cnr Rosedale and Airborne Roads, Albany,
Auckland 1310, New Zealand

Penguin Books Ltd, Registered Offices: Harmondsworth,
Middlesex, England

First published in Viking by Penguin Books Canada Limited, 1996
Published in Penguin Books, 1997
1 3 5 7 9 10 8 6 4 2

*Publisher's note: This book is a work of fiction. Names, characters, places
and incidents either are the product of the author's imagination or are used
fictitiously, and any resemblance to actual persons living or dead, events, or
locales is entirely coincidental.*

Manufactured in Canada

Canadian Cataloguing in Publication Data

Casper, Claudia, 1957-
The reconstruction

ISBN 0-14-025387-4

I. Title.

PS8555.A778R4 1997   C813'.54   C96-931448-5
PR9199.3.C38R4 1997

Visit Penguin Canada's web site at **www.penguin.ca**

For my early mentors
Helen Patterson
and
Greta Greisman
may their memories always be blessed

The process of reconstruction is like
a dissection in reverse.

—*John Gurche*

If little penis worms ruled the sea
I have no confidence that
Australopithecus would ever have
walked erect on the savannas
of Africa.

—*Stephen Jay Gould*
Wonderful Life

Acknowledgments

I would like to thank my husband and first reader James Griffin. This book would not have been possible without him. I owe a large debt to scientific artist, John Gurche, for his generosity with his time and his vast knowledge of hominid reconstructions. Thanks to: Larry O'Reilly, Chief of Exhibits at the Museum of Natural History, Washington DC; my charming dentist, Pierre Vigneault; artist David Dorrington; and my editor, Meg Masters, for her fine editorial touch. I'd also like to thank my parents, Mary Lou and Don Miller and Gordon Casper, and my friends, Marilou Appleby, Nora Blanck, Barb Hart, Steve Osborne and Maureen Moore.

A special thanks to Howard White, winner of the 1991 Stephen Leacock Award, writer, poet and publisher extraordinaire, for his undogmatic, essential advice.

The author also gratefully acknowledges the receipt of a Canada Council Explorations Grant that helped in the research and writing of this book.

THE
RＥCONSTRUCTION

ONE

"Wider please."

Her jaw ached but she obeyed, stretching her lips back further. She blinked up at his face. *I could bite your fingers off.* His eyes were a blurred blue concentration behind the saliva-spattered lenses of his glasses.

Margaret imagined what he saw. A tiny, detailed, oral world: particles of food being broken down by saliva; coffee stains near the gum line; fillings and caps and root canals that gave her a dental history unique enough to identify her body should she be disfigured in death. The inflamed slippery tissue of the tender pink gums and a floppy velvet tongue trying spasmodically not to get in the way, not to lay itself protectively over the areas he probed. Everything wet and glistening and red and imperfect. When he prodded with the curette she could smell the foul little odours that sometimes escaped.

The decay.

She wondered if dentists still enjoyed kissing. Did they still want to slip their tongues into a lover's mouth and explore the wet soft private place, did they still want to wind tongues sinuously like two snakes trying to penetrate each other's skins? Could dentists repress their daily observations of oral decay when it came to sex?

To kissing?

A narrow room with a low ceiling. The blue shadows of fir branches and lace curtains moving on the wall, a man's breath, his tongue moving supplely inside her mouth, his skin hot and surprisingly smooth against hers.

That night no longer seemed real. It seemed implausible that those lips had touched the body sitting now in the dentist's chair, or that her fingertips had pressed on his skin, that those moments—finite, discrete—existed objectively in her past. It seemed implausible that that night was not a dream. She didn't know his last name or address. She knew only that his first name was Phillip.

"You can close now."

Dr. Adin walked over to his cabinet and held an x-ray of her lower right jaw up to the light. He selected several tools from a cabinet drawer and they clinked metallically as he dropped them onto his stainless-steel tray. The throbbing pain had subsided as soon as she entered the front door of his office, as though the tooth sensed it was now in good hands.

Margaret looked out the window. A silver-haired woman waited at a bus stop across the street. The woman stared vacantly into the road and took no notice of people joining her at the stop.

Margaret remembered her childhood dentist's office,

which looked out over a cemetery. Her wisdom teeth hadn't erupted yet but all her adult teeth were in. It was summer and the window was open. She heard chickadees chirping and bluejays screeching and children calling to each other on the way home from school. The dentist pencilled notes on her chart.

"Well young lady," he said presently, "you have a cavity."

"But I thought you couldn't get cavities in your permanent teeth," she'd cried. "Aren't they supposed to last the rest of your life?"

"Only if you take very good care of them," he replied sternly.

She'd felt panicky. If she failed to brush her teeth, they might decay before she grew up. She was barely a teenager and decay had already taken root in her body.

Dr. Adin adjusted his hygienic mask. "Open please," he said through the white cotton.

Using a clamp carrier he picked up a metal clamp from the tray and jostled it over her molar, then released it. The clamp gripped the tooth, then slipped down slightly onto her gums so the serrated metal clamped the soft tissue. She winced.

She remembered her adolescent face, blurred by hormones, in the bathroom mirror. A heaviness had come over her, a kind of depression or passivity. She felt too heavy to run or jump. Often she felt too exhausted to brush her teeth. She'd go to bed, too weary even to take off her clothes, and curl up and quickly sink into unconsciousness. The next day she'd go to school wearing the clothes she'd slept in.

Weeks would go by. A sense of doom would build,

and then one day she'd be horrified by what she was doing. She'd rush to the bathroom mirror to examine her teeth, expecting rotten brown stumps, yet miraculously they'd gleam back at her, still white and even. And she would turn over a new leaf for a while, brushing and flossing three times a day.

People were always surprised when she said she had bad teeth. "They're so white and even, they're so beautiful. You have a lovely smile."

"They're full of cavities," she'd answer.

Dr. Adin snipped a small hole in the middle of a black latex dam. He stretched this opening over her tooth and pushed down, driving the edge of the clamp further into her gums. She gasped and gripped the chair's arms. Then he took some dental floss and forced the latex down between her teeth. She moaned.

"Did that hurt, Margaret?"

She took a deep breath. Relax. Soon this moment will be over. She nodded.

The dentist's assistant sprayed air on the frozen tooth. It felt like a cold electric shock.

Where pain is involved, waiting begins.

Margaret recrossed her ankles with the left foot on top, trying to divert her attention from her mouth. She looked out the window again at the woman standing at the bus stop, staring down at the asphalt. An expression of anguish suddenly passed over the woman's face, after which she seemed to become self-conscious and glanced round nervously to see if anyone watched her.

Pain changes time. You wait always for the present to end. The bus arrived and occluded Margaret's view of the stop. Hope lies in the quick termination of minutes.

You can spend your whole life just waiting for the next moment to be over.

The drill bit contacted her enamel and an unpleasant burning smell filled the room. Then he shone a light into her mouth. Time waiting for its own extinction. Her life was permeated by a kind of continuous background hum of low-grade emotional pain. She wasn't aware of it really, except that she remembered feeling differently as a child. Puberty had been like a disease for her. A disease she'd never really recovered from.

The drill whined like a giant mosquito. It turned decayed enamel into dust and made way for itself to move deeper.

The bus pulled away and the bus stop was deserted. She blamed Jane Goodall. That weekend she'd been reading a chapter on the sexual behaviour of the chimpanzees at Gombe Stream. The boisterous mating scene around a female in estrus, all the males converging on her pink, swollen bottom, restlessly lining up, had filled Margaret with envy. When she'd realized she was envious—she'd put the book down and wept.

Her sexual isolation inside her marriage seemed absolute. The quick thrust of a male chimp seeking to reproduce his genes seemed a level of pure sexual desire she herself could never hope to attract. She felt like a tree whose fruit was rotting on the branch.

John had stood by the front door, garment bag in hand, his face affecting the same wooden expressionlessness as her own, his voice intoning the same leaden bitterness. An hour after he'd left, her tooth began to throb; the pain clung to her all weekend long like sinew to a meat bone.

After packing the hole in her tooth with amalgam, Dr. Adin removed the latex dam and the clamp. His assistant vacuumed around her molar, causing more sensitivity shivers. The nozzle sought blood, pulp, shards of enamel among the saliva.

He held a carbon paper between her upper and lower teeth. "Bite… Grind… Open."

Her mother's voice, *Close your mouth. You'll catch a fly.* Margaret glanced at the office window. Open, but screened. In the garden sometimes, in the evening when Margaret kneeled down to pull up weeds, her lips would part slightly with effort and tiny flies did occasionally dart inside her mouth. What attracted them? The warm breathy darkness? Were they overcome by tiny impulses to self-destruct?

Her mother never seemed actually concerned about a fly really entering Margaret's mouth, nor did she seem concerned that her daughter might look moronic sitting slack-jawed and staring. It was more as though she was just mouthing something her own mother had said to her, a warning she'd never really understood the point of but repeated in the vacuum of any genuine maternal concerns of her own. Her mother had vaguely gone through the motions of motherhood, imitating what she imagined a good mother should be.

"You can close. We're done for today. It looks like we'll be seeing lots of each other this summer," Dr. Adin concluded cheerfully, as though he thought she might welcome this news.

"There are eight more cavities that I can see without x-rays. In six the decay has probably penetrated to the root system. Two are wisdom teeth, so they can be extracted. The other four will need root canals, and it's unlikely enough healthy enamel is left to do fillings. You'll need caps." He looked down at her chart. "You also have two smaller cavities but they can wait. We'll just keep an eye on them... You're on a dental plan?"

She shook her head. His cheerfulness changed to concern. "Mmmm. A root canal and cap run around $900, $1,000. The extractions will be around $200 each. The smaller fillings probably $180. In total you're looking in the neighbourhood of $5,000."

"I can't afford that right now." She took a deep breath, trying to quell tears. "What if I have the rotten ones pulled?"

"You can't do that," he said sternly. "The other teeth need support. You'd have to wear bridges and they're expensive too."

"What if I have them *all* pulled?" she asked. An end to decay. Perfect, white dentures. "How much would that cost?"

The dentist looked down at her in horror. "You're too young! No, I wouldn't advise that. You have such a pretty smile! I'd refuse to do it!"

She looked away. Her throat tightened and tears started again. She envisioned her face without the structural support of real teeth, the flesh around her mouth sagging and puckered, the jawbone weakening. She imagined a floppy gummy smile—defenceless and pathetic.

"Extraordinary stress can cause this kind of sudden decay," he said kindly, perhaps inquisitively. "It weakens the enamel." His white hair rose in unruly wisps like towering clouds on a windy spring day. His cheekbones were high and Slavic. The image of her toothless grin, accompanied by his gentle tone, snapped her last threads of control and she wept outright.

He gave her a box of tissues and sat down. "Your other teeth are actually in quite good shape," he said, offering consolation.

Undesired. Discarded. A mouth full of rotting teeth.

Her weeping did not abate and Dr. Adin grew uneasy. His next two patients were waiting in the front room, rattling their magazines nervously and shifting positions in their chairs as the sound of sobbing reached them.

"Margaret, it's going to be all right." He patted her shoulder. "We'll fix your teeth. You can pay in instalments, something you can manage until you're back on your feet."

Meekly, gratefully—spent—she nodded. She blew her nose, pushed her hair out of her face and stood up. She hadn't realized she'd been clenching her muscles during the whole appointment. She was stiff and her clothes were damp from perspiration.

"Make an appointment with the receptionist. Remember, twice a day," he said, holding up the dental floss as though to remind her of her part of the bargain.

TWO

The irritating drone of a neighbour's lawn mower penetrated Margaret's sleep on Saturday morning and brought in its wake a brief memory of the dentist's drill. She slid back into her dream.

She's in a country cottage. There's been a big storm and all the lines are down. It's getting dark outside. She wants to turn a light on, but no matter how gently she turns the switch, it won't catch and the light doesn't go on. She tries other lights and none of them work either. She is scared at the thought of being alone all night without lights. She picks up the phone to see if the telephone lines are down too. A male voice speaks her name as though across a great distance. He says he won't be able to fix the lines until tomorrow and she thinks, *I don't want him to know I'm here alone in the house*, so she says, "We're fine," hoping he'll believe a man is with her.

The voice wants to know if she can pay.

An angry, frustrated sound—lawn mowers. She'd perspired while sleeping, in places where skin touched skin—the inside of her legs, her armpits—and the side of her head that lay on the pillow. It was going to be an unseasonally warm spring day.

Now that her husband was gone who could confirm for her every day that the world was real? Who was there to witness her in her cotton nightie twisted round clammy knees, who to smell the morning air blowing in from the sea? Why stop dreaming?

She sank back to sleep.

She woke again in the afternoon. The lawn mower was silent now and she rolled onto her back. Another interminable day in an interminable series, nothing melting into nothing, silence into silence. She tried to fall back to sleep but the comfort of unconsciousness evaded her and she supposed the sleeping pills had worn off.

When she'd got back from the dentist on Monday she'd switched on her answering machine and turned the volume down to zero. She'd taken sleeping pills in the intervening nights and often during the day, too, waking only to eat, go to the bathroom or watch sitcoms and talk shows in the evening. The past eight days, Margaret thought while examining the light fixture on the ceiling, had been like a Surrealist film where the hero's profile is shown in shadow—eye open, eye closed, eye open, eye closed; waking, sleeping, waking, sleeping, day and night passing in an eye blink, occasionally a tear escaping the closed eyelid, the closed shutter.

She rolled back onto her side. A perfect blue sky hung

outside the bedroom window. Without warning tears began streaming down her cheek and round her nose. A wordless moan rose from her chest, naked and raw, so animal that even in her pain she was shy hearing it.

When the weeping passed she lay as before, staring out the window. She couldn't understand why, if they no longer loved each other, the prospect of divorce should hurt so much.

THREE

It hurts so deeply because he never loved you.

She opened her eyes. Spring clouds like amorphous white balloons bobbed across the blue sky. Sunday morning. She closed her eyes.

Looking back now she saw that it had started the first time he'd insisted the lights be turned off. They'd had sex mutely in darkness and afterwards he'd been unusually affectionate and solicitous. Then he stopped touching her breasts, except occasionally as a kind of courtesy, and finally he stopped touching her at all. He bought her a long-sleeved, high-collared nightgown and asked her to wear it when they had intercourse. He fabricated a sexual fetish—"You look like a nun," he said. At other times it was a ghost. The ghost of desire.

She rolled onto her back and opened her eyes again. Dead insects had accumulated in the ceiling light fixture.

She could see their threadlike feelers and legs through the frosted glass. The last three years he'd had sex with her once a month, out of duty, with soft desireless caresses, penetrating her reluctantly, holding himself up on his fists, his face turned away.

"It's not you," he offered as consolation one night. It was his medical practice. Being confronted with the human body, day in and day out. When he looked at people, shook their hands, said "Hello, how are you," he was overwhelmed by repulsive physiological impressions: rattling mucus in the chest, the clammy pungent smell of genitals, ear wax, ragged skin near the cuticles, pimples on the buttocks, dark hair follicles on the backs of arms rising to goosebumps, the odour of warm urine, vomit, sweat, faeces, rot. When he looked at people, their whole biological history rose before his eyes, from the bloody mess of their birth to the morbid sweet smell of their infirmity. He had to strain now to hear what people were saying over the roar of their bodies. Other people, friends from medical school, his mother and his sister, had been irritated by his air of preoccupation, his inattention to their conversation. Margaret tried to understand and be sympathetic.

She'd brought up the subject of children a year or two after they were married; he'd wanted to pay off his student loans first and get established in his practice. She asked about children again a few years later and he was frank. "I can't risk being repulsed by my own child. I couldn't bear that. The smell of that genetically new skin, milky vomit, yellow diarrhoea. I would be unable to show affection. I couldn't do that to a child."

But you can to me. She felt like the shell of a woman.

Bodiless. A mute pair of eyes watching from an internal desert.

She put a foot over the side of the bed and lowered it onto the cool wooden floor. Then the other foot. She stood up. Her joints felt as though they were held together by thread, her bones suspended in the air like a floating mobile. She clicked and creaked over to her chest of drawers like a fragile, somnambulistic exoskeleton.

The mirror revealed oily hair full of rats' nests, kinked at weird angles. She hadn't changed her clothes since Monday and they smelled strongly of skin oils and stale perspiration. She took them off and put on a clean oversized T-shirt and went down to the kitchen. She opened the fridge door and looked inside. Sour milk, coffee cream, all the usual condiments—mustard, relish, jam, etc.—and a pastry box containing a lemon meringue pie. She never ate food like that, old-fashioned bakery food. She'd bought it for comfort and consolation. She cut a big piece, mentally listing all the ingredients that were nourishing—citrus, carbohydrates, eggs, vitamin C, cornstarch. It tasted like cardboard and refrigerator ozone. She made coffee. The first sip warmed her mouth, then her throat.

She carried her coffee into the studio. She hadn't looked inside this room since Friday night when John had come to take his possessions. He'd found a town-house to rent. Her studio had lost a lamp, a small Persian carpet, a large cactus, and there were gaps in the bookcase that the remaining books had collapsed into.

One of the things she'd been avoiding by sleeping the past eight days away was working on the hummingbird. Even before John left, she'd avoided it. It repelled her in some way. But she was out of bed now and wide awake and she could not afford to procrastinate any longer. She'd checked the calendar, "Monday, April 4—Del. hummingbird." The thing was due tomorrow. She should have phoned the guy at the aviary and told him it was going to be late. She wanted to phone and tell him that she was very sorry but she couldn't do it at all. That she thought it was a very bad idea in the first place to build a giant hummingbird, that the request was oxymoronic since the essence of a hummingbird was to be small and fast and blurred and the idea of creating a giant one negated the very qualities that gave it hummingbirdness. It was just not possible to build a giant hummingbird that would "appear lifelike."

But she needed the money more than ever and so she hoped that, because it was only intended to be suspended from the ceiling of the new souvenir shop and would not be part of any scientific display within the aviary proper, its surreal qualities might be considered quirky, intriguing, some kind of artistic statement.

Appear lifelike.

Removed from life by one. Not-life appearing to be life. She thought of science fiction movies—ectoplasm, alien incubations, demonic succubi, silicone ooze transforming itself into credible representations of human life on earth. Not-life appearing to be life. The back of her throat began to ache as it always did when she was about to cry.

Her life.

The aliens in those films were metaphors for how people really felt about themselves. Strange souls inhabiting body shells.

A tiny stuffed hummingbird sat brilliantly on the worktable. She'd found it after a fruitless search through all the taxidermy shops listed in the Yellow Pages. It had been in a pawn shop, recognizable as a hummingbird only after she'd blown off a thick coat of dust.

She liked the beautiful stuffed thing and thought of it as the "real" hummingbird, though it wasn't really real either. It was a shell too, the shell of a real hummingbird whose hummingbird soul had hovered briefly over its still-warm body, then departed. A taxidermist had carefully sliced open its skin and removed all the flesh inside, transforming it into an emerald feather coat for a tiny fairy king. The taxidermist had then sewn it back up, filled the coat with stuffing, implanted tiny glass eyes, glued its tiny feet to the lacquered stand and set luminescent wings up in the air, poised as though it were caught in slow motion. Time-held. Pinned forever to the present.

Beside the mounted bird on the worktable was the huge blank presence of the giant hummingbird. It looked, with its smooth white skin of plaster, like a giant eggshell with the foetal head, wings, tail and legs growing on the outside. The eyeballs were covered with saran wrap and masking tape. Wire hoops jutted out where the wings would be. It looked so heavy and white. Its whiteness seemed to connote pure fear and absolute burning hatred for everything that caused that fear. It was stranded, wingless and blind, on the wire frame she'd built to keep it upright while she worked, and its white paralysed bulk, its malevolent fear, dominated the room.

She hovered at the doorway, hesitating to enter. The hummingbirds—small and giant—watched her nervously from glassy eyes at the sides of their heads, ready to take off should she move. There was still so much work to be done. Sanding, all the painting, the wings needed to be finished, its beak wasn't set right. Each of these tasks required thousands of tiny decisions and the thought of even one such decision exhausted her. She couldn't even lift her foot past the threshold into the room. She felt like a statue, with no live nerves to transmit messages from her brain to her muscles and instruct them to move. The lines were down. The present moment fell continuously away before her and devoured her puny impulses before a decision to act even formed.

The giant hummingbird stared out at the world through the saran wrap; its will to see was frantic and unflinching, its anxiety intense. It was desperate to know if enemies approached, if it was hunted. By not finishing the wings she'd left it disabled. It foundered on the table, struggling helplessly, trying to see her clearly, see what sadistic creator had reduced its flickering emerald beauty to this white, gravity-stricken, inanimate silence.

She wanted to get the thing over and done with and out of her house, but since she couldn't even bring herself to go into the room she decided to escape to the museum. She often went to the museum on Sunday, sometimes first to the art gallery and afterwards she treated herself to a steak sandwich and a glass of wine at a nearby bistro. She liked being in an anonymous crowd, participating in a shared culture with strangers, eavesdropping on their comments, observing faces and body language. Even so, she often felt a little pained being publicly alone—unclaimed. But the overall feeling of freedom, of being able to live in her own thoughts and act purely on her own whims, to watch people who were too occupied being with someone else to look consciously around them, compensated for it.

She got dressed and stepped out of the house into the breezy April day feeling a little like a taxidermied animal herself, whose soul, mute and anxious, still inhabited the stuffed dead body.

FOUR

Bones as big as buildings. Large unwieldly joints assembled like a child's Meccano set. A giant sloth reared up, exposing a pelvic girdle wide enough to give birth to a sumo wrestler, a rib cage big enough to house a child; it pawed lethargically at the air. If it could, it would bring down clouds, like deer shot in mid-air. Enforce the law of gravity. Bring the sky to the ground.

The dark-brown tibia of some lumbering dinosaur whose pinhead bobbed at the end of a neck long and muscular as a python. What huge plants travelled down that esophagus to fuel its thundering motion? The tibia was six feet tall and shaded brown and black like a very tarnished penny (if time had a colour...), its concave curves and convex knobs the sensual structure of a history of wordlessness and slow turbulence, where Homo sapiens was still too random a possibility to be a twinkle in anyone's eye. The dinosaur bones were like a beautiful hallucinogenic mystery, a creation worthy of an omnipotent God.

The small dark rooms of the museum rumbled with the silence of the extinct bones.

Margaret heard a whimper and turned to see a young boy clutching his mother's leg. The mother tried to pry him loose—"They're just bones Tommy, they can't hurt you. They aren't alive."

Across the room tyrannosaurus rex loomed, jaw gaping open, tiny thalidomide arm stubs sticking out from its chest. The child whimpered louder and begged his mother to take him away. He didn't believe it was dead, couldn't believe in the inanimateness of such huge bones; and the thought of it being alive, running after him, standing over him with that cupboard-sized jaw caused his small heart to despair. He would not be comforted and his mother finally gave up and carried him out.

Margaret progressed through the halls, moving from the prehistoric toward the present, and noticed that the skeletons became smaller and more delicate, as though a creator had reversed the usual process for sculpting and had built giant crude maquettes as practice for later, smaller originals. The gargantuan rib cages, thundering legs, huge stone-toothed jaws were becoming less evident and in their place came a profusion of delicate skeletons: crouching, cowering, grazing, poised to flee. The more recent bones were lighter and had a frail, desiccated look, like the exoskeletons of dead insects.

They reminded Margaret of Giacometti's statues— tiny purposeful figures telegraphing small personal intentions in a huge silent space. Subjectively alone, they were connected to one another through spatial relationship only. They had a whimsical fragility, implausible as physiques meant to survive in the real world.

Margaret entered a marine room where murals of ancient sea life decorated all the walls and the lighting was dim and blue. The huge skeleton of a prehistoric whale was suspended from the ceiling, its vertebrae curved like a sickle, as though it were diving down, jaw open, sharp carnivorous teeth to the front of the mouth and, at the back, teeth that were serrated very oddly and looked like miniature art deco buildings. Floating behind and below the rib cage, unconnected to any other bone, was a vestigial pelvic bone.

The plaque explained that whales, and all other sea mammals, had been land animals who returned to the sea—possibly, in the whale's case, because their skeletons could no longer efficiently support their tremendous weight. The bone structure of the whale's flippers still showed a flattened-out elbow joint and five trailing, elongated fingers.

The words *returned to the sea* filled Margaret with an unexpected nostalgia.

She sat down on a banquette and wondered—had there been a wistful look back, memories of the sound of birds, the feeling of the sun on skin, the pressure of gravity, the touch of a breeze, feet on solid ground? A pull toward the land?

Once exiled, there can never be a complete return home. Something is always being left behind, a slight memory, and there is always a yearning, however repressed, for the life in exile.

People drifted by Margaret's banquette. Adults murmured to one another; children exclaimed insistently to their parents, usually more to get attention than out of true wonder at what they saw. The burble and chirp of video displays echoed intermittently through the halls.

She remembered another afternoon in the museum, gazing at the Neanderthal burial scene. She'd felt someone watching her and when she looked up she almost laughed out loud because he was so startlingly handsome. He didn't smile, but continued to stare at her. He seemed shorter than he actually was because his torso was long and his head large. He made her think of an amaryllis, its huge exotic bloom supported by a leafless stalk, excessive in its most sensual parts.

She remembered seeing Phillip naked. He looked lean and strong, like someone who practised yoga. He had almost no body hair. She remembered his chest, ribs showing through bands of muscle, waiting to press down and touch her. Her hands on his stomach, the muscles of his abdomen taut. She remembered his hot skin in the cool room.

His eyes were an intense burning blue, yet his gaze also had a kind of coolness, a friendly detachment. He seemed interested, gently appraising, inviting a reciprocal appraisal. There'd been an ironic self-consciousness in the way he'd walked toward her across the room.

Why remember Phillip now? Almost a year had passed since their encounter. Only one night, no last names, no addresses. She'd made it clear that their intimacy would be bounded by the beginning and end of that evening. She would not see him again after she got dressed and left.

She hadn't understood yet that her marriage was ending, and she was very clear that she didn't want an affair. But on some level she must have given herself permission to take one night and see what it was like to be desired again, to remember herself before John. She'd returned to her marriage and more or less erased the night from memory.

But there can never be a complete return.

In the next hall a little girl sat exceptionally still in front of a video monitor. An animated mudfish told her how life first moved from the sea onto land. Margaret watched the girl. She looked eleven or twelve years old. Her hands were tucked under her thighs, elbows out, toes pointed in. She was banging her heels against the wooden bench and her mouth hung slightly open.

Margaret remembered the video from her last visit to the museum—the sappy characterization of the mudfish recounting his own story as though it were the plot of a Walt Disney movie. Yet the video had made her think. It made her remember swimming in the warm lakes of Ontario, how wonderful and free she used to feel in the velvet water.

She would forget about her parents sitting on the dock and dive under the surface and swim out as far as she could without coming up for air. All her flying dreams were of swimming through air. Immersed in the lake, all frustration and loneliness fell away; she was pulled by no other desires. In those perfect moments she had everything she wanted; she could float forever.

As she watched the young girl's absorption Margaret wondered what she made of the story. Was she thinking that she was descended from a fish? Was she wondering what physical mutations had occurred to make that happen? The video ended. The girl stared at the empty screen for a moment then got up and walked over to a display of freshwater fossils.

A group of nine or ten people edged into the underwater hall. They had deep suntans and some wore T-shirts with various references to Texas. From the middle of the group Margaret recognized Frank Rice's voice. He was the museum's Chief of Exhibits and he often escaped his office to roam the museum, eavesdropping or giving impromptu tours like this one.

"The architecture of this wonderful museum is simple—a central rotunda from which the halls radiate like the spokes of a wheel, offices and research laboratories on the outer rim." He was tall, with the graceful awkwardness of an amateur basketball player, slightly dishevelled, rosy-cheeked, buoyant.

"As you meander through these halls, it may seem to you that each display follows logically on the one before and that each one is complete and scientifically accurate. Museums create an aura of permanency and stability and even authority. The truth is, here at the National Museum, we're continually improvising. Tinkering, revising, fiddling, updating. I liken the process to evolution itself where every species, no matter how old and stable, is becoming something else, has been something else. The museum is no different than the life you see around you. Transient. Change made concrete.

"We humans," he added, as though it were an afterthought, "are prone to think of ourselves as the final product of evolution. We think of the species preceding us as part of a teleological progression whose sole purpose is to evolve into Homo sapiens. Because we think of ourselves as the goal of evolutionary change, it's easy for us to think the world around us is permanent and stable and forget that we too, however slowly, are either evolving into another species or heading for extinction."

The group was getting restless. One heavy woman nudged her husband and they sidled away to look at an ancient sea turtle. Frank recognized Margaret, waved and signalled for her to wait.

"Well *I'm* just getting warmed up, but you people are here to see the whole museum. I'll leave you to explore. If you have any comments or suggestions please drop me a line." He handed out business cards, then strode over to her.

Normally Margaret would have been pleased to see him, but today she didn't feel up to making casual conversation. She smiled.

"Good luck to bump into you. I was going to phone you anyway. Do you have a couple of minutes?"

Frank led her past a security guard down a long corridor. On one side dark-green filing cabinets lined the wall, on the other doorways opened into tiny offices where desks and shelves were piled high with a miscellany of birds' eggs, stones, animal skins, books, microscopes, gurgling fish tanks, mouse cages, bones, casts and moulds. Someone had a radio tuned to a rock station playing what sounded like The Clash.

"Did you ever meet Neill Hansen when you worked on that last project for us?"

She nodded. She remembered him quite well because she hadn't really liked him. He was obsessed with the details of his work and his obsession seemed to go hand in hand with undisguised disdain for everyone else not similarly obsessed.

"He did the Neanderthal bust in the Physical Anthropology Hall." They side-stepped a stack of boxes with Latin names scrawled on the sides. "And now he's working on a new series of hominid reconstructions for us."

They turned left down a short wide corridor that led to a huge hall. The wall between the corridor and the hall had been completely knocked down. The sound of drills and objects being crashed about gregariously made it difficult to hear.

"This is the back of the old Marine Hall!" Frank shouted.

The toxic smell of burning plexiglass made Margaret try to breathe as shallowly as she could. The hall was illuminated by dark-blue light intended to create a deep underwater effect. A torch aimed at the rivets on an old bathysphere caused an arc of bright orange sparks to rain down. Someone called for a hammer.

Margaret felt drawn to the room, to the energy of the men working together. Their reality seemed more secure than her own, less arbitrary, less tenuous. Frank touched her elbow, indicating they should turn to the right and continue along another corridor.

The next hall was empty. Wires, sockets, plumbing lay bare; new drywall was stacked in the middle of the floor. Frank unhooked a chain across the entrance and ushered her in.

"What you see," he lifted his arms and circled the empty space like Zorba the Greek, "is the new Hall of Human Origins. I've been lobbying our board and the government since I started this job five years ago. What we've got now is pathetic. See that line?" He gestured at a wide rough band halfway up the wall with wires and pipes sticking out. "There'll be two floors. The top floor will be home for the hominids and the bottom will be used for Native American Culture, which is also desperately in need of more space.

"The museum has caseloads of good fossil casts, from Johanson's First Family to Raymond Dart's Taung skull, and I'm having glass display cases built for them. We'll move the Neanderthal burial scene here, such as it is, and Neill's bust. Work's already started on a three-dimensional computer-animated short depicting a day in the life of Australopithecus afarensis, Homo habilis and Homo erectus, and we're building a small theatre to screen it in. But at the rate Neill works it's going to take him years to complete the hominid reconstructions, and I need a new display for the opening next fall. It's got to be ready on time because I've had to fight hard and I don't want to give the board any excuse to cut this project back.

"You've worked on a couple of projects for us now. The miniature dinosaur environment you did was excellent. You work fast and you have the background in human anatomy with your sculpture. What I'm about to propose, however, will be fairly challenging. Scientifically speaking the territory is uncharted—you'd have to do more of your own research and more scientific guesswork. You'd have Neill as a resource person and supervisor—he has an unparalleled knowledge of comparative primate anatomy and a solid understanding of paleoanthropology."

Frank stopped talking and appeared to be waiting for some kind of answer.

"What is the proposal exactly?" Margaret asked eventually.

"Of course. The display I want completed by the fall requires full body reconstructions of a male and female Australopithecus afarensis. That's the same species as Lucy." He looked to see if this reference meant anything to her.

"The fossil named after 'Lucy in the Sky with Diamonds,' right? Yes. I remember learning about it in an anthropology course. It was found in Ethiopia. Donald Johanson. The remarkable thing about it was not only that the skeleton was quite complete for something so old, but also that it had already evolved structurally for walking erect, but its brain was still not much bigger than a chimpanzee's."

"That's right. Our display will centre on the Laetoli footprints. You've heard of them?"

"Mmmm. Vaguely. No, not really."

"The Laetoli footprints are amazing. They're one of the most magical finds in paleoanthropology. They were discovered one day when some scientists from one of Mary Leakey's digs had an elephant dung fight. Three and a half million years old, there they were under soil and sediment. Footprints of three human ancestors walking erect across a bed of ash spewed out by a volcano. It rained and the rain turned the ash into a natural kind of cement. The footprints are even older than the Lucy skeleton, but they almost certainly belong to the same species. They're absolute proof that Australopithecus afarensis walked erect, at least some of the time.

"Neill has already started on the reconstruction of the adult male. I'm hoping you have the next five or six months free to do a reconstruction of the adult female. He'll familiarize you with the necessary primate anatomy and your work will be based on Johanson's Lucy skeleton. There is a large difference in size between the male and female but structurally they are very similar, so you should be able to use a lot of Neill's research."

"Are there any reconstructions of Lucy in other museums?"

"I think there are a few. One in London I believe, New Mexico, New York—but none have been done with the level of research and attention to science that Neill is bringing to his work. I don't think they'll be hard to improve on."

Frank walked over and picked up a chocolate bar wrapper someone had tossed into the hall. He scrunched it up and held it in his hand.

"The great thing is next week the museum is hosting a symposium jointly with the universities on modes of locomotion for Australopithecus afarensis, and one of the speakers is bringing some original fossils of a female. They'll be stored in our labs for a few days. The chance to see one of these fossils firsthand without having to travel to Africa is rare, because of course now they all return to their country of origin."

Original bones. Margaret imagined them in the dry powdery earth of an excavation, slowly unburied, lifted gingerly out. "Who are you?" the paleoanthropologist in khaki shorts and shirt asks the bones, hair unbrushed, face hot and dusty, hand spectacularly aware of contact, the hard dusty feel of an ancestor. "Who am I?" The bones answer question with question.

"So are you interested?" Frank asked.

"Yes," she said and added, smiling, "I'd get to keep my teeth after all."

He raised his eyebrows but did not ask. "Good. There's a meeting of the Hall of Human Origins Committee at nine Friday morning. Can you come?" She nodded. "The budget is as usual restricted but we could offer you the equivalent or perhaps a bit more than last time. I might be able to squeeze some kind of advance if that's helpful." He looked at her intently.

"How *are* you?" he asked. She looked evasively out the door. "You've been unusually quiet."

Margaret hesitated. He would be the first person she'd told.

"My husband and I are splitting up. But really I'm fine. It just takes a little adjusting," she said lightly, trying to smile reassurance.

He gave her shoulder a little squeeze, hesitated, wondering perhaps if he should say more, but decided to accept her reassurance.

"Well all right. See you Friday morning. Take care of yourself."

They had walked across the empty hall to an entrance that led back into the museum's public space. Frank lifted the chain, invited her to duck under, then scissor-jumped over himself, coins and keys jangling. He strode off through the crowds with his loose-limbed gait, tossing the candy wrapper into the wastebasket from an imaginary free-throw line. He turned and waved to her.

Margaret didn't know what to do now. She didn't really feel like wandering through the museum any more, but she didn't feel like going back to an empty house either. She decided to look for the reconstruction of the Neanderthal Neill had done. She didn't remember seeing it on other visits to the museum.

Why hadn't she married someone like Frank? Cheerful, curious, generous, *fun*. No—wrong landscape. She would never fit into Frank's world. She and John were both serious, heavy, like characters in German movies, both not *fun*, both hungry.

The bust was in a small alcove where Native American History ended and Anthropology began and it drew her eye immediately. It was of a completely different order from the reconstructions for the Neanderthal burial scene, which seemed crude and toylike in comparison. Neill had left the grey clay unpainted and had not added hair, yet it seemed more real than the painted, hairy specimens.

Something about its massiveness made Margaret want to touch it. It was sensual, its lips suggested a kiss to her, a caress, and its contours aroused a kind of hedonistic pleasure in her that was oddly intensified by its facial expression. The Neanderthal seemed surprised and pained, as though he'd just realized he was the last one of his species.

FIVE

Margaret suddenly grasped the side of the bed. She felt as though she were falling, as though all the nerves in her body were blocking out the tactile information that there was a bed underneath her. She was plummeting down a black hole. *Where am I?* 1:12 a.m. No John. She drifted back down to sleep.

Small dinosaurs cavort in the dust at her feet.

They crane their long necks. Their heads are cool and smooth and round as a dog's nose and they brush against the bare skin of her ankles. A tyrannosaurus rex runs on miniaturely powerful legs. It ignores a tasty apatasaurus on its right and aggressively charges her ankle, leaping into the air with open jaw. Its mouth is open so wide it can't see where it's going, even though it's already airborne toward her flesh...

A garden, lush and green and damp with mist. She is

sitting on a moss-covered stone beside a magnolia tree. A snake is coiled around the trunk, emerald-green and brown. He offers her the nozzle of a hookah. She takes the pipe in her mouth and sucks smoke in and only then realizes there is no way to exhale. Her body fills with smoke like a balloon, growing bigger and bigger, and she floats up above the trees.

She is growing quite anxious because if she lets her breath out now she'll whoosh down to the ground so fast she'll be dashed to pieces. The smoky air explodes out of her and *whoosh*...

A single-celled being. Tiny creatures with waving cilia swim by. An amoeba projects a foot and traps one of the tiny creatures. It secretes a substance that breaks down the creature's outer membrane. Then the amoeba absorbs it. With great effort Margaret manages to grow a little bigger. The ground shakes. A June bug looms over her then veers suddenly to the right. It attacks a worm and the worm struggles to keep the June bug from killing it.

Her body expands and shrinks as though it exists in a manic zoom lens. She can't hold a stable size even for a second and helplessly fluctuates from microcosmic to gigantic.

SIX

She woke.
The hummingbird was due.
She went back to sleep.

In the afternoon she got up because someone was phoning her repeatedly. The answering-machine was on and the volume was turned right down because she didn't want to hear the caller's voice, or John's, intoning their message. Still, the phone rang a couple of times before the machine intercepted and those rings were making her anxious. She unplugged the phone, then she went back to bed.

One thing she'd miss about marriage was the feeling of public accompaniment. Of being beside someone. She'd enjoyed having John's parents over for Sunday dinner for example, not because their company was particularly agreeable, but because she liked the feeling of being hosts together, of working side by side. She loved the moment in a movie theatre when the lights had just gone down and the opening credits were rolling and John was beside her, facing the screen. She'd glance at his profile in the reflected light. In the early days she would swing her leg over his and hook her foot under his other knee.

She remembered sometimes being overcome with sudden happiness when the two of them walked down the sidewalk together. She'd fall behind him, then take a couple of running steps and jump up on his back, wrap her arms round his neck and kiss his cheek. The first couple of times he chuckled indulgently and carried her past a few houses before stopping to let her down. Then he'd just stand there patiently waiting for her to slide down again. Then he started complaining, "My neck! It's straining my neck, Margaret. You don't know what stress it causes having an adult woman hurtle up behind you and hang herself on your neck when you're not pre-pared." And she had let go obediently, believing it was his neck. The last couple of times he just snapped, "Christ don't do that! I thought I explained it to you. My neck can't take it." She'd felt shame but she didn't want to apologize. She no longer believed it was his neck.

Now she questioned why she'd kept jumping up on him after he'd made it clear he didn't like it. Had she been so wrapped up in her own passing joy that she didn't care if his neck hurt or not? She did think the pleasure of receiving her affection should have tran-scended any discomfort she might inadvertently have caused. What was a little neck pain compared to the upwelling of true love?

The thought that John might never have loved her had hurt, but she was beginning to suspect something even more difficult. She was beginning to suspect she might not have loved him. She'd loved him in the sense of indulging an intense affection, of wanting to be near him, of wanting him, but she doubted she'd ever considered him separate from her own needs. And when his needs didn't coincide with hers she'd resented them, felt wounded by them, abandoned.

If she hadn't loved John, had she ever loved anyone?

That night she watched TV until two in the morning, took a couple of sleeping pills and slept again.

The next morning—Tuesday—she woke early. Ten mornings without John and now she was no longer surprised by his absence beside her in bed, no longer searched confusedly for an explanation.

She dressed quickly and went down to the kitchen. The sound of her sandals clacking on the wooden stairs echoed through the house. She never remembered hearing her own movements in the house so distinctly before, though of course she'd often been there alone. There was silence when she stopped to turn the thermostat up, then her sandals made a softer clatter on kitchen linoleum. The hummingbird. She needed the money for the dentist. And for the mortgage. She just wanted to get the damn thing out. It was such an unpleasant creature.

She poured cereal into a bowl. She poured milk on it. The flakes seemed too dry, despite the milk, too papery and brown. She tried to scupper a couple with spoonfuls of milk. Already she could feel her will to work on the hummingbird fading. She looked out the window at her garden. Random clusters of crocuses were spent, the shrouds of their blooms glued filmily to their leaves. Among the compacted drifts of decaying wet leaves yellowy-green sprouts had broken through. The ground seemed to rumble softly with subterranean growth. Margaret imagined worms industriously depositing brown coils of earth at the mouths of their holes, clearing out their tunnels for spring, preparing for the onslaught of pale roots poking through in a lightless search for nitrogen and other nutrients. Tiny pigmentless slugs tumbled out of slug egg or womb, anticipating marigolds and lettuce.

Her flowerbeds were usually well tended but last year she'd neglected them. Chickweed appeared in sporadic light-green clumps. Yellow dandelions drew sunlight down on their heads. Runners of grass laid claim to unoccupied earth.

She went outside. The sun was warmer than she'd expected for April. Its heat penetrated her clothes. She was struck by the freshness of hearing sounds not generated by herself—birds singing, the diffuse rushing sound of free air, car tires on asphalt, a lawn mower running over a stick. She felt reassured by them, relieved that the world existed outside of herself.

On the stairs of the back porch was a columbine she'd bought just before John left. It had enchanted her, an old-fashioned flower from the time when ladies wrote long letters to one another and were friends for life.

She saw that one of the blooms was open, and she crouched down to look more closely. It was colourful and exotic and reminded her somehow of a nun. Perhaps because of its wings, the flaps and tendrils all sticking out crisply at angles. The flower's sex was in the centre, a bouquet of yellow seeds on sticky stamens cloaked by a hood of yellow petals which were capped by deep-red wings, the airborne part, the red fairy's hat. A tiny brown bug was taking liberties among the seeds, wandering from one delicate cluster to another. Sensing her presence it scooted out of sight into the hidden roots of the stamens.

The plant had survived several weeks being watered only by rain, but it hadn't rained in a week and the earth in the small pot was dry and had shrunk from the edge. She put on her gardening shoes and an old gardening hat and carried the columbine to a spot between two clumps of irises. She knelt in the small world of shadow the hat created round her. Above, last year's rosehips knocked dryly in the breeze. Delicate burgundy leaves sprouted from green branches. Last summer its huge red roses could only be seen from the second floor because neither she nor John had pruned. They'd both stopped doing much around the house. The lawn got mowed but not weeded or aerated. Shingles weren't repaired, eavestroughs weren't cleaned. The rosebush now stood over ten feet high and had become a chaotic tangle of the quick and the dead.

She dug several trowelfuls of dirt and piled it to the side, picking out larger stones and bits of crockery. Every spring it seemed a new assortment of broken china and stones surfaced on her flowerbeds. She remembered how she'd first learned why this was so, but she didn't remember where she'd come across the story, or if it was apocryphal.

Two lovers in the Soviet Union, desperate for privacy, went out into the country. They found a field lying fallow, and as they wandered looking for a spot to spread their blanket they stumbled across a huge marble head breaking through the soil among the grass and wildflowers. They made love by its right cheekbone, excited by the voyeurism of its stone gaze, then informed officials at the city hall of the nearest town that a statue was rising out of the field.

It was Stalin. Twenty years earlier villagers had carted it out to the field, dug a huge hole and buried it, forever, they thought. But now it had floated back up to the surface. They were uneasy about its reappearance until they learned that stone was lighter than earth.

The hole for the columbine was almost deep enough when she noticed something writhing at the bottom. It was a half-worm, its severed body frantically searching for the rest of itself. Even as she recoiled and wondered nervously where the other half was, hoping it was not anywhere near her, she felt anguish for the worm and thought there must be pain. The sight of the pinky brown end waving in the air, not knowing in which direction to travel, was unbearable. She lifted it onto the trowel and tossed it behind the irises. If birds didn't find it first, the worm could regrow its lost half. She tossed some more earth over it and tried to forget it was there.

There was no escape from pain. Even here, in the peace and beauty of the garden.

Half a self lying every morning divorced on the mattress: an arm, a leg, an eye, an ear—a divorced Noah's ark sailing to the end of life with only one of everything, its past and future amputated. Her house half-filled with furniture, half the necessary kitchen utensils, half the pictures gone, half of everything missing. Divorce was very physical. She felt so vulnerable now even walking down the sidewalk, or talking to friends. She was at the stage before the missing parts started to grow back, the writhing, confused stage. Root, living terror.

She pried the columbine from its pot. A white web of roots held the soil in the shape of the pot. She placed it in the hole and found that the hole needed to be deeper and wider at the bottom, so she lay the columbine on the grass and began scooping more earth out. Something whitish fell in. A tiny bone. It was porous and light, no knobs or joints, slightly curved. A rib.

Gently she scratched the wall of the hole where she thought it had fallen from until she found another whitish object. As she excavated around it with her fore-finger, the roots of the iris tubers tickled her knuckles.

The second bone was a tiny skull with the upper part of a beak attached. Robin-sized, she thought. The skull was filled with dirt—no maggots or flesh that Margaret could see. The fine bone around the eye sockets and at the base of the skull had broken and chipped, but other-wise it was intact. Two pea-sized holes about a quarter-inch apart made her think perhaps it had been killed by a BB gun.

She imagined the bird at night, scaly feet holding a branch deep inside a fir tree, watching shadow and wind play with each other, tucking its head against its breast to sleep. The fragile skull whispered of a terror-stricken moment, a sad ending. She put the skull aside on the grass.

She dug another hole and planted the columbine, sat-urated it with water then pressed earth firmly around its base. She left the first hole open so she could come back later and look for more bones. She wanted to clean the dirt out of the bird's skull and look at it more closely, but also she felt ready, finally, to enter her studio and begin work on the hummingbird.

As she carried the tiny rib and skull back into the house, an image floated through her mind of a skull with a columbine planted inside the cranium. The intricate flowers bloomed through the eye sockets, and its roots grew out through the neck: the past containing the present while the present gradually eroded it and turned its losses into dust.

The air in her studio was dormant and smelled of plaster and clay and glue. She put the bird's skull on the filing cabinet. A few clumps of wet dirt spilled out. The skull seemed so delicate and fragile, so alive in contrast to the hulking, mummified form stranded on her worktable.

She decided not to listen to the messages on her answering-machine but just to phone the director of the aviary and tell him she was still intending to deliver.

"To not even have the courtesy or the professionalism to call and tell me it would be late is unacceptable. I can tell you right now you won't be working for me again. When *will* it be ready?"

"Tomorrow," she answered impulsively. She hadn't really figured out how long the work would take. "Tomorrow afternoon."

"Call me when it's done," he said and hung up.

She didn't know how to begin, how to approach the bird's whiteness, its blank skin. She began to talk herself through each step with short plain instructions.

"Pry open the paint cans... Where's the screwdriver? What colour do you need first?... Find the mixing jars… Clean the airbrush nozzle."

The trick would be to mix a hot green and fleck it with turquoise and gold. Glowing. Average body temperature 105 degrees Fahrenheit.

"Up to 114 degrees," she murmured to herself. "How hot would its body feel in your hand?"

Their tiny chokeberry hearts beat five hundred to twelve hundred times a minute. The wings flutter so fast they look translucent to the human eye.

"Fill the airbrush. You need a mask unless you want green-speckled lungs."

Why do they need to move so quickly? Flowers aren't going anywhere. They have the highest metabolism of all birds. They eat more, relative to their body weight, than any other vertebrate.

Why? They move fast so they can eat a lot. They eat a lot so they can move fast. There is no purpose. They might survive just as well eating less and flying slower.

The reason must be—in order to be hummingbirds. As though evolution's purpose—no, it doesn't have a purpose—evolution's *effect* were to create as much variety as the earth could support. Difference for its own sake. For the sake of beauty.

It was all flesh and blood though, all integument and bone and sinew, all the same clay fired with the same spark.

"Keep your hand slow and steady. Apply evenly." Her arm was tired and she rested.

A metabolism too fast for memory. A hummingbird's present is gone before it can snag onto the past and be remembered. Hummingbird moments vanish as they occur—hot and impenetrable. They burst through time, embodiments of the ephemeral. They live only slightly longer than insects.

She began again, fading the green slowly toward the wings. The rhythm of the work absorbed her. She mixed colours for the belly—buff, soft brown, whites. The afternoon passed timelessly. She sprayed black under the beak and made it blend into the green. She switched to oil paints and brush for the brilliant fuchsia gorget. A bejewelled bird. When she finished the neck she set the brush in turpentine and looked up from her work. It was dark out.

After dinner and with a fresh cup of coffee she returned to the studio. She hesitated at the doorway.

Painted, with the eye unbound, it was amazing how different the bird looked. The white spot behind the eye seemed to accentuate the bird's anger, even malevolence—a glittering vindictiveness. The truth was hummingbirds were very aggressive. Thirty-five percent of their waking hours were spent in belligerent displays, swooping down on each other with long sharp claws eager for each other's flesh, beaks poised to poke at the other's eye. On such a large scale it was impossible to hide its true nature.

She set her coffee down and walked round to the other side of her worktable, where the bird's eye was still bound in plastic and tape. The covered eye made the model look completely different—vulnerable, tragic, as though, like Oedipus, it had been struck down by fate.

The bird's duality reminded her of John. Sarcastic, hostile, disappointed—above all disappointed. It never occurred to him to try to change what was disappointing him—his practice, her, himself; he just sank into resentful hostility.

Then the covered eye—underneath the plastic and tape another side of John facing her. Three years ago she'd called a cab and rushed him to Emergency; he was gasping with pain, sweating, dizzy, he didn't know what was happening. He was rushed into an examining room and the next time she saw him he was lying on a trolley in a green hospital gown with an IV hooked up and a clear plastic tube running out of his nose. He looked right in her eyes. They'd given him some morphine and he was sinking into a calm euphoria, but he still knew he was in danger and helpless. He looked at her with complete trust; she would look out for him. There was no doubt and no measurement of this bond. It was just there.

They'd had a couple of poppyseed squares from a European bakery for dessert. As she watched the poppyseeds zip out his nose and down the tube, she realized he did have her absolute loyalty; she would be vigilant until he was through this. She was surprised because the appendicitis attack happened when their marriage already seemed dead. They weren't talking any more, except to make observations about the newspaper, the weather, their food.

She removed the plastic from the other eye and painted around it. When she thought of John she blamed him for her loneliness, for the pain she was in, for her inability to face much more than getting out of bed each day, for her bewilderment and fear. But blame implied choice, and she wondered, did he have a choice? Could it have been different?

For example, she had chosen to marry John of her

own free will. She had thought she could get what she needed from him. But in retrospect the choice was made blindly; she had no control over and little insight into what impelled it. She didn't know in advance what the outcome might be. Free choice was still subject to contingency; it didn't mean you were in control of your destiny. But if you weren't in control how could you be responsible for the outcome? And if the choice was always mostly blind, how could you blame anyone? How could you say either of them was responsible for the failure of the marriage? Still she felt guilty. And still she blamed John.

Resentful. Malevolent. Helpless. Afraid. One side struggling to see, struggling for insight and control, the other side not caring, angry and looking for revenge.

By midnight she was ready to start the wings. She'd already constructed the individual spines of each feather and attached them to the wing bone. She spread a bolt of purply-taupe silk gauze over her worktable. She would stretch it between the spines of each feather and cut an overlap which she would glue underneath the next feather. Then the whole wing would be painted with satin-finish varathane and the curved tip of each feather shaped from the stiff gauze with scissors. The effect she hoped to achieve would be of gossamer flight, a slightly blurred impression of speed.

She was tired, yet the hours of uninterrupted work had left her feeling peaceful and a little light-headed, almost giddy. She sifted the gauze through her fingers, letting it fall in shimmering folds on the table. She had an impulse to drape the fabric over her shoulders, which she did and, having done that, found herself wrapping it around like a toga. She went to the bathroom to look in the mirror, expecting a glamorous reflection, a goddess. *Mirror, mirror on the wall…*

The material was so light and thin that she looked more like a fly wrapped in a web. She took the end that hung over her shoulder and wrapped it round her face. She looked like a creature from the spirit world, silent, mysterious, boneless, a mummified bride, hovering before the mirror. An androgynous voice began to speak from her, as though the unconscious had come up for air, or an oracle were throwing seeds of the future into the wind.

"*Where you come from, that is where you'll return.*"

"From dust to dust?" she asked her image.

"*No. Only the present is real. Even a bone is only a dream. The dream of a skull, a skull dreaming.*"

"All that is solid melts into air?" she quoted Marx.

"*No,*" replied the cocooned oracle from her veiled and softly bound mouth. "*Who are you? No one. There is only one being. People are variations on a theme.*"

"The collective unconscious?"

"*You are a collection of fragments of that being. You must not worry about being separate; it doesn't matter.*"

"God is one?"

The oracle departed, leaving a silence deeper than the mere absence of sound. The gauze fell from her face and she felt silly swathed in the hummingbird's prospective wings.

SEVEN

"**A** museum is a gathering place for dead objects."
Frank Rice poured ice water into his glass from a
jug on the table. "Everything here has been stolen from
its real context and placed in a kind of limbo, deprived
of its natural right to decay. Preserved. And turned into
a static dead object.

"Why do people go to museums? They go to see natural wonders. They're drawn to strange, slightly macabre
relics, like mummies. They want to see the secrets of the
past. They come to be enlightened. They come for a religious experience. They come to discover some esoteric
truth about the world.

"How do we satisfy their desires?" Frank opened his
eyes a little wider. The meeting room was small and
dingy. The paint on the walls was darkened by grime
and age, the finish on the floorboards had long since

worn off and the grouting round the windowpanes had chipped and cracked. The meeting table was solid oak while the chairs everyone sat on were a miscellany of plastic kitchen chairs, desk chairs and lab stools.

In attendance were the chairman of the board and eight members of the Human Origins Committee: Frank, Frank's assistant, a staff paleontologist, an exhibit designer, a staff writer, a representative from a 3-D computer animation house, Neill Hansen and Margaret. Neill and the writer seemed bored, as though they'd heard this speech before, while the designer, the 3-D guy and the paleontologist seemed interested, if somewhat confused about where it was leading.

"We create stories around the artifacts. We recreate the natural context of our artifacts and we place them in history, so that when visitors leave they feel as though they've seen and understood the thing itself. We bring dead objects back to life through the imagination, through *story*."

Margaret leaned her head heavily into her palm, her elbow propped against the table. Her eyes had puffy bags beneath them. Her shirt was wrinkled, her socks didn't quite match, her earrings were silver when gold would have done better, and her lipstick was smeared in one corner of her mouth.

I can barely hold my arm straight to support my head, she thought. *I need sleep. I must look like hell.*

You are no one, the oracle's voice still echoed from Tuesday as though some ghost were wandering across her synapses. It was not her own voice yet not exactly someone else's either.

She felt unattractive and rumpled and insecure. Her

grandmother on her father's side, who prided herself on her continental elegance, had said about her granddaughter, "You're *attractive* dear, not beautiful but attractive," and though Margaret had understood it was meant as a criticism she'd been content with the assessment. She had long wavy light-brown hair and brown almond-shaped eyes that in sunlight were shot with streaks of green and gold. Her mouth was large though not voluptuous—slightly voracious looking. Her lips were quite red. She wasn't glamorous, yet she wasn't rugged either. More like a hard-angled Pre-Raphaelite.

She wondered if she'd be adequate to the task of reconstructing the australopithecine, and she was already sensing aloofness and contempt from Neill. Her insecurity had started yesterday as she'd overseen the transfer of the giant hummingbird into the aviary's truck and she'd known it wasn't very good. It looked too lumpy and egg-shaped to be capable of flight, and it also looked vindictive and nasty. She wasn't surprised when the director phoned to say he couldn't use it, and if he couldn't use it, he couldn't approve the issue of a second cheque. He didn't ask her to fix it or do another one.

"Footprints," Frank grabbed his chairback for emphasis, "in the hardened ash of time. These will be the basis for our story, as most of you already know." Frank took a deep breath. Neill looked out the window with an irritated sigh. "Three of our ancestors walked across the Laetoli plains 3.6 million years ago, just after a volcano had showered them with ash. This ash contained carbonatite making the ash harden to a natural cement when it rained, leaving us this incredible record of their passing."

Dust into dust, echoed the voice. Ash into ash. No one into nothing. She imagined walking naked across a bed of light flaky ash—poof...poof...poof...soft clouds rose and settled. Everything around her was covered in ash—ash trees, ash stones, ash grass.

"The smaller hominid, which we are guessing was female, paused at one point and turned slightly to the left. This moment of hesitation..." Frank hesitated, searching for words, "is so poignant, pregnant, communicating a feeling of doubt or uncertainty in that creature across three and a half million years—it's an incredibly evocative moment."

Only the present is real, the voice intoned like an oboe solo rising out of a symphony orchestra. Only the moment, the hesitation, the empty space between impulse and action. Margaret felt her feet stop for a moment to gaze at the ash world around her, all colour transformed to grey, all texture feathersoft, almost softer and lighter than air.

"It seems that the 'female'," Frank continued, "and one of the two larger individuals which we are presenting as an adult male, might have even been touching each other in some way as they walked, arm in arm, or one with its arm around the other. The footprints are very close beside each other and vary on their path from side to side almost identically. For the purposes of this display, however, we are choosing to place the female, in her 'moment of hesitation,' with the male a step or two ahead on the original path. The third set of footprints that lie under the 'male's' we will refer to only in the storyboard. We will not do a reconstruction for them because they are somewhat indeterminate and frankly, we don't have the budget. Angela has some ideas about the footprints." Frank gave the floor to the exhibit designer.

A footprint is like a dream, the past insinuating itself into the present. A footprint is a trace of being, left behind like Cinderella's glass slipper. Margaret continued walking in the world of ash while the exhibit designer explained her idea for an interactive display where people could "walk in the footsteps of their ancestors."

Neill cleared his throat. "I have a problem with the display. If we have an adult male and an adult female travelling together they will look like a couple, which is almost certainly misleading. No other great ape has a monogamous mating system, and for that matter 80 percent of *human* societies are polygamous. Furthermore, and this is the strongest argument against it, the degree of sexual dimorphism is much too pronounced in afarensis. The male is at least one foot taller than the female and nearly twice the body weight. Monogamous pair-bonding is found only when the male and female are close in size."

Neill spoke with an unpleasant belligerence, as though expecting irritating or silly objections.

"What about a consort situation?" Margaret asked, then instantly regretted speaking. She was not up to any kind of articulation this morning. "Like chimpanzees."

"What's that?" asked the writer.

"The male forces a female who's in estrus to go off alone with him for several days so he can mate exclusively with her. The females are almost always reluctant to go and have to be bullied. They hang back and try to return to the group. Perhaps this model might provide one explanation for the female's 'moment of hesitation.'"

"I doubt most people are capable of distinguishing the subtle differences between a consort relationship and a modern nuclear family," Neill said contemptuously.

Margaret shrugged and retreated back to the ash world she'd been day-dreaming about. She veered left, away from the track of the male. Raindrops plopped silently into the ash and beaded like mercury before dissolving. The grass underneath the ash was straw-yellow and grazed to the bone. The raindrops augured a change of season, a metamorphosis from grey to green, a billion plump shimmering bodies sacrificing themselves to the dust, and out of this—a brief growing season, enough food for a female hominid to survive another year. A bird flew across her path into a tree and caused a small flurry of ash to float to the ground.

Who are you? the voice asked, and Margaret couldn't tell if it was she who was being addressed in the meeting room or the australopithecine in her ash world.

"I agree with you completely, Neill. You make a strong argument and your points can't be ignored," Frank said. "On the other hand, I don't know how to solve the problem unless we scrap the footprints as the founding principle of the display, which I'd be really reluctant to do. If there's a way to clearly establish a consort relationship over a monogamous one, maybe that's a way to go. With the footsteps following almost the exact variations parallel to one another, it will be hard to justify placing the male at a completely separate point in the tracks. Let's look into other ways we might dissociate the male and the female so they don't appear to be travelling together.

"We've got a tight schedule. Neill's almost finished his preliminary research and he and Margaret should be ready to start their reconstructions by next week. The 3-D computer animation will also have to progress quickly to be ready by fall."

After the meeting Neill suggested Margaret accompany him to the lab where he could demonstrate his recent research in the comparative anatomy of chimpanzees, gorillas and humans. Margaret agreed on condition that she could pick up two coffees from the cafeteria on the way.

The lab was a large room in the basement with stainless-steel tables, sinks, lots of counter space and walls of huge storage drawers. Neill opened a vacuum-locked door to a freezer room.

There were shelves along the walls holding various-sized bodies wrapped in plastic. Neill peeked under the plastic of one, then wheeled a steel trolley beside it. At the end of the refrigerated room he took hold of four chains hanging from an H-shaped joint that ran on two ceiling tracks. The crossbar of the "H" moved sideways so the chains could be pulled to either side of the room. Neill pulled the chains to the body beside the trolley, put hooks attached to each chain through an eye at each corner of a canvas sling underneath the body and winched the sling up. He moved it over the trolley, lowered it and detached the hooks, then wheeled the plastic-wrapped body out into the lab.

A row of plaster casts of chimpanzee heads caught Margaret's eye. It was as though dying had been the culmination of some long, excruciating labour. Their faces were scrunched up and folded in on themselves in a perpetual grimace, their brows collapsed over their eye sockets, their snouts pushed forward, teeth clenched, lips parted. They looked as though they'd been holding onto life fiercely and it had been torn from them.

"How did they die?" Margaret asked.

Neill shrugged. "Some were pretty old. About half from disease. I had one that drowned in a moat."

The lab had the sharp, oily smell of formaldehyde, though Neill's corpses were frozen not preserved.

"I only work with frozen cadavers," he said. "Formaldehyde changes the tissues. I can't get as accurate measurements."

The smell reminded Margaret of the first time she'd seen a cadaver. On her second date with John in the medical school lab. He was doing a dissection and she'd asked if she could see the corpse. This was the term before her anatomy course at art school. She remembered the snap of latex as John got his surgical gloves on.

The corpse was a woman in her early fifties. He had already dissected and reassembled her so he merely had to unfold the skin and lift the organs out. He laid them on the woman's chest and told Margaret how they worked. She imagined having her own organs laid on her body, outside, after she was dead.

John inserted a probe in the womb, then through the cervix and out the vagina—to shock her perhaps, but no, she thought, he really just wanted to show her how everything connected. He kept checking with her to make sure she was okay and she kept saying she was fine. She really did feel privileged to have access to the cadaver. Was she shocked?

No. Yes. She wouldn't let herself be. She was determined not to be squeamish.

The woman was slim yet Margaret had been surprised how greasy the body was; there seemed to be deposits of yellow fat everywhere. Neill opened the female chimp and removed her digestive organs to show Margaret the form of the thorax which was more conical in chimpanzees and Lucy than in humans. He explained how the form of the thorax influenced the shape of the muscles of the trunk. The chimpanzee's fat looked whiter and there was much less of it.

"The papers I gave you include photocopies of my dissection notes," Neill said. "You can come anytime and take her out, but obviously put her back together when you're finished. I've taken casts of most of the layers of the dissection. Some are here and the rest are in my studio."

Margaret was still tired and unable to concentrate on what he was saying. She drifted back to her own thoughts. She remembered when John had uncovered the woman's face. Her head was shaved. There were lines where the skin had been cut: one incision started at the bridge of the nose and went over the top of the head to the base of the neck, another circled the whole crown going across the brow, one went from the corners of the mouth to the base of the jaw and another went from the back of one ear along the scalp to the back of the other ear. The woman's expression had not been like the chimpanzees' at all; it was calm—not peaceful so much as neutral.

The dissection of the face shocked her much more than John's probe poking out of the vagina. The deconstruction of the woman's face seemed a violation.

John peeled back the skin of the cheek and named the muscles and tendons of the face. He carefully lifted an eyeball from its socket and pointed out the nerves feeding back to the brain. He lifted the muscles of the lips and chin to show her the roots of the teeth. After all that lifting of layers she felt as though she'd lost something forever. Like the moment in a science fiction movie when the latex mask of what one thought was a human being is peeled off and an intricate computer is revealed inside. She felt duped, fooled by appearances, by skin, by faces, into thinking humans had a unique identity, a self. In some way *she* felt violated.

John folded the woman's face back together and it regained its dispassionate expression, but for Margaret the woman had become an organic machine, her face a flesh mask.

Neill was now describing how the pelvic bone of Australopithecus afarensis was evolutionarily intermediate between a chimpanzee and a human. Margaret tried to listen but she couldn't concentrate. She told Neill about the morning she saw her first cadaver.

"It was a Sunday, and afterwards John had arranged a brunch to introduce me to some of his friends.

"The lab had brains in plastic ice-cream containers, a heart in an old Corningware dish with the little blue flowers, there were legs and arms wrapped in green garbage bags and I thought it was very surreal. I didn't think I was bothered by it until brunch. It was *dim sum*, which I'd never had before, and everything was coated in this white slippery dough and filled with indeterminate bits of animal meat. When we left the restaurant I started burping and the burps had a strong aftertaste of formaldehyde. I couldn't stop. I burped until I went to bed. I guess they were kind of hysterical burps."

She laughed. Neill, irritated at being interrupted, responded with a begrudging "Hmmm."

"It was her face that really bothered me. When you cut up the face and show the mechanics, it's as bad as thinking of the soul as just a bunch of chemical responses in the brain. There's something very empty and depressing about it."

Neill did not encourage Margaret to go on. He wrapped the chimp back up in its plastic and asked her to hold the freezer door open. He wheeled the trolley in, transferred the chimp to its shelf and winched the cadaver of a gorilla onto the trolley.

A woman in a white lab coat leaned in through the door and told Neill his mother was on the phone.

"You can see what I've done if you want," he said after they had wheeled the trolley out. He handed her a scalpel and left. She sat down beside the gorilla and yawned.

Even frozen there was a slight smell from the gorilla's hair. Where had it come from? Since it was frozen it must have been from a zoo or primate centre. Not from the wild. Not killed by poachers. She'd read about poachers killing gorillas just to cut off their heads and hands as trophies to sell to tourists. The hands were made into ashtrays. Gorilla hand, palm up, supplicant, someone stubbing a cigarette out on its palm in a mimicry of torture. It reminded her of images from the Holocaust, lampshades made of human skin, piles of human teeth harvested for gold fillings. She'd heard recently that the lampshades were apocryphal, but it seemed irrelevant because the image expressed so precisely what was being done to Jews and Gypsies, communists, homosexuals and other "enemies" of the Nazis.

She wondered about the gorilla hand ashtrays, if they were apocryphal too, but it didn't matter.

Humans were strange. To want such trophies in one's house. One's own artifacts. Like a shark's jaw, or a fossil. Something powerful brought down. Dead hands. Hands that held death. Hands that touched death. Explored other people's sick bodies. Those hands had touched her body.

Had she dreamed it? John touching her breasts for the first time that afternoon. He'd come up to her room in the rooming house for tea. They'd kissed. Or rather he kissed her. Passionately, while she was still tasting formaldehyde and burping. They were sitting on a sofa. He unbuttoned her shirt, asking first if it was all right. She said yes, but she hadn't really thought about it. He cupped her breasts in his trembling hands. Had they trembled? Something about him trembled. He leaned forward and put his lips over her nipple and looked up at her and it disturbed her to have him looking up at her that way, perhaps because it was so submissive, or so childlike. Despite her recurring burps, it didn't seem to occur to him that she might still be thinking about the corpse, that images of dead body parts in plastic bags and food containers might be juxtaposed in her mind with his foreplay. She felt guilty that at such an intimate moment all she could think about were the stiff yellow mounds that had been peeled away with the skin of the chest when he'd opened the rib cage.

On their next date she confessed what she'd been thinking and he withdrew, calmly, without reproach, and didn't try to touch her for a while. She appreciated his reserve. After a few more dates she'd finally kissed him.

For their honeymoon John's uncle had invited them to stay at a guest cabin on his ranch. They swam in a river whose water was red from the earth, red and opaque so she couldn't see her toes or legs when she was treading water. She remembered John's leg rising to the surface. Wanting him to touch her in the red water. The sensation of skin touching skin underwater, one sensation layered on top of the other, warm on cool, floating in lighter gravity.

They found a spot on the bank, in the mud. She remembered wanting him closer and closer, wanting him inside her skin, under her skin, wanting to cut herself open and wrap her flesh round him, wanting to give herself totally over to him, to lose herself and drown all pain and fear.

They dropped acid that trip. An old high school buddy of John's had slipped it to him at their wedding. She'd never taken it before and John hadn't since high school. They laughed about the gift because it was so out of character for them, but they took it because they felt carefree and adventurous and like doing something different together. She remembered laughing hysterically about some minnows swimming upstream, nicknaming one of them "Rocky" and this being very funny.

Neill returned from his phone call and they began examining his dissection of the gorilla. She glanced down at one of its arms, the one that hadn't been dissected. It lay by the animal's side and looked alive, as though he might wake up soon. The hand was palm up, fingers curled over, thumb lightly turned in, the hugely callused knuckles visible. She felt sad for the gorilla who was gone and for its life, which could not have been sweet in gorilla terms. She felt an urge to place her hand inside his and hold it, kindly, forever.

Her husband's hands. Hands that later forgot themselves and began performing examinations instead. Once he'd actually started taking her pulse without thinking, then dropped her hand. *Does this hurt? Does this hurt? Do you feel any pressure here?* She hadn't answered truthfully then as she'd laughed.

EIGHT

S he had a strange dream.

On the passenger side of a truck's cab sits a skinny truck driver in his fifties with strawberry-blond hair. His boss sits beside him in the driver's seat. The driver's telling the boss, who has grey hair and wears an elegant white dinner jacket, that he and the boss's mistress had sex. He's somewhat sheepish but he doesn't think the boss is going to be really upset because it happened during an errand they were doing for the boss, and they didn't do it out of lust but out of despair, out of a shared sense of submission to the boss, and out of bored compassion.

The boss, however, takes out a gun and shoots him in the head.

Then he telephones his mistress at her hotel room. He tells her, "I'm picking you up in fifteen minutes. Do a good job on your make-up. I want you to look perfect." She has platinum-blond hair and brown eyes.

The mistress is Margaret, yet in the dream she always thinks of her in the third person—"she" never "I."

There are four people in the boss's limousine: the boss, Margaret, another woman who is possibly a prostitute and another man who is a middle-of-the-road rock 'n' roll singer and reminds Margaret of Billy Joel or Phil Collins.

The boss orders her to take off her shirt. Her naked breasts are beautiful and warm and tanned. The boss tells the other man to touch her breasts if he wants, and so he reaches back from the front seat and caresses them.

The experience is very erotic for Margaret. The excitement of a stranger…the forbidden…the beauty and heat of her own body.

The boss tells her to put her shirt back on. He tells her to fix her make-up. It must be perfect. And suddenly she realizes he's going to kill her. In retrospect she realizes that she already knew when he told her to take off her shirt in front of another man. Even earlier, in fact, when he phoned her and there was more menace than usual in his voice and an absence of words, of sex, just the command. He meant to kill her then. She gets her purse from under the front seat, takes out a compact mirror and lipstick and begins applying it to her lips.

She sees her eyes in the little mirror and in them the sudden comprehension of the reality of what she is doing—this moment—carefully moving lipstick over her skin, making the red outline of her mouth faultless so that in a few hours, after she is dead and her lips are cool as clay, they will look beautiful. She is putting lipstick on, conscious that it is for the last time.